Pat Sweet was born in Dundee. She obtained an honours degree through the Open University, and a post-graduate degree with the Department of Government, University of Strathclyde. She has worked as an income tax officer, advertising sales executive, local news reporter, lecturer, research fellow and evaluation consultant. She now writes full-time, lives in Glasgow and has two grown up children. She has just completed her second Cat O'Connell mystery.

TROUBLED
WATERS

Pat Sweet

Published by VIRAGO PRESS Limited August 1995
20 Vauxhall Bridge Road, London SW1V 2SA

First published by Virago Press in 1994

*A CIP catalogue record for this title
is available from the British Library*

Printed and bound in Great Britain by
Cox & Wyman Ltd, Reading, Berkshire

For my mother, Mary Muir

Another Day

Being a single parent, it took me years to persuade myself that I wasn't personally responsible for the breakdown of society. My next discovery was to twig that while failure is always possible, death is a certainty. And time runs out. When my son left home two years ago to see the world, I left a city law practice to become a private investigator. I also gave up thinking of myself first and foremost as a mother.

Now forty-five, still mobile and reasonably sane, I live alone near central Glasgow in a small attic flat which doubles as my office. Business is slow, but I try to look on the bright side. Optimists have more fun than pessimists. And fun is something I've decided to have a little more of in my life.

I drew up into my parking place opposite the sandstone tenement, a tiny part of which I call home. The buildings were stone-cleaned and repaired three years ago, so the crescent looks pretty spruce. A strong Residents' Association makes sure it stays that way.

The private gardens out front are tended by a gardener. I

dig deeply into my pocket every three months to pay my share of his hefty bill, and for the cleaning of the communal hall and stairs. The next time one of these jobs is vacant I'm thinking of applying.

My only other contribution to the general ambience is two window-boxes. Since I live up in the roof, I'm the only beneficiary. But it earns me Brownie points for effort.

I heaved my bag from the car and up the stairs, road-up signs imprinted on my eyeballs. Sunday isn't my favourite day for driving. I punched in the alarm code. At least I hadn't had any uninvited guests.

I dropped the bag in the hall and went into the sitting-room. It's a fair size, with cream walls, a pale coffee coloured carpet and a clutter of books, paintings and plants. The sofa and armchairs are built for sprawling in and take up most of the floor space.

The only discordant note was the heap of unopened mail beside the computer on the desk in the corner. It had been lying there so long it was starting to curl up at the edges, and there was a new lot behind the door.

I ignored it and walked over to the window. The city spread out before me, a twinkling carpet of lights. I gave a satisfied sigh. My view on paradise.

The phone rang. I made a dash. I have no plans to buy an answering machine. I get little enough peace as it is, without having to return calls.

I caught it on the second ring. I've got faster since my new neighbour started to complain about the noise I make living. Planting the receiver against my ear, I looked at the clock. 1.00 a.m. That should please him.

'Hello,' I said, 'Cat O'Connell here.' When that voice boomed in my ear I wished I hadn't bothered.

'Caithlin! Where the hell have you been? I've set up a contract for you. And contracts, in case you have forgotten, mean money.'

I leaned resignedly on my elbow, the receiver glued to my head. I didn't want to talk to Stanley; he depresses me. Unfortunately, he is married to one of my best friends. He is also my bank manager.

'Good of you to phone, Stanley,' I lied.

'Well?'

'Well what?'

When Stanley started to speak to someone whose brain had atrophied, I checked that I was the only person on this end of the line.

'Have you received a letter about a possible contract, Caithlin?' he finally managed to get out. I could have spelled it quicker.

I took the receiver from my ear and peered into it, trying to make eye contact. Stanley MacDonald is a pain. How Doreen has managed to live with him for fifteen years is one of life's great mysteries. The only reason he's still my bank manager is that I'm never out of overdraft long enough to transfer my account.

'Look, Stanley, I've been away for a few days and haven't had a chance to go through my mail yet.'

'Out on the tiles again?' he sniped. 'Given up work, have we?'

A fuse lit in my head. I'd spent the last week on a ratty proposal, for a miserly fee. 'Listen here, Stanley, I don't need this hassle. Anyway, have you any idea what time it is?'

There was a silence, then I heard rustling and whispers. Stanley sighed as if it cost him. 'All right, Caithlin. It's late. I apologise. Now go look for the letter.' There was another pause; I could visualise Doreen at his shoulder. 'You know we worry about you,' he said grudgingly.

I gave a sour grin. Stanley worried about two things: Doreen and money, and not necessarily in that order. But what really irritated me was his Caithlin this and Caithlin that. I've been Cat since the age of three, and I detest being called Caithlin, and he knows it.

'I haven't been through my mail yet,' I said tightly. 'I'll get back to you.'

'Never put off till tomorrow what you can do today.'

'I'll get on to it,' I snarled, and clattered the phone down. Stanley and his proverbs: they're so banal they'd strip wallpaper off a wall.

I marched into the bathroom. I feel guilty about Doreen. If I'd stayed home that summer fifteen years ago, I might have saved her from her hormones – and Stanley. I stepped under the shower and thumped the gauge, and was suitably grateful when some warm water descended.

Doreen and I were best friends at school, and have stayed that way ever since. No matter what. In my so-called adulthood, I've been married and divorced, raised a son, and lost a father. And there are days when I think I'm just beginning to get the hang of living.

My father died five years ago, and my mother went to live with my sister Clemency and her husband Raymond. The three of them get on famously in deepest Kent. That's around six hundred miles away, and it's not far enough.

The problem is Clemency and me. She is two years older and chalk to my cheese – in every way.

I have dark hair, going grey, that grows like field grass in summer, and looks it. Every time I face up to a mirror, my eyes, dark blue with black lashes, seem to be taking over. And they're supposed to be my best feature.

Clemency's blonde hair curls in the right places, and if a strand of grey has the nerve to push out it's instantly doused. Her blue eyes are softer than mine. I think she's trained them.

Nothing much has changed over the years. I'm still tall and thin, she's still petite and cuddly. It's just that our bodies are beginning to lose the battle with gravity.

Clemency, I snorted, a misnomer if ever I heard one. The iron paw inside the velvet mitt. If she ever decides to move up to Glasgow, I'm emigrating.

I dived for a towel and dried myself quickly. Clean, awake and hungry, I wolfed a slice of brown bread and two peaches, and picked up the mail and sat down to go through it.

The first thing I looked for was my son Allan's handwriting. He was now in Australia, and I hadn't heard from him for four weeks. I sighed, nothing. Another week, and I'd be hitting the panic button. I forced myself back to business.

I may not like him, but Stanley is never less than accurate

on matters of finance. If he said there was a money earner in the midst of this pile of bills – there it would be.

I got it, eventually: an American oil company, Yukon Discovery, invested heavily in North Sea Oil and was prospecting a new strike. 'Recent incidents', the letter said guardedly, 'have led us to believe that a confidential expert investigation would be a useful adjunct to our negotiations. You have been recommended as being likely to assist us in this matter. If it is convenient, we would suggest a preliminary meeting with you at 10 a.m. on May 10th, at the above address.'

I looked up at the calendar. That was tomorrow, in Dundee. I had nothing on that couldn't wait, and since when could I afford to ignore the prospect of work?

But why had Stanley put my name forward? What I knew about the oil business could be written on a postage stamp, several times over. Should I go?

I looked at the growing pile of bills. Did I have a choice?

When I got out of bed five hours after crawling in, I had to force myself to bend and stretch. Some mornings I add a jog, but this wasn't going to be one of them. I showered and wrapped up in Martin's bath robe. Sighing, I pulled the collar up and held it against my cheeks; missing him wasn't getting any easier. I made a pot of Darjeeling and refused myself a cigarette.

Breakfast over, I dived into my wardrobe and pulled out a dark suit: a purple wool mix with a pencil skirt and long jacket. While I was in there, I looked at my clothes: dismal stuff, must be my psyche. I closed the door.

I got the Mini moving without too much trouble, cruised on to Great Western Road and sliced determinedly through the commuter traffic to take a devious back route, longer, but more fun than sitting nose to tail.

I emerged on Hyndland Road alongside high red sandstone tenements, turned sharp right towards Dumbarton Road, right before Partick Cross, then on to the expressway and the motorway. Straight through more or less from here.

I took a passing interest in the number of K-reg drivers

with a mobile phone stuck to their faces, and wondered what they had to talk about. Realising they were all men, it led me to contemplate sexual differences. Since there are worse heartaches, this soon palled.

I tried to work out what this contract involved, how Stanley had come to hear of it, why he had put my name forward, and what he stood to get out of it.

I knew that he liked being thought of as a fixer, a man with contacts, and that he prided himself on knowing the best people. But he'd pronounced me certifiably insane when I gave up being a lawyer, so what had changed his mind?

I grinned. For Stanley to put work my way, I must've crawled to the bottom of the ladder. Might even be close to getting a foot on the first rung.

With the new motorway sections, I was soon skirting Perth. I swept right towards Edinburgh, took the slip-road to the left and over the Tay, and on to the straight to Dundee.

It's been a long time since I lived in Dundee, but one thing still rankles. In the Nethergate, right beside the Church of St Mary, is a post-war shopping centre. It shouldn't be there. I figure that the person who allowed it to be built was an Englishman with a grudge.

I tore my eyes away, moved on into Reform Street, and weighed up the cost of parking on a double yellow. A van eased out in front of me and I zipped in before the space cooled.

Deciding that a shiny face didn't inspire confidence, I patted powder over the offending area and applied lipstick. Then I wet a finger and ran it over my eyebrows. That was me. Now for Yukon Discovery.

The address led me to a road off Reform Street, and a narrow doorway lined with brass plates. At the end of the half-tiled entrance hall, there was a small cage lift. I walked straight past, trudged up two flights and came to a glass-panelled door with 'Yukon Discovery' emblazoned across it, in red letters outlined in gold on a blue background.

Bright is what it was. I'd lay bets that if they slapped that logo on all their equipment, nothing would get mislaid – I squeezed my eyes tight and opened them again – or stolen.

The receptionist looked up and took my measure, red lips curving into a professional smile. 'Good morning,' she intoned. 'May I help you?'

I stated my business, gave the contact name and sank into the voluminous settee. Whatever problems Yukon Discovery may have, cash flow didn't appear to be one of them.

The decor was blindingly fresh, pale grey walls with cream cornicing picked out in gold, and deep red plush carpeting. The furniture was new, reproduction Edwardian, and the computing system was state of the art. Large colour photographs of oil rigs hung in heavy gold frames around the walls, each with an identifying sticker at the side.

The door across the way opened. A stockily built man in a Savile Row style suit walked briskly across the room, hand outstretched, smiling as if he was glad to see me.

His short blond hair was tightly curled and showed a scattering of grey. His features were regular – in other words they didn't strike me as being out of the ordinary – but his eyes were a clear blue, and sharp as buttons. I could tell that his internal information processor was logged on and working smoothly.

'Ms O'Connell? Edward Tomlinson. Good of you to come.' His voice was surprisingly deep, with the flat vowels of the deliberately accent free. 'Tea? Coffee?'

I stood up and discovered our eyes were on the same level. I was wearing heels so that must make him around five ten. I had my hand pumped up and down and managed to say coffee before I was rushed along the corridor.

It crossed my mind that if he did everything at this speed, his relationships with women would be short-lived; or confined to business.

Into the inner sanctum. More Edwardian repro, but it suited the proportion of the room. The desk looked used: it was scattered with papers, three telephones and a computer. I locked on to the shrewd eyes. It was a fair guess that this disorder was only on the surface.

Coffee arrived via the receptionist. She turned out to be his secretary, and must have run all the way. I took a sip, enjoyed the kick, and waited for Tomlinson to open play. He'd given up hurrying.

Keeping a weather-eye on me, he rifled leisurely through a bundle of papers, pulled out a heavy document and placed it on top. I had the impression he had known exactly where to find it. He was just taking his time, weighing me up.

'Ms O'Connell. Let me explain the company situation. I opened this office two years ago, when I became the European director of Yukon Discovery' – his eyes twinkled becomingly – 'and was spending more hours up in the air than on the ground. And business is still growing.' He waved at a colour print of an oil rig. 'We started by prospecting and building rigs, but have diversified considerably. My reason for contacting you involves a new strike.'

I dislike people wasting my time and I don't see why I should waste theirs, so I came clean. 'Mr Tomlinson, I know nothing about the oil business. If the work that you have in mind requires specialised knowledge, I'm afraid I won't be able to help.'

He smiled coolly. And the nothing out of the ordinary impression I'd had of his looks started to disappear, fast: each feature was clear cut, and disciplined.

'It requires a certain expertise. But I am reliably informed that it is an expertise that you can offer. Anything you need to know about the oil business, I can tell you.'

I smiled back. I was getting conflicting signals. He was friendly enough, but there was aggravation in the air. 'What exactly are you looking for?'

He leaned back in the leather swivel chair and made a steeple of his hands: 'I want a spy. I need to know who is doing what and why. And I need to know soon, very soon.' He leaned across the desk. 'I'm told that you can be relied on to get this sort of information, quickly and accurately.'

Mentally cursing Stanley, I gathered up my bag and briefcase. 'The price for accurate information, Mr Tomlinson, is confidentiality. That means I can't name names, or point the finger. I provide an analysis based on hard facts and substantiated details. Not tittle-tattle. And I'm not a management spy.'

He fixed me with a stare that stopped me in my tracks. 'Let's not be too hasty, Ms O'Connell. I am well aware of your track record.' He looked as if he had started sucking a lemon. 'Perhaps I phrased it badly.'

I sat back down. 'You could try rephrasing it.'

He sat in silence for a long moment, distaste digging deep grooves in his cheeks. 'I'll be quite frank. I wasn't in favour of approaching you. Nothing personal, I hasten to add. I just don't think a lone operator has much to offer.' His eyes were like ice. You didn't need to be Einstein to know that he was seriously upset. His mouth got even tighter. 'But in the States, as you are no doubt aware, businesses take a different view. In this case, being the only English' – he quickly corrected himself – 'British representative on the board . . .'

I got the picture. Tomlinson had been out-voted by his American colleagues and he didn't care for the experience. The good news from my point of view was that it looked as if a contract was on the cards, if I wanted it.

My mind ticked over; I had to consider the drag factor here. I studied Tomlinson. In my work, executive antipathy is a fact of life. But you can get too much of a bad thing. To accept a contract when all the cards were stacked against me would be suicide. And I have no suicidal tendencies, professional or otherwise.

I stared steadily across the heavy desk. 'I'm sorry you feel that way. But I won't know whether or not I'm interested until I know more about the situation and' – I stressed the words – 'your board's expectations.'

He got my message, looked at his watch and said coldly, 'I have several calls to make, Ms O'Connell. May I suggest we meet in an hour's time for lunch, and discuss this in more detail?'

That suited me. And his choice of eating place wasn't bad either. I smiled. 'I look forward to it. I'll see myself out.'

I left him standing at his desk, looking less than pleased but not unduly troubled. On the way past, I gave his secretary a nod. Liking her answering smile, I made a mental note that she would be one of the first people I spoke to, if this went ahead.

Food
For Thought

I crossed the Tay Road Bridge into Fife and took the coast road to St Andrews. I drove slowly through Tayport's tight grey stone buildings and on towards the flat of the estuary and Leuchars, and started to enjoy my view of the Tay.

I had decided I could fit in a walk along the beach before heading inland to the restaurant of Tomlinson's choice. I needed to think. I was at a crossroads, in more ways than one.

I was going to have to decide soon whether to continue my hand-to-mouth existence doing work that I enjoyed, or get a proper job and have a regular income again.

I was also going to have to make up my mind about Martin. I'd asked for time to think things over, but I kept finding excuses for not contacting him, since I still hadn't been able to work out what I wanted, and why. What was there to say?

I started to unwind a bit when I came up to the Old Course and saw the hoardings advertising the Dunhill. I don't play golf, but I like the bustle it brings to St Andrews. Town, gown, and golf make a good mix.

I turned left at the golf shop and crept along looking for a space. It was car after car, end on, and I was nearly off the front before I finally found a slot. I parked, changed shoes and jacket and locked up. The wind hit me in the face. I scrabbled down to the beach, got on to firm damp sand and began a fast walk.

I couldn't pretend that I wasn't interested in Yukon Discovery. For a start, I was curious to find out what sort of equation international contacts and big profits brought to company operations. And maybe I rather liked the idea of being a burr in Tomlinson's flesh.

I stopped and scuffled thoughtfully in the sand, and looked back along the wide sweep of the bay, deserted apart from a distant walker and scampering dog. An outing here as a child had been a big deal. I smiled. It still felt like the edge of the universe.

The sun was bright with the pale gleam of early winter, and the sea a rippling dark blue, frilled with white breakers; very calming. An east coast beach always has that effect on me, which probably explains why I live in a city in the west.

I took another gulp of brisk east coast wind. No effort was required. It blew itself all the way into my lungs. When I finished gasping, I made up my mind.

I would phone Martin when I got back. I was just getting used to my freedom and wasn't in any hurry to give it up. I was going to have to tell him so. I'd give my friend Joy a ring too. The way things were going that part-time research job she mentioned might keep the wolf from the door.

Deciding that I'd been sufficiently aerated, I checked my watch. Time to go back. I retraced my steps and started to look forward to my lunch.

I'm a punctual sort of person, one of those pain-in-the-neck types that get irritated if they're kept waiting – and show it. I drew up at the inn dead on time.

It's in the middle of nowhere, but I have never seen the car-park without a show of quality cars. I usually come in a fancy car, too. Somebody else's. Today, my faithful heap drew up between a Jag and a BMW and shook to a standstill.

*

Tomlinson was waiting for me in the cosy chintz furnished reception area that doubles as a bar. He had the corner seat beside the log fire, and got to his feet when I walked in. He looked like a philanthropic millionaire who'd been forced to meet one of the masses. Courtesy is all.

He shook my hand firmly. 'Ms O'Connell. Let me get you an aperitif.' He glanced at the glass in his other hand. 'I'm having Kir. What would you like?'

Prospective employers usually prefer to think they are hiring modest social drinkers, so I side-stepped my first choice, straight MacCallans, and opted for a dry white wine.

Drinks in hand, we settled down to a bit of casual chit-chat. Serious business, by mutual and unspoken consent, was reserved for table, where there would be a space between ourselves and any big ears.

It was a useful fifteen minutes. I discovered that Tomlinson had been raised in Yorkshire, his father had worked in the steel industry, and times had been tough but happy. Since taking his degree, he had worked in the oil business around the world.

This had cost him his marriage. His wife had got tired of moving from place to place, and divorced him four years ago. He didn't seem too upset about it.

All interesting stuff; the only trouble was that he winkled out more about me than I had been prepared to tell. Why should I mention that I'd been divorced for eight years, and rabbit on about my reasons for starting up on my own? Beyond me.

And I was beginning to suspect that he was hard-nosed as hell under his urbane exterior. Warning bell number one.

We wandered through to the back room, past the little alcoves of pink-clothed private tables laden with gleaming cutlery and shining crystal, to a secluded one of our own beside the patio doors. This man was an organiser. The nearest table was ten feet away.

The order placed, Tomlinson looked at me steadily. 'Let's get down to business, Ms O'Connell. Yukon Discovery has a problem, and the main board is divided on how to deal with it. That in itself isn't novel, for us or any other business; but some important decisions have to be made, and made soon, and there is a feeling that these can't proceed until we have a better idea of the extent of the problem.'

I nodded, breaking off when a tiny but exquisite prawn and lobster salad was placed in front of me and begged to be eaten. Tomlinson seemed surprised when I started. I wondered how long he planned to sit and look at his.

Not long. He forked a mouthful and swallowed it in the same movement. 'On the surface, it seems pretty straight-forward. It's either a personnel difficulty, with somebody upset by recent changes trying to get their own back, or we have a case of industrial sabotage.' His gaze hardened, warning me not to argue.

An argument was the last thing I wanted – bad for the digestion – but I was getting impatient for a few facts. And I didn't understand why Tomlinson was being so close-mouthed. Unless he was having second thoughts about hiring me.

He started to give me a run down on the oil business, and the sort of problems that could arise. I listened carefully. Our plates were whisked away, and the main course arrived with a flourish. I got stuck in. The food was scrumptious, but I wasn't here to enjoy myself.

'What has actually been happening?' I asked, between mouthfuls. 'And how long has it been going on?'

Tomlinson looked at me sourly, as if he had read my mind and didn't like it. 'The board introduced a new policy six months ago, with widespread changes in training and safety, as a pilot scheme in the Scottish branch. The intention was to extend it throughout the company. Trouble is, the feed-back we're getting is bad news.'

'So, why isn't this new policy being dropped?'

'Because not everybody is convinced that it's the root of the problem,' he gritted. 'Sabotage is a strong possibility. In which case, once it's dealt with these new plans can go ahead.'

He finished his chicken fricassee and raised his eyes to mine. I felt as if I'd been blasted with dry ice. 'There is a lot of prestige and money involved here, Ms O'Connell,' he said quietly. 'And people can play dirty.'

I digested his last remark along with the crumbs of my vegetable pie.

There was playing dirty and playing dirty. I hoped he wasn't suggesting physical violence. Outrageous lies and vicious slander I could cope with. Well, I was beginning to get used to. But I didn't like the idea of lead piping. Or worse.

I took a sip of wine, chose cheese before the pudding, and stared at Tomlinson. Pleasantries are a small price to pay for a good meal, but we were running out of time. And I wasn't much wiser than when I started.

I asked myself the question. Do I play safe or not? Since that sounded as if I was adopting a sensible approach, I allowed myself thirty seconds more consideration than it deserved, and still I nearly blew it.

'You've given me a nice press release,' I said bluntly. 'Isn't it about time you gave me some facts?'

'That sort of information would be very useful to our competitors,' he snapped. A second later, cold humour gleamed in his eyes. 'If they aren't already aware of it.'

I munched a portion of Stilton. He was starting to look as if he had added things up. Was he going to opt for the man on the spot exercising his judgement and to hell with head office, or was he going to be professional? I counted to ten before I took up the cudgels.

'I treat all information as confidential, Mr Tomlinson. So far, all I know is that Yukon Discovery has some unspecified problem that may be down to a personal vendetta, or industrial sabotage. That's just not enough for me to work on.'

He spooned up some chocolate mousse. I tried to stop my hand shaking as I reached out for my own spoon. There was no point getting mad, better, as they say, to get even.

Finished, Tomlinson dabbed his napkin to the corners of his mouth and stared across at me. 'Three things.' He held up one finger. 'One: there seems to be a lot of ill-feeling, but it's all under the surface, and that's the kind that can blow up. Two.' A second digit joined the first. 'The training scheme in new routines doesn't seem to be working. After six months, most of the men don't know any more than they did when they started.' The third finger popped up. 'Three: there have been a number of accidents, avoidable accidents. Is it sabotage? We don't know.' The blue eyes zeroed to frost. 'One of these at a time? Maybe. All of them at the same time? No way. Too much of a coincidence.'

I was inclined to agree. And I felt that we were finally getting somewhere. Was I interested? I thought so. But there was something that had to be thrashed out first. I said yes to coffee and sat back. He looked at me quizzically.

I got straight to the point. 'I'll need unrestricted access,' I said, calmly. 'Access to papers, people and places.'

His eyes turned into steel bolts. 'Obviously, any relevant papers will be made available to you.' He leaned across the table, looking as if he was having a hard time keeping his temper. 'And I'll arrange any meetings and visits that you think are necessary.'

I sighed. Some things never change.

'I am afraid that's not feasible, Mr Tomlinson. One reason is that I don't know ahead of time who I want to talk to, or what I want to see. Another is that I have to be seen to be independent, free to follow up leads as and when.' I shot him a smile as a pacifier. It didn't seem to work, but I persevered. 'You'll appreciate that anything less makes it look as if it's just a PR job.'

Tomlinson looked as if he didn't appreciate anything of the kind, and cared even less. He appeared to be grinding his teeth. Maybe there was something wrong with his coffee.

'Do you mean to tell me,' he said heavily, 'that you expect to wander around the sites and offices of Yukon Discovery, going where you like and talking to whom you like? And' – his lips widened into a passable snarl – 'you expect to lay your hands on business papers, as and when you see fit?'

What could I say? He'd put it in a nutshell. 'Yes,' I said.

'Well, let me tell you, Ms O'Connell, if I have any say in the matter, hell will freeze over first.' His accompanying glare made it quite clear that he did have a say in the matter – and it would.

I stood up. 'In that case, Mr Tomlinson, we don't seem to have anything else to discuss.' I thanked him for lunch and took myself off.

When I looked back, he was biting savagely on the end of a cigar. It made me realise just how badly I wanted a cigarette.

I got in the car. Passing isolated houses, stuck beside steep, winter-bleak fields and bare trees circled by raucous rooks, I reached the straight and aimed for Stirling. I would pick up the motorway there. Whether I would have been quicker taking another route was a question I didn't intend to bother my pretty little head about. I had more important things to consider.

I knew that Tomlinson controlled the European end of Yukon's operations. Now, that might not sound much when it's said quickly, but it involves a lot of countries, a lot of money, and it was growing. A pussy cat wouldn't last long, and Tomlinson looked as if he was on top of things. So, he was no pussy cat.

He was also against one-man – or one-woman? – operations. And he had made it clear that he didn't intend to have anyone wandering around his patch, without him knowing exactly where they were going and who they were talking to.

It didn't look promising. But this was nothing new.

I specialise in company investigations. I've been involved in a couple of cases of industrial sabotage, but more often it's straightforward review of management practice. Straightforward? That's a laugh.

One of the problems is that executives rarely welcome my attentions. The inept ones are scared they'll be found out, the others think they know more than I do – about everything. Either way, the end result is the same.

The first move is to make sure that I'm kept in my place – at the bottom of the heap. The second is to try to fix it that I have to tell them everything I'm doing, before I do it. That way they can exercise their superior intellect and judgement, and run the investigation.

This is where a difference of opinion arises. I happen to think that if I'm doing the investigating, then I run it. That means unrestricted access and no management interference. Pedantic is one of the milder terms of abuse I've had thrown at me for refusing to compromise on this.

Tomlinson wasn't the first and wouldn't be the last to try to fit a bridle and blinkers. But until this was thrashed out, I wasn't about to consider myself hired.

As if this wasn't enough to be going on with, warning bell number two was ringing. I tried to work out why.

Maybe it was the maverick quality about Tomlinson that was unsettling. Despite his polish, I suspected that the uncivilised side to his nature wasn't as deeply buried as it should be. And I didn't care for the way he stared at me when he thought I wasn't looking.

I slowed down for Moodiesburn and was overtaken by a manic driver who didn't recognise thirty signs when they were crowding the pavement. After a moment's self-righteousness, I got back to the case in hand and started to count my blessings. I found one. I wouldn't have to buy any food today.

I brooded. The financial crunch time was getting closer. If I had been willing to bend a little, I could have tied up that contract and had money in the bank. The alternative, life as a 9-to-5 employee, rose up like a spectre and I winced.

It started to rain, a regular west of Scotland downpour. Sheets of water drummed on the car and bounced up from the road, reducing visibility to fifty feet. I turned on the wipers and slowed down.

In a defensive urge, I said my favourite four-letter word, loudly, and prayed that it might be magically transmitted through the ether to Stanley's ears. I knew it would upset him – unladylike.

Turning off the motorway, I swished along the curving St George's Cross slip-road, passing tree-tops, feeling as if I was flying. The arrival on Great Western Road was abrupt.

Lined by four-storey tenements with ground-level shops and bars, the road was wet and jammed. Parked cars had pushed the traffic into one lane each way. There's never a traffic warden around when you need one.

I found myself stuck between a delivery lorry and a bus, listening to water sloshing on the roof. As I inched forward in first, I decided that what was required that evening was a little conviviality. I ran through some of the possibilities, and tried to pretend I had the luxury of choice.

When I parked outside my abode ten minutes later and made a run through the rain for the door, I still hadn't come up with anything.

A Change
in the Weather

She was waiting for me. Her door shot open as if spring loaded. I didn't even get time to wipe my feet. My neighbour Miss Hilda Alison Green, HAG for short, stood in her doorway, a Fury incarnate. I was only grateful the other two couldn't make it.

She's in her eighties and denies it. She is also around five feet two inches in height, and insists she has been five foot six all her life and nothing has changed. Every time I see her she is bristling with disapproval. Like now. I often wonder why I don't hate her.

HAG crossed her arms, pushed up her bust, and fixed her schoolma'am eyes on me. 'That man was back,' she sniffed.

I stood, the water dripping down my face, and stared, bemused. The floral apron was the type that wraps round in two parts, one under, the other over, with two ties secured in a bow at the back. Sleeveless and low-necked, the apron showed the bright blue sweater she was wearing underneath. Everything had been ironed to within an inch of its life.

She had on the red mop cap she uses when she's dusting. Fascinated, I finished the check-up by looking at her feet.

She was wearing an oversized pair of lime-green floppy socks.

An octogenarian hippie. Lord save us.

'I told him you were out, but he still went up,' she said accusingly. She peered at me to see how I was taking this information. I tried to concentrate. Her frown deepened, presumably to emphasise the gravity of the situation. 'He told me he was leaving you a note.'

The clue came in the disparaging he, and I saw the light. She was saving me from a man. Or from myself. Or both of us from each other. It all depends how you look at these things.

I shook my head to clear it. But what man? I wasn't exactly getting knocked down in the rush. I came to the conclusion that I needed a hint.

Since an expression of guilt speeds up communication with HAG – something to do with her Presbyterian upbringing – I tried to look contrite. I must have succeeded, because she blossomed immediately.

'He still has that noisy old blue car,' she said, her voice doom ridden.

There was only one person that could be. I was delighted, but knew better than show it. 'You mean, Dr Grant?' I stressed the doctor bit, to make the point that Donald was a respectable member of the community.

She frowned on, having none of it.

HAG has no immediate family in the area; I think she's scared them off. But she has a coterie of friends: tiny white-haired body-builders, who meet regularly to indulge in the verbal slaughter of acquaintances and the youth of today. Youth, by their definition, being anyone under sixty.

Since HAG's dusting usually precedes one of their get-togethers, I decided to make myself scarce. I started up the stairs, two at a time. 'Thanks, Miss G,' I shouted back.

Her door slammed. I grinned, dumped the bags and picked up the note. Scrawled on the back of a used envelope was 'Dinner at Franci's? Tonight at 8? Explain later. Lots of L. D.'

I hadn't seen Donald since he had moved to Aberdeen six

months ago, although he'd phoned once to tell me that he was being worked into the ground. I hummed round the flat, tidying up.

He's the exception in my life – a lover who became a friend. I know this is supposed to happen all the time. People say it does, anyway. But not to me.

I poured myself what I choose to describe as a small dram, and drank it reflectively. Given my experiences with the opposite sex, it doesn't surprise me that I am in no hurry to get involved with anyone again. Even Martin.

I looked at the glass. If I put some more whisky in it, I could drink it in the bath. So I did.

As I steeped and supped, Yukon Discovery receded from my mind, along with thoughts of the money I badly needed. Tonight, worry was being relegated to the back burner.

Dried, I slipped on a tight black dress and tore at my hair until it stood out from my head, stiff with fright. When poverty is hammering on the door, a little style is required. I phoned a taxi.

In the restaurant, Donald and I flew into each other's arms, hugged, and stepped back laughing. When I got a proper look at him, I had to work to hide my surprise at how tired he looked. And he'd lost weight.

Donald's broad frame never carries excess flab. He eats like a horse and burns off the excess calories by rushing around, this was the first time I'd ever seen him verging on slim.

He smiled teasingly, and looked more like his old self. 'Good to see you, Cat. You're looking terrific. Got a new man in your life?'

'A man is the last thing I need, Donald,' I countered briskly. I may be a lukewarm feminist, but I have my pride.

His lopsided smile blew the months away. 'Sure.' He held me close and whispered in my ear. 'But you're cooking.'

I clung to him. He held me tighter and we swayed together. I burrowed my face into his shoulder and a shiver ran through me. I almost groaned aloud. He was right.

I unravelled myself, and tried to look cheerful about it. 'It's good to see you.'

'And you.' He gave me a lingering kiss on the cheek. 'It's been too long.' He took my coat and handed it to a waiter. Gripping my elbow, he led me to the table. 'I've got a lot to tell you.' His tone of voice made me look at him. His face was grim.

'Are we talking serious?' I asked quietly.

'Put it this way, Cat. I think you'll find what I have to tell you . . . interesting . . .'

Since this was our synonym for all hell's broken loose, or it's as serious as it can become without involving war, pestilence and famine, I sat down carefully. I had no appetite. Even if I had arrived with one, I would've lost it on the spot.

I closed the menu thoughtfully and laid it down. 'I'll settle for something light and tasty, like a bottle of Pouilly-Fumé.'

I watched him as his brown eyes flicked over the menu. He raised them indifferently as he stated his choice and ordered the wine. This wasn't the laid-back Donald I'd known for twenty years. This was an uptight, worried man, with a bitter twist to his mouth.

Donald ate solely for nourishment, keeping conversation to the have you seen or heard variety. I kept him company by swigging the Fumé. I imagined it was bringing a sparkle to my eyes. It certainly felt like it.

I squinted at the bottle and tried to gauge how much was left. I hoped he would tell me what was wrong soon, because I was rapidly approaching the stage of sympathetic stupor. The next stage was coma.

He poured himself a glass of wine, leaned on his elbows and stared across at me. 'I've got to tell somebody what's been happening, Cat, and you're the best person I can think of.'

His eyes were red-rimmed with exhaustion. I reached across impulsively and took his hand. He gripped mine tightly and gave a wry grin.

'Okay, from the top.' He took a drink and sighed. 'When I started six months ago, I was based in Aberdeen. There wasn't a great deal of work: routine checks for insurance, injections for personnel going overseas, that sort of thing.

After a few weeks, a month I think, I was posted off-shore. You know, the usual two weeks on two weeks off.'

I sat up straight at that. 'I didn't know you were on the rigs. Or even that you had anything to do with oil. I thought you were on contract to a big business conglomerate?'

'Sure,' he agreed, dryly. 'It's called Yukon Discovery. Small in North Sea Oil perhaps, but business-wise they don't get much bigger.'

This came as even more of a surprise. I stared fixedly across the table. If Donald had mentioned the name of the company before, I would have remembered it. So why hadn't he?

A thought struck me. Had it been deliberate?

What was going on here?

He rubbed his eyes. 'It's been a funny business from the start. Too much secrecy about routine matters. I suppose I should have been warned.' He gave a wry smile. 'I've never agreed with you on that, have I? That secrecy's an open door to malpractice. Well, I think I'm becoming converted.'

He gazed earnestly at me. 'I'm sorry to be such a bore. But it helps to talk about it. Particularly when I'm beginning to think that I'm simply overtired, and imagining things.' His eyes blazed with a little of their old fire. 'The problem is that there's been a number of accidents. Avoidable accidents. And they're being brushed under the carpet.'

I sat up even straighter. Coincidences always have that effect on me. Tomlinson hadn't gone into detail, but he too had spoken of avoidable accidents.

The hair at the back of my neck twitched ominously and a rush of cold ran up my backbone. I don't know about anybody else, but I trust my internal trouble diviner implicitly, and it was telling me, in triplicate, that there was trouble afoot.

What was worse, it was beginning to look as if everybody was doing their best to deliver it to my doorstep. And I could live without it – easily.

I glared mutinously over at Donald. Why me? After all, he's six foot two and brawny. I'm a five seven bundle of bones. I registered the greyness of his skin and felt guilty.

He didn't know I'd been approached by Yukon Discovery, so how was he to know that he was putting pressure on me. I picked up the bottle and let the last dribble slide into my glass. It was my turn to sigh.

I took myself in hand. 'What makes you say that things are being brushed under the carpet?'

'I've formally requested that these incidents be investigated – three times in the last two months – and nothing's been done.' He looked at me sharply. He seemed to find something in my expression not to his liking. 'I mean a thorough investigation of the company, Cat. The police have done what they can but unless,' his eyes shadowed, 'until, someone is killed, it's out with their jurisdiction.'

I wasn't following Donald's logic, and wondered if he was getting things out of proportion. Accidents are never good news, but they do happen – accidentally. Was there something else he wasn't telling me?

I must have looked puzzled, for he burst out.

'I think there's some skulduggery going on. And it's big; maybe even spread throughout the company, or it will be, if it's not stopped.' His eyes suddenly took on an anger that I never thought would be turned in my direction. 'Okay, I know. You think I've gone bananas as well.'

This was getting out of hand.

'Wait a minute, Donald,' I said quickly. 'Remember me?' I tapped myself on the chest. 'This is your old friend, Cat. Stop looking at me as if I'm the enemy.'

He gave a nervy laugh. 'Sorry, Cat. I guess this is really getting to me.' His eyes looked haunted. 'I'm here on sick leave. Enforced. They're trying to make out that I'm suffering from stress; that I'm not fit to do my job.' He held my gaze. 'I've been set up. Somebody wants me out of the way, because I've been nosing around.'

This was bad news. Enforced sick leave due to stress would be no help in getting another post. Doctors were expected to cope with stress; not just their own, but everybody else's as well. If they started having nervous breakdowns, the NHS would cave in, medical consultancies would disappear.

I saw Donald look away as if he couldn't bear to see the expression in my eyes. I knew how he felt. There are times when we all need blind, unquestioning loyalty, no matter how unreasonable. Anything less and something dies.

And if I'd been the one it might die on, I wouldn't want to watch it happen either.

I studied him, ticking off the symptoms. His eyes were bloodshot, his skin grey and clammy, and his hair needed a trim. He looked all in. There was no doubt about it, he was exhausted, stressed out. And with the dangerous working conditions on rigs, it wasn't unreasonable for a company to insist that he took sick leave.

But if he said he'd been set up, I believed him.

'Well, they've managed to get you out of the way, temporarily,' I said. A slow grin started at the corners of his mouth. I grinned back. 'We've got lots to talk about. First, a good night's sleep, at my place.'

I glowered impatiently at his raised eyebrow. Where did he get the energy to play games? 'Stop trying to pretend that I'm making advances,' I said ill-temperedly. 'It just strikes me that if you're in trouble, that might be safer. And it will give us a chance to talk things through.'

'I agree. Let's go.' He had the bill paid in minutes and led me at a fair lick out of the restaurant.

As he hailed a taxi, I had a good look at him. He seemed rejuvenated. Could lust be rekindled from ashes? I shivered. Maybe I was about to find out. The trouble was I wasn't sure that I was in any condition to meet the challenge. I raised my eyes to the heavens and got into the taxi.

We crept upstairs, giggling. Must have been the wine. Part of me hoped that we weren't making too much noise, in case we disturbed Sanderson, my boorish new neighbour. The other part didn't give a fig.

Donald collapsed laughing on the sofa, and when the telephone rang I fell over his feet trying to get to it.

'Ms O'Connell? There's no need to answer. Just listen.' The male voice was a harsh growl. I started to sober up, rapidly. 'A little advice for your friend, the good doctor.'

The caller sneered, 'Yes. We know he's with you. Tell him to stay away from things that don't concern him. Or he'll end up getting hurt. Badly hurt. We don't give two warnings, Ms O'Connell. Believe me.' The line went dead.

I believed him as well. It must be my night for it.

I stood holding the receiver, feeling like an undertaker who had called at the wrong house. My mind couldn't make sense of what I had just heard. And I didn't blame it.

I turned to tell Donald, getting ready to laugh when he wrote it off as a hoax. He was stretched out, fast asleep. Great help. There was something to be said for looking on the black side, after all. Less chance of being disappointed.

I took off his shoes and loosened his collar and belt, and covered him with a quilt. Then I undressed, slipped on a robe and made a mug of lapsang souchong. I curled up in an armchair, my hands shaking.

Hoax or no hoax, that was as clear a threat of violence as I'd ever heard. And I hate violence. It scares me. Even as a child, I only got into a physical fight when it was unavoidable. Like when the alternatives were to move home or have plastic surgery.

I thought about it a bit more. That phone call certainly confirmed what Donald had said. Something was going on at Yukon Discovery, and he was being targeted.

He must have stumbled into something pretty big to get this much attention. The anonymous caller knew exactly where to find him. And he'd talked of 'we'. So who were the others? And were they company men or outsiders?

As for Tomlinson. Did he know more than he was saying? Maybe he was against an investigation because he had something to hide – not just because his nose had been put out of joint.

In the morning, I would get the full story from Donald: dates, names and places. That would be a start. And when I saw Tomlinson again I would have some idea of the sort of questions I should be asking.

For I knew I would be seeing Tomlinson again. I figured he'd have to swallow his aggravation and offer me the contract. It would be foolish of him to openly buck the decision of his board, when he could quietly undermine me later. And he didn't give the impression of being a fool.

But assuming I was right, what was I going to do about it? Did I really want to work for Yukon Discovery and its representative on this part of the earth, Tomlinson?

After some more thought, I decided this wasn't the issue. It was simpler than that, much simpler. To be precise, it was an either–or situation.

Either I follow my instinct to avoid trouble and refuse the contract, or, I get stupid and want to chase after answers to some awkward questions, and accept.

I fell asleep knowing that I wasn't that stupid.

An Evil Hour

When I came to, I was curled up in the armchair covered by the quilt and it was nearly lunchtime. Donald had left a note. Too lazy to get up for my glasses, I waved it in front of my face until the words swam into focus.

'Something very important to do in Aberdeen. Explain later. Love. D.'

When it registered, I sat bolt upright. What was so important that he had to dash off without telling me? And to go back to Aberdeen, when he was exhausted and supposed to be on sick leave?

I didn't like what I was thinking. But it wouldn't go away. He was off investigating. I could feel it in my bones.

And I hadn't had a chance to tell him about that phone call. Now I didn't know where to contact him. All right, the call was probably a prank, in which case it didn't matter. But even the remotest possibility that the caller meant what he said had me worried.

I threw off the quilt, stood up and tightened the belt of the robe, and made for the phone. There was something to be said for not going to bed at night. Makes it easier to get up in the morning.

I drew blanks.

I tried his parents, and had to back-step daintily because they hadn't seen him for weeks. They wouldn't have been delighted to hear that he had been in Glasgow and not visited them.

I tried three of his friends. The two that were in hadn't seen him recently and said to tell him it was about time he called round.

I was getting desperate so I called Donald's girlfriend, Anna-Marie, her of the platinum hair and pneumatic body. I needed to be desperate to call Anna-Marie. I was never able to talk to her for more than five seconds without wanting to pull her hair, out by the roots. She didn't need it anyway, just keeping an empty space warm.

The phone was ringing. I fretted and wished she would hurry up and answer. There was a click as it was picked up.

'Hello. This is Anna-Marie speaking.' The voice was breathy and vaguely mid-American. 'Who is calling?'

'Cat,' I said urgently. 'It's Cat O'Connell, Anna.'

'Anna-Marie,' she corrected, sugary sweet.

I breathed heavily and capitulated. I needed information more than a fight. 'I'm sorry to trouble you Anna-Marie, but it's important that I get in touch with Donald. Do you have an Aberdeen number where I can contact him?' She took so long to answer I wondered if she was practising her pout.

'Donald?' she said coolly. 'Donald Grant?'

If she'd been in the room, I would have spat in her eye. How many Donalds had she been sleeping with lately, for God's sake? 'Yes,' I snarled.

'No, Donald isn't with me,' Anna-Marie snapped, the mid-American twang out the window. 'I don't know where he is, and I don't care. If you must know, I found out he was seeing someone else.' There was a moment's silence. 'Some teuchter from up North,' she screeched. And slammed the phone down.

I smirked and hung up. Every cloud has a silver lining.

But even good news has its limitations. And this wasn't getting me any nearer finding Donald. I thought about who

I could call next, and talked myself into leaving it for a couple of hours. By then he might contact me, or reappear.

Stanley came on the phone. He said that Tomlinson had been in touch and would be phoning me later. That the contract was on if I managed to behave like a normal human being long enough to sign it. And did I realise that I was overdrawn again, and he didn't recollect giving permission.

I held the phone away from my ear. When he got tired waiting for me to get aggravated, he rang off.

I showered, dressed and caught up with some paperwork. I should have sent out a few looking-for-work letters but didn't. On the way to the post, I stopped by to ask HAG if she needed any groceries.

The door edged open, and HAG's face peeked out, a little above the doorknob. The parchment skin extended into a sharp nose, on each side of which was a fierce eye, and I could see the whisper of combative whisker across her upper lip.

She was wearing a large brown sweater, brown trousers and a pair of furry boots. She seemed tired. She shivered suddenly, as if she was feeling the cold.

Worried, I took another look, then tried not to smile. The old devil; hung over more like. She and her cronies must have been at the sherry bottle.

Her hand appeared with a piece of paper. I took it. It was a grocery list. I marvelled. Is this woman fey, or is she fey? My mouth was still open when the door shut.

I went shopping, a browse over fruit and veg piled high on a pavement stand, and a quick visit to the small local general store that smells of spices. This didn't take too long and I enjoyed it. As usual HAG's list was short, so I added some extras. We never discuss these extras.

The nearest we got was in the early days, when she tried to wrap them around my ears. My defence was that I was trying to curry favour. Since nothing more has been said on the matter, it seems that this meets with her approval.

I rang her bell, the door swung open, and her bag trolley was abruptly pushed forward. Although she still looked a bit shaky, her eyes were like gimlets as she watched me load up.

'I hope you've been careful with the eggs,' she fussed, checking the box to make sure. She glared as if refreshing a bad memory. 'That was a terrible time you came in last night. Was that man with you?'

I worked away in silence. She had that look on her face that demands an answer, but she wasn't going to get one.

'And there was another man up at your door, when you were at the shops.' When I still said nothing, she snorted, 'Men. Wouldn't see them in my road.' She disappeared into the gloom and the door swung shut behind her.

I hadn't been paying much attention, so it took me a minute to realise I wasn't getting my cup of tea. I was in the dog-house, again. I smiled.

I was still smiling when I turned on the radio for the news. It was a couple of minutes before the hour. I chopped busily at fresh basil.

By now I had seen the error of my ways. I was preparing a supper that I would enjoy while I was waiting, or that Donald and I would both enjoy when he returned. After I had given him abuse for treating me as if I was one of his women.

I tuned in. The clipped voice of the announcer said, '. . . a blue Rover has been recovered from Aberdeen harbour. Reports of a body have yet to be confirmed. News has come through of the latest million pound purchase . . .' I switched it off.

I felt as if a fox had broken into the hen-house, and I was the only hen in residence. I took a few deep breaths and stuck my head between my knees. I don't suppose it would've helped the hen much either.

I sat up and told myself to calm down, and think rationally. I was jumping to conclusions here. All because of that phone call. Why decide that it was Donald's car that had been dragged from the harbour? There were thousands of blue Rover cars, all over the country.

I reached for the telephone. Rationality is a great thing, but sometimes there's an inner voice that tells you things you can't reason out for yourself. Mine was trying to attract my attention. And I thought I should listen.

I phoned a reporter friend. Said yes, it would be good to get together one evening, catch up on our news. And, by the way, had she heard anything more about the car pulled out of Aberdeen harbour?

She had. She had the number and the news that there was a body, presumed to be that of the car owner. Of course the police wouldn't release his name until he had been formally identified. Confidentially though, the name she'd been given was . . . umm . . . Grant. D. Grant.

I thanked her for her help.

The deep ache started to spread through my stomach, pushing icy fingers into my chest. Shivering with cold, I wiped the tears furiously away and tried the number again.

Answer dammit. Doreen wasn't in. I'd tried twice. Martin had to be in. He just had to be. I pressed the L for re-dial. The phone rang again. It was picked up.

'Martin Black.'

'Martin, Mar—' I choked on the words, trying hard not to cry.

'Who is it?' Martin's voice was sharp with concern.

That made me worse. 'Martin,' I wailed. 'It's Cat.'

'Cat!' He sounded as if he couldn't believe it. 'What the hell's happened? Are you hurt? Where are you?' He shouted down the phone. 'For God's sake, Cat, will you answer me!'

'At home,' I whimpered.

I wanted to crawl into a dark corner and pull a rug over my head, and stay there, for ever. The pain reached my chest. I thought it was going to burst. I panted to ease the agony. It was like childbirth, without a future.

'Wait there!' he shouted. 'Don't move. I'll be right round. Cat, are you listening?'

I couldn't answer. I looked at the receiver as if it was a new invention and hung up. Sure I'd wait. I'd no plans to go anywhere. I curled up on the sofa and hugged myself, tight.

The pain was expanding. My heart hurt – dull-hot.

When the bell went I walked woodenly through and opened the door. Martin stood on the doorstep, crisp and efficient in his lawyer's garb: a sparkling white shirt and neatly knotted tie, black jacket and striped trousers, and the black cashmere overcoat.

I used to mix with this attire every day of the week. Now, I felt as if I was in court about to face an interrogation.

Martin is in his late forties and looks ten years younger. Married once, he doesn't talk about it, other than say it was his fault the marriage broke down – and that's a hang-up if I've ever heard one. I began to wonder why I'd called him.

He looked me over, his eyes worried. 'What the hell's happened? Are you all right?' He shut the door and put his arms around me. I stood and shivered, icy cold, unable to speak. He urged me forward. 'Come on.'

He walked me to the sitting-room and sat me down, and went straight to the kitchen and made a mug of sweet tea. He stood over me until I drank it. Then he took me to bed.

I cried a lot. I told him what had happened in great gasping sobs and cried some more. He wiped my tears. I blew my nose. He wiped my tears again. I finally snuffled into silence.

He reached for me and eased me astride him. I fell asleep, eventually.

I'll never need anyone the way I needed Martin that night. But the minute I wakened, I knew that something had changed. I slid my eyes sideways and looked at the room. I felt like a visitor.

Martin's lawyer's pin-stripe had been dumped on a chair. There was a pair of knickers and a bra lying on the floor, on top of paperbacks. Other than that, it was reasonably tidy. But whoever lived here didn't bother much about decor.

I stuck a foot out from under the covers and tested the temperature. It was refreshingly cool. In bed, it was like Dante's Inferno.

Martin was still asleep. When he turned and tossed his arm over me, my whole body started to ache. I felt as if I'd spent the night being bounced off a wall.

I slipped out of bed carefully, showered with the door

shut, and tip-toed back through for a cup of tea. I had a hammer of guilt in my hand and I started to beat myself mercilessly over the head with it.

If it had been hard going with Martin before, what was it going to be like now? After making out I wasn't ready for any commitment, suddenly I treat him as if he was the answer to my dreams.

I'd dropped myself right in it this time. Nice one, Cat.

My waist was grabbed in a pincer grip. 'Gotcha.' I rose into the air.

When I landed, I snapped, 'You shouldn't sneak up on people like that, Martin.' Since this only made me feel more guilty, I took a deep breath and concentrated on filling the kettle.

Finished, I made an effort to be friendly. 'Would you like some tea?'

He smiled gently, his eyes focused on me. 'Please.' He pulled the towel more closely round his midriff. 'How do you feel?'

I poured the water into the pot, feeling as honourable as a snake in the grass. I was grateful to Martin, but that look on his face was beginning to get irritating.

'I'm fine. Honest,' I said sharply. I pushed a mug towards him. 'Here, take this.'

When the phone rang, I grabbed it. It was Doreen.

'I've just heard. Cat, this is awful.' We listened to each other breathing for a while. 'I'm coming right round,' she said quietly, and rang off.

I turned and tried to meet Martin's eyes. Being awash with guilt, this was difficult. 'I appreciate it, Martin. Your being here, I mean. Very much. I don't know what I would've done without you.' I meant every word. But I wanted him to go away.

'That's all right. Don't worry.' He reached an arm around my shoulders. 'I'll sort things out, arrange a car, flowers, and so on.' He looked at his watch, and smiled as if he'd won a national lottery. 'I'd better get to the office. Two meetings this morning.' He pressed his lips against my cheek. 'We'll talk later, darling.'

I ran it past myself one more time. He'll arrange this, that and the other, and, 'We'll talk later, darling.' He was referring to a funeral, Donald's funeral. But who would've guessed?

If I'd been a dog I would've bared my teeth.

When Martin finally made for the door, groomed and civilised, a pillar of the establishment, I held up my cheek to be kissed. And added depression to my grief and guilt.

Doreen appeared ten minutes later. She let herself in and rushed into the kitchen, where I sat hunched up on a stool, drinking more tea. We looked miserably at each other.

She was white-faced but as beautiful as ever, wide blue eyes and fine features. A natural blonde, she has the look of someone who wakens each morning with a song in her heart. Even now, with her eyes red from crying, she still had that sparkle.

Slipping off her wool jacket, she hung it on the back of a chair. She was wearing a cream silk blouse, tucked into a neat pair of tailored trousers that showed off her slim figure.

Her gaze was disconcertingly direct. It always is. It reflects her practical approach to life. She focused it on me, full strength, looking for the hurt so she could kiss it better. We grabbed each other tight. I hung on for dear life.

When I'd calmed down, I told her what I knew. It wasn't much.

She heard me out in silence, then looked at me in disbelief. 'Oh, Cat. It's bad enough that Donald . . . But . . . but this is awful. You're not serious.' Her eyes were twin circles of horror. 'You don't really think Donald's been . . . been murdered . . .?'

Her voice trailed away and the sentence hung in the air. Before I could answer, she said briskly, 'You'll have to go to the police, Cat. Let them deal with it. That's their job.'

I felt like saying, I know that, think I'm daft?

I stopped myself in time, and mulled things over. Doreen watched me carefully, as if she thought I was on the verge of rushing across the room and throwing myself out of the window.

I kept coming back to the same conclusion. I'd nothing to

go to the police with. Only a phone call, the content of which I was beginning to think I'd imagined. And there wasn't a lot they could do with that.

Anyway, the police were quite capable of deciding for themselves whether there were any suspicious circumstances. The only problem was this could take time, and I was beginning to feel decidedly draughty round the gills. Whoever made that call knew my name, and where I lived.

But whatever had possessed me to tell Doreen?

I was furious: me and my big mouth. Doreen is a loyal friend, but she shares her life with Stanley. Not that she tells him everything, but she would tell him something like this. And I didn't think he should hear it. Probably have me locked up, if the police didn't get to me first.

'I didn't say he'd been murdered, Doreen.' She gave me a 'who're you trying to kid' look. 'Well, I didn't mean to,' I said hurriedly. 'I wasn't thinking straight. I just meant that the job put unnecessary pressure on him.'

Surely that was non-committal enough.

The phone rang. I didn't know where to turn, but since I couldn't escape and Doreen was still looking at me as if I was ready for the funny farm, I picked it up. It was Tomlinson. He didn't sound any happier than I felt.

'Ms O'Connell, I understand that you are still interested in working for Yukon Discovery.' He took a patient breath. 'Well, I've thought it over and decided to offer you the contract. Perhaps you'll be good enough to arrange an appointment with my secretary, so that we can sort out details: your fee, etc.?'

I felt my hackles rise. Tomlinson must have heard about Donald, but he was acting as if nothing had happened.

'Thank you, Mr Tomlinson,' I said icily. Doreen's eyes widened. I moved the phone out of her reach. 'But I have more important things to . . .'

The receiver buzzed in my ear and I gave it a shake. I'd been cut off. Then I saw Doreen standing with the power point in her hand.

'What the hell do you think you're doing, Doreen?' I raged.

'Stopping you making a fool of yourself,' she said calmly. 'Now go and have your bath and get dressed. I'll make a bite to eat. Then we'll talk.'

I was ready for a fight.

I looked stubbornly at her, thinking about it, but decided she wasn't the person I should be fighting with. There were better ways of excising my pain. And getting to work on finding the people responsible for Donald's death would be a good beginning.

That was when I really started to think.

Not Waving

By the time I sat down for breakfast I knew that I was taking the contract. It was the only chance I had of finding out whether Donald's death had anything to do with his work for Yukon Discovery. I would arrange to meet Tomlinson, sort out the details and get some background information.

The first thing I wanted to know was the management structure of the company, and the names and duties of personnel in Scotland. Once I had that clear in my mind, I'd know where to start.

Cooler now, I planned on. I needed to find out how the Aberdeen set-up fitted in to the larger picture, and how much Tomlinson knew about Donald's work there, who he worked with, and who he reported to.

I'd look into Donald's personal life as well. After what he'd told me about Yukon Discovery, I had no compunction about including this in my paid-for time.

And if Anna-Marie was right about him having another woman, I had to find her. She might be able to tell me what had been happening over the last few months.

'Cat.' It came again, louder. 'Cat.'

I looked up. Doreen was sitting at the other side of the breakfast bar, one hand under her chin, giving me her professional GP stare. It took me back.

She and Donald had trained together, which is how I met him. In those days, we'd all been carefree twenty-somethings, newly qualified and ready to set the world to rights, confident that we could do it.

Doreen's gaze has developed its stringent quality over the years, as she fought her personal battle against society's injury and disease. Now it was concentrated on me. I was being examined for signs of incipient emotional collapse.

I glared back. Just because I was in pain, it didn't mean I'd gone soft in the head.

Her blue eyes grew sharper. She was going to look after me whether I liked it or not. 'Black coffee isn't enough, Cat,' she said firmly. The toast rack came winging over to my side. 'You've got to keep up your blood sugar level.'

I wasn't remotely interested in my blood sugar level, and nearly said so.

'I know,' she said gently, as if she'd read my mind. We exchanged glances and smiled. It certainly feels like she knows what I'm thinking sometimes.

We ate in silence. Neither of us cared to talk about Donald. That would come later. I didn't thank her for being here. That was understood.

I poured more coffee. 'How well does Stanley know Edward Tomlinson? Is he just a banking contact, or do you meet socially?'

'Both.'

There are times when I wish Doreen wasn't quite so economical with words. I tried to encourage her to spit out a few more. 'Have they had many business dealings? How often do you see him?'

She stopped me with a half smile. 'I think they've done quite a bit of business together,' she said carefully. Her eyes warned me that I'd have to ask Stanley for details. I shrugged, that was OK. 'Socially? Well, we've met at a few parties. The usual crowd. You know the sort of thing.'

I did. Gatherings of local worthies, most of whom don't

— 40 —

believe in allowing their thought processes to get in the way of their convictions. I held my tongue. I feel bad enough when my brain says such things, when my mouth says them I'm in deep trouble.

I pressed on. 'What do you think of Tomlinson?' I prepared to listen carefully, for Doreen is a fair judge of character, but she took her time answering and I started to get restive.

'I think he's ambitious, very ambitious,' she said finally. 'And he likes the good things in life. But I get the impression he doesn't allow himself to relax often enough to really enjoy them. I also gather' – she looked pointedly at me – 'that he is generally regarded as tough but fair.'

I would have phrased it differently. Like hard-nosed bastard.

'All these questions, Cat. You're not? Not today?' Doreen looked at me and sighed, 'I see that you are.'

She sat for a moment reading the tablecloth, then got up and started to stack dishes. 'Eat with us tonight. I'll expect you at seven.' She held up a firm hand. 'No arguments. You can get on with whatever you're doing today. I'll make sure that you have a decent meal at the end of it.'

I wasn't keen. To be in Stanley's company once a year is a sacrifice. And I only do that because I love Doreen and wouldn't miss her birthday. Any more is an undeserved penance.

But I had questions for him, and Doreen being around might stop us going for each other's jugular – maybe. In any case, if I was set on finding out what had happened to Donald, personal antipathy would have to take a back seat.

'Thanks,' I said. 'That'll be good.'

If Doreen was surprised at how easily I gave in she didn't show it.

'I have to get to the clinic, Cat.' Jacket on and half-way out the door, she hesitated, walked back, and fixed me with another analytic stare. 'You'll do,' she decided. 'Remember. 7 o'clock.'

She leaned over and gave me a hug. I hugged her back, gratefully.

*

My first visit was to the university library. I ploughed all the way up to the top floor, where I expected to find government papers, and some information on North Sea Oil.

I used the microfiche to narrow the search to companies, investments and recent strikes. The mound of material and statistics got me confused. But since this happens a lot, it doesn't worry me. I ferreted on.

I left after two hours. My head buzzed with details I would probably never have any use for and would forget soon anyway, but I was well satisfied.

At least I had an impression of the general set-up I was going to be immersing myself in, and a better idea where to find more detailed information as and when needed. Company records could wait until I had read through Yukon Discovery's PR releases.

I went back to the car, ripped the parking ticket off the windscreen and tossed it disgustedly on the passenger seat. Sometimes I think I drive a marked car. Paranoid? Could be. I gritted my teeth and drove off.

I toured George Square searching for a meter. The second time I crawled past the bronze monuments of Victoria and Albert and their stylish mounts, I was feeling decidedly crabby.

I looked past the islands of flower-beds and lawn, to the central, tall fluted Doric column bearing the effigy of Sir Walter Scott. Beyond that, at the east end of the square, the patriarchal bulk of the City Chambers loomed above the Cenotaph.

The loud toot up my back end returned me to the painful present. I engaged first, smartish, and turned to the right, away from the dull frontage of Queen Street Station. A second later, I saw a space and zoomed in.

I nipped across the square, dodging the human traffic, and made my way to the post office with the overdue parcel of wool for my mother. She is a keen knitter with a preference for Scottish yarn, and it makes me feel good to do little things to please her. The fact that Clemency is her favourite is neither here nor there.

The virtuous glow was still with me when I made my last

stop before heading home, for a box of computer paper. My stocks were low, and when I'm working on a case I put information on disk, religiously, and print out from time to time.

I've learned the hard way that findings must be recorded daily, even if they don't seem important at the time. It's only too easy to forget details, or to recall them wrongly, even in the short-term.

And since there's no way of knowing what is relevant until things start to come together, the safest way is to start by trawling and trying to make sense of it later.

I may also, depending on the contract, send in regular reports. One way or another, I use a lot of paper. As usual I went for the better quality; another idiosyncrasy that I can ill afford.

I drove back quickly and was staggering upstairs with the box, when I heard clumping feet heading down. I recognised them. They belonged to my boorish new neighbour, Sanderson the flat-footed security guard.

He'd moved into the flat below me three months ago. Since then he's plagued me with complaints about my late night comings and goings. A frantic social life I have, according to him. I should be so lucky.

He rounded the corner and stopped when he saw me. A big man running to fat, his heavy breathing bulk filled the stairway. His pudgy face screwed up in anticipation and the covering pink sheen spread. I sighed and waited. He lowered his brows over his piggy eyes and gave a grunt of satisfaction.

'Miss O'Connell,' he said stentoriously, 'I have just put a letter through your door.' He trumpeted his throat clear, his cheeks flushing red with the exertion. 'Telling you,' he peered maliciously, 'that I intend taking a petition around these flats, to complain about the hours you keep and the noise your men friends make when they come visiting.' His lewd little eyes gleamed that he knew what went on when they did.

Sounded as if somebody was having fun. Certainly wasn't me.

He lifted his chins. 'What do you think of that then?'

I contemplated telling him, and thought the better of it.

One shove from him and I'd be bouncing back the way I'd come, box and all.

I glowered and backed carefully to the landing and stood against the wall. If he started anything here, I could drop this ton weight on his flat feet. And he'd be the one rolling down the stairs.

We glared at each other malevolently.

'Right then,' he blustered. 'Just as long as you know.'

He sidled past me and I got a strong whiff of sweat mixed with a deadly aftershave. Paint stripper stuff. He stomped on down. When he was safely on the next landing, he shouted back, 'You can't say you haven't been warned.'

I leaned against the wall, shaking with anger. Sanderson is one of those people who makes unpleasantness an art form. It's not all on the surface either: his mind is as repulsive as his body.

I shuddered and trudged on. My next moment of delight was going to be when I phoned Tomlinson, for I had no intention of working through his secretary. I panted upwards, musing on the fact that some days don't get any better.

When I got in, I dumped the box, threw Sanderson's letter in the bin, unopened, and checked the rest of the mail. Still nothing from Allan. That boy deserved a clip on the ear. The pink, scented envelope stood out from the business mail like a red light in suburbia.

Just to make sure, I took another look at the handwriting and checked the postmark. My heart sank. Clemency. No doubt about it.

I wondered what I'd done wrong. Forgotten mother's birthday? Clemency's? Raymond's? Mine? I shook my head, didn't think so. I decided a management decision was called for and tossed it back on the pile. Nothing that couldn't wait.

The coffee was soon ready and I allowed myself to sit and drink it with my feet up, then reached for the phone.

'Ms O'Connell?' A friendly sound entered the cool secretarial tones. 'Please hold. I'll check if Mr Tomlinson's free.'

I said I would, and waited for the inevitable. It didn't take long.

'I'm very sorry, Ms O'Connell. Mr Tomlinson is engaged

at the moment, but he has asked me to arrange an appointment for you tomorrow. Would . . .?'

I interrupted as pleasantly as I could, and was glad I'd taken the trouble to read the name plaque on her desk. 'Thank you, Ms Jordan, that's very kind. But it would be helpful to have a word with Mr Tomlinson. He has my number. When it's convenient, perhaps he could give me ring.'

There was a silence, then she said, 'I'll give him your message, Ms O'Connell.' It was probably my imagination, but she seemed amused.

I put the phone down and decided to get things organised. I'd given up on thinking for the time being, my brain needed a rest, so I concentrated on routine.

I took the remnants of paper out of the printer and fed in the new fanfold. Next, I selected and labelled three new disks 'Yukon Discovery'. One would be a working disk, the other two would be back-up copies.

Computers are wonderful, but occasionally they get temperamental and lose, destroy, or mulishly refuse access to stored material – at least mine does. And since it is a curious fact that such disasters rarely occur if a back-up exists, this habit is not merely prudent, it makes life easier.

The second back-up disk is extra insurance. I carry it with me wherever I go. I was raided once, by experts, and my hard disk was wiped clean and my back-up took a walk. I shivered at the memory. Never again.

I checked the time. It was a little after six, I'd have to hurry. A bath would have been too soothing, so I showered quickly, dressed and carefully applied make-up. Moral support. I needed it, knowing that I'd soon be sitting next to Stanley. And I'd be expected to eat.

The phone rang. I went back to answer it. I listened in silence, said thanks, swallowed hard, and hung up. I checked the evening paper. It was there all right.

I patched the eye make-up, and phoned a taxi. The only thing Stanley isn't mean with is his drink.

I crunched up the driveway to Stanley and Doreen's west-end villa. Square built, with a stone porch edged by half pillars and tall well-proportioned windows, it's an impressive pile – and better than he deserves.

I often think I'd have liked to have been a bourgeois Victorian. The self-satisfaction must have been very reassuring. I patted the stone lions – here's looking at you kids – and tugged the brass bell-pull.

Doreen welcomed me with one of her warmest smiles. My heart lifted and I gave her a hug. We wandered through to a bedroom and I laid my coat on the bed.

Doreen was wearing a silk dress that shimmered over her curves and the deep blue made her eyes look even larger and darker. I admired the dress, and her. She didn't notice.

'How are you feeling?' she said quietly.

I looked at her. 'As well as can be expected. How about you?' I didn't mention what I'd read in the paper; she'd probably seen it.

She shrugged, her eyes bright with tears. 'It's not easy.'

'No,' I agreed, 'it isn't.' For something to say, I added, 'I hope you haven't gone to any trouble.'

This was silly. Doreen always goes to a lot of trouble, which is why she's such a fantastic cook. We both produced a weak laugh, and she linked her arm into mine and walked me from the room.

'We have another guest tonight, Cat. Stanley thought it would be helpful.'

Stanley, helpful? I refrained from comment.

We strolled comfortably through the cavernous hall. Stanley is partial to a luxurious life style, which is one of the many reasons I don't like him. I noticed that it had been redecorated, crimson flock on beige; a chinese restaurant from the sixties. Jesus. I stole a look at Doreen. Would I ever understand how she could live with that man?

I heard voices as we neared the sitting-room and began to feel happier. A change of company was just what I needed. When we reached the doorway, I stopped abruptly. Stanley was standing at the window with Tomlinson, giving vent to manly chuckles.

Doreen had the grace to look abashed. 'If you're going to take that contract, Cat, you're going to have to work with the man. This is one way of oiling the wheels.'

I had to admit that Doreen was talking sense. The only difficulty was that she was labelling the wrong man as the problem. Stanley's an even bigger pain when he has an important guest to look after. And with his connection to Yukon Discovery's millions, Tomlinson would definitely come into that category.

What I had to look forward to was an evening of syco-phancy. Terrific.

Being too late to do anything else, I uncurled my lip and studied the pair of them. It was an education. I hadn't realised they had quite so much in common.

Both men were dressed in sharply pressed grey slacks, white shirts with club ties and dark blue blazers. They had healthy golf-aired faces with sharp eyes that didn't always smile at the same time as their mouths, and they were almost the same height. Each clutched a whisky tumbler carrying a hefty dram.

If I'd been pushed to identify a difference, I might have suggested that a certain shift of Tomlinson's eyes, and the way he held himself, pointed to a harder core. But it was touch and go.

I walked in and produced a friendly smile. 'Stanley. Good to see you.' I knew that he knew that I was lying, but what the hell. I offered my cheek for the ritual kiss. The sum total of my feminine manners.

Stanley gave me a gentlemanly peck. He carries off this sort of thing better than me, more practice. 'Delighted to see you again, Caithlin.' He delivered the look he uses to butter up rich widows. 'You're looking very pretty tonight. Lovely dress.'

I scowled. Stanley would stare a man straight in the eye while he was cutting his legs off. And pretty? Bloody cheek. Did he think I was a poodle or something?

Stanley indicated Tomlinson and smiled. 'It's time you two met each other socially.' He took a firm grip of my arm and led me forward. I took a firm grip of my temper and let him off with it. 'Caithlin,' he said in a poncy voice, 'allow me to introduce Edward.' He gave me a look that said, Smile.

I smiled. 'Hello, Edward.'

'Hello, Caithlin.' Tomlinson didn't look too happy either, but he was clearly going to take it like a man. 'This is a delightful surprise.'

Caithlin, from him as well. My fuse grew shorter. Stanley stuffed a dram in my hand and fed me a warning look: any trouble from you O'Connell . . .

I don't give a puff for Stanley, but I wanted that contract. I took the glass with a smile that was sweet enough to put Stanley into shock, and turned to Tomlinson.

Dredging up my social manners, I engaged in a little cultivated conversation. I discovered that he loved Scotland, played bridge and golf, and thought our theatres were excellent. By the second drink we were beginning to act as if we liked each other.

With Stanley adding his tuppence worth, this stretched out until Doreen called us through for dinner. When we sat down at table, I thought heavily of the hours that lay ahead.

Tomlinson had turned out to be pleasant, even witty. But Stanley was on his finest proprietorial form, and I just didn't know how I was going to bear it.

I glowered at Doreen. After this, I would view any future invitations from her with the gravest suspicion. Then I'd refuse.

She smiled sweetly back at me and held out a basket. 'Bread, Cat?'

So Refined

As usual Doreen's food was superb. I discovered an appetite I didn't know I had. Anyway, having my mouth full stopped anyone expecting me to speak.

I zipped through a plateful of mushroom soup and demolished several hunks of home-made bread, and was ready and able for the vegetable lasagne that Doreen had prepared for me.

I'm a near-vegetarian, usually the only flesh I eat is fish and I've got a feeling that's going to be off my menu soon, so I'm not the easiest dinner guest in the world. But she never seems to mind the extra work.

Stanley surpassed my worst fears, producing a stream of increasingly boring golfing stories for our delectation. Tomlinson laughed heartily and added a few of his own. His were only marginally better.

Doreen kept eyeing me mischievously and passing food in my direction. She looked as if she was having fun. I was glad somebody was.

I ate and listened. The food stopped me getting too morose. I discovered that Tomlinson banked with Stanley and had been introduced by him to the golfing mafia.

I wouldn't have been surprised to hear that some of Yukon Discovery's money was channelled through Stanley's bank as well, but this wasn't mentioned. That would come under the heading of business talk, which in Stanley's world is kept to the port.

I sat back, replete but sour.

Stanley was still talking. 'Edward is moving into a new flat in Dundee, Caithlin. A conversion in one of the old jute mills. Very nice. Very nice indeed. He likes it.'

I looked at Tomlinson wondering whether his mouth had seized up, since Stanley was doing his talking for him. He gave a brief amused smile and said nothing.

Stanley yapped on. 'You used to live in Dundee, Caithlin. You'll remember the mills when they were working.'

'I do,' I said. 'But I was lucky enough not to have to work in them.'

Tomlinson looked interested. Knowing me and Stanley, I decided it was safer not to pursue the subject. I picked up my spoon and dug into the cherry glacé.

'The mills are sadly missed in Dundee,' Stanley announced, putting on a face that claimed to know what it was talking about. 'They provided work for a lot of people. Now half the city's unemployed.'

This man just doesn't know when to leave well alone.

'The only people who miss the mills are the ones who made money out of them,' I said sharply. 'And that wasn't the people who worked there.'

Stanley's eyes narrowed and his mouth turned into a tight bun. He looked as if he was putting a curse on me. I dared him to try it.

Doreen said quickly, 'Stanley, you're neglecting our guests.'

'What?'

She raised a helpful eyebrow, 'The wine?'

'Oh. Yes.' He stopped glaring at me long enough to pick up the bottle and start to top up the glasses. 'Sorry about that.'

I waved my hand over my glass, dessert wine, yuch. But Stanley knows that. Maybe that was what made my mouth open. Or maybe I'm another one who doesn't know when to leave well alone.

'In some of these mills, the dust was so thick you could scarcely see, never mind breathe,' I said, 'and the noise . . .' I leaned forward, aiming straight for Stanley. 'Do you realise that people had to mouth messages to each other? How would you fancy that for ten hours a day? And coming out at the end of the week without enough money to live on?'

There was a deathly silence. Stanley's jaw tightened until I thought it was going to crack. I dug happily into my pudding.

'I'm inclined to agree with you, Caithlin,' Tomlinson said quietly.

Stanley looked appalled. In his book, dinner parties were happy occasions with lots of *bonhomie* and mutual back-scratching. And the rocking of boats was *verboten*. He had also, it has to be said, momentarily lost control of the conversation.

But it takes a lot to faze him; I'll give him that.

His face rearranged itself into a smile. 'You're getting into politics now, Caithlin. And you know what they say about politics and religion.' I wasn't sure that I did, but I knew I was about to be told. 'Not a suitable subject of conversation in mixed company,' he said archly. 'Chesterfield.'

I glared at Stanley. Chester who? But I was pretty sure the daft bannock had got it wrong. I looked at Tomlinson and discovered that he was another one who seemed to be enjoying himself. How do they do it?

Tomlinson's smile broadened. 'Will you be playing in the golf match next weekend, Stanley?'

Stanley cheered up on the spot, and started to explain how he was personally going to ensure a club win. 'My partner and I will play off last, of course. That'll scupper their weak pair.'

I went back to sleep, sitting upright.

Doreen produced coffee and chocolates and whispered, 'I'm going to disappear, Cat. You have things to talk about.' And vanished.

This didn't please me either. I had questions for Stanley and Tomlinson, but not at the same time. Even with the best intentions, and I don't credit Stanley with having any of those, they would influence each other. Once that happened there was no going back.

I sighed. The best I could do would be to try to keep the conversation as general as possible. And the way things had gone so far, I wasn't sure that would be possible.

Stanley produced the port, and his avuncular expression narrowed to business mode. He took a deep draw on his over-sized cigar and leaned back, oozing complacency.

'Right, Caithlin.' I looked at him, then at the cigar. He was definitely stripping the bank of its assets. Stanley puffed out happily and eased a fragment of ash against the ashtray. 'Doreen says you have some questions for us.'

I took a sip of coffee. 'Not really,' I said. 'At least, not at the moment.' They both stared at me. I studied the oil painting on the opposite wall.

'It's a bit short-sighted, surely, not to take the chance when you've got us both here together,' Stanley said tightly.

Now I knew he was getting really mad. He'd forgotten to say Caithlin.

'Precisely,' I said.

Stanley shot a look at Tomlinson, as if he wasn't quite sure how far to go. After all, he'd recommended me for the contract. It would look a bit odd if he suddenly started treating me like an idiot, as was his wont. I tried not to smile.

'I understand what Caithlin's getting at,' Tomlinson said, unexpectedly. 'She doesn't want to muddy the waters.' I looked at him in surprise. I couldn't have put it better myself. He turned to me. 'I presume this means that you are going to accept the contract?'

I hesitated. I was beginning to like Tomlinson. But he hadn't found the time to return my call, and a little politeness goes a long way.

'I'm sorry I didn't have a chance to get back to you this afternoon,' he went on. 'But I've arranged to be in the Glasgow office over the next two days.' He picked a card from his wallet and handed it to me. 'Our address. I've kept an hour clear tomorrow morning at ten o'clock. Would that be convenient?'

I thought so, said so, and slipped the card into my bag.

'One other thing,' Tomlinson said awkwardly. 'I hadn't realised that Dr Grant was such a good friend of yours. That was a dreadful thing to happen. I'm very sorry.'

This took me by surprise and tears came to my eyes. I looked down, furious with myself. When I got myself under control, I stared hard at him.

'Another avoidable accident, would you say?'

Tomlinson stiffened, the relaxed demeanour going up like a puff of Stanley's cigar smoke. 'An unfortunate accident, certainly,' he said, his voice like steel. He wasn't going to give an inch. 'We'll have to wait for the results of the autopsy before we know what happened.'

The temperature joined him at zero.

I could have told him about the phone call from my reporter friend, and that I had the results of the autopsy – accidental death from drowning – and that I didn't believe a word of it.

But this was neither the time nor the place.

I looked up. The glare Stanley was handing out would have set fire to wet loo paper. Written all over the scowling face was, There you go again, O'Connell, blowing it.

I managed to hold my tongue. All he can think about is business. But one of these days Mr Stanley MacDonald was going to be on the receiving end of a few home truths. And I was going to be the one making the delivery.

Stanley got to his feet. 'Well now. What say we have a comfortable seat and a nightcap?' He ushered us towards the sitting-room as if he didn't have a care in the world. 'Doreen'll be through in a minute.' He slapped Tomlinson heartily on the back. 'Another malt for you Edward, or can I tempt you with a brandy?'

Tomlinson still hadn't defrosted. 'A brandy would be excellent, thank you, Stanley,' he said stiffly.

Very refined. I wondered if I was going to get anything. Like glass, finely ground.

'Caithlin?' Stanley barked.

'Brandy,' I said sweetly.

Fortunately, Doreen chose that moment to come back in. Tomlinson and I vied with each other to tell her it had been a wonderful meal, and that she was a superb cook. All true.

We settled down to an uneasy conversation and sipped the brandy. By the time I finished mine, I was feeling the beginnings of a mellow glow. It was time I left, before I started to enjoy myself.

I stood up, both men leapt to their feet, and I said thank you and goodbye very civilly. Doreen came with me to get my coat.

She helped me into it. 'Am I right in thinking that things didn't go too well at the end?' She handed me my gloves, tutting, 'You and Stanley are the limit. You behave like children.'

I knew who the child was all right. And it wasn't me. But why should I be the one to carry the bad news? I gave her a kiss, and said sleepily, 'Night, Doreen.'

She held my hands, her eyes searching mine. 'Take it easy tomorrow, Cat. You've got to rest. Especially with the funeral the day after.' So she had read the death notice. 'I'll come with you,' she whispered. 'Stanley's getting a car; I'll let you know the arrangements.'

'I'm going to visit Donald's parents tomorrow,' I said inanely. 'I didn't like to disturb them today.' We stood in silence, then I remembered. 'Martin said something about getting a car.' I heard Stanley's shout with a feeling of being let off the hook. 'There's my taxi,' I said quickly. 'I'll phone you.'

In the taxi, I sank back, sagging with relief. What an evening. And tomorrow wasn't going to be much better. But the next day would be harrowing. Maybe Doreen was right, and I should try to take things easy.

I paid the driver and started belligerently up the stairs. The way I was feeling right now, if Sanderson popped out of his cage and gave me hassle there'd be a rammy. I turned each corner looking for trouble, but all was quiet. He must have known.

I locked up, kicked off my shoes and hung up my coat. I thought about it and decided that the whisky bottle was better left alone. I finished undressing, cleaned my face and my teeth, and crawled into bed.

I read for a few minutes but couldn't concentrate. I switched off the light and lay back, and tried to close my mind to the pictures from the past that were searing into my brain.

I got to thinking about the results of the autopsy. The police would have examined the site of the accident. If there were any suspicious circumstances, they would have notified the Procurator Fiscal's office. And if the post-mortem examination had found any marks or contusions other than those that might be expected, they wouldn't have released the body.

I squirmed uncomfortably. All the signs were that Donald's death had been an accident. But how had he managed to drive over the edge of the quay in the first place? And why hadn't he got out of the car? Surely he had enough sense to wait until the water level stabilised.

Had he been drinking? I tossed that idea around and decided it didn't pass muster. Donald drank, yes, but not to excess, and certainly not when he was likely to be driving.

There was also the small matter of the threatening phone call. Hardly an everyday occurrence. And what about his car? Had it been checked over for mechanical faults? Such as brakes that had mysteriously stopped working.

I had to give up finally and pad through for a couple of pain-killers. I gulped them down with a glass of water and went back to bed. And took up tossing and turning where I'd left off.

Troubled Waters

———

I allowed myself plenty of time. Apart from the fact that I was nursing a hangover, getting a meter in the city centre at this hour in the morning is like finding gold dust in slurry.

After circling three times, I found a spot in West George Street. I got out, fed the meter the small fortune, and made my way to the address on the card. Long way round as it happened.

I passed the Hatrack, a tall narrow façade of delicate stone with an expanse of glass and fantastic detail, and got ready to cross over St Vincent Street, a galleon in full sail.

I kept a careful eye on the traffic lined up at the lights. Four lanes, all itching to go, and all aiming at me. One of the first things you learn around here is how to show a quick pair of heels.

I sped across at an angle towards a towering modern block, Rennie Mackintosh style. It was an amiable contrast to its older, staider neighbours. But Glasgow is a city of contrasts, a great squatting cauldron that occasionally erupts. And warm, funny and alive.

I toddled on. This time Yukon Discovery was encased in a vast new edifice, with startling protuberances and a dark glossy surface. Very impressive – if you like that sort of thing.

The lift smoothed me upwards and opened silently on to a square hall, with strategically placed pot plants and hi-tech sofas. I had no difficulty deciding which door to aim for. The red, gold and blue logo blared out like a bite that had gone septic. I closed my eyes and pushed on through.

Inside they'd stuck to the same colour scheme, pale grey walls and red carpeting, but instead of Edwardian repro the furniture was starkly, and expensively, modern. More of the large colour photographs of rigs, this time encased in smooth gold frames. Everything fitted as if it had been designed at a hefty price. It probably had; they could well afford it.

I was expected. When I gave my name the receptionist stood up, smiled warmly, and asked me to follow her. She was pleasant, efficient, and nice to look at. They choose their secretarial staff with care in this company.

I ambled along behind her, wondering when I was going to walk into an office like this and find a hunky young man ensconced behind the desk. And him leaping up and asking me to follow him. Should I live that long.

Tomlinson stood up when I came in. He hadn't cheered up any, and there was a glint in his eyes that said it wouldn't take much to get him going. Since I wasn't feeling too good-natured myself, that suited me just fine. I showed my teeth in a smile.

He walked over and offered his hand. 'Good morning, Caithlin.'

I took it, shook it, and decided there was no time like the present. 'Cat,' I corrected. 'My name is Cat, not Caithlin. Good morning, Edward.'

'I'm sorry,' he said crisply. 'But I thought Stanley called you Caithlin.'

'He does, and I don't like it.' I glowered. Did he think that was funny?

'Cat,' he said, not a smile on his face. From his expression he'd added two and two and got four. 'I'll remember that in future.'

He gestured to an inner door. 'We'll work in the committee room. More space to spread out papers. Aileen here,' he nodded at the receptionist, 'has put together some bits and pieces, and she's trying to cancel my 11 o'clock appointment. I think we're going to need more than an hour.'

I thought so too. I moved straight into the committee room, curious to find out what had been put together. It was another large room, with a long table seating twelve, fourteen at a pinch. On it were several neat piles of paper. At the end nearest me was a silver tray carrying a coffee pot, two bone china cups and saucers, and a row of attractively quartered, crustless sandwiches.

'Coffee, all right?' he asked. When I said it was, he waved me to a seat, poured two cups, and pushed a three page document in front of me. 'The contract. If it's acceptable, we'll get it signed and out of the way.'

I read it through. Carefully.

The money was good, about 15 per cent more than I'd intended asking for, so there was no argument with that. One month, renewable. I didn't like this so much. These things took time. There again, I might be well sick of Yukon Discovery in a month and want out.

Weekly written reports, expenses claims and meetings were asked for. This I liked even less. It was the same old story. Tomlinson was cracking the whip so that I didn't forget who was boss.

I was about to point out that reporting for the sake of it was a waste of paper, and that I had better things to do with my time, when Stanley's scowling face swam to mind, the same shade of red as my bank balance. He must be having an out-of-body experience. I sighed, and turned the page.

I double checked the important bit. The question of access had been dealt with as 'open access to all relevant papers and personnel'. Tomlinson had left himself a loophole by the use of the word 'relevant'. Who was going to decide what was relevant? Him or me?

There were two ways of looking at this. I could accept it at face value and hope no difficulties arose, and if they did that we could negotiate. Or I could hold things up by arguing about it now.

I decided to opt for the first. If it came to the crunch, I could always walk away. As long as I kept my nose clean that could cause problems for him with his board. And I didn't doubt that he could work that out for himself.

I signed and pushed the paper over to him. He gave me a keen look, picked up the pen and scratched out a signature. If he was surprised at the lack of argument he seemed happy enough to take advantage of it.

That didn't bother me. I don't mind being underrated. In my line of business, it can be useful.

'Okay, Cat. Let's get started.' He almost smiled. 'These papers', he pushed a bundle over, 'give details of the company's organisation and personnel. These', another bundle followed, 'concentrate on the Scottish set-up. You can take these with you. You'll need time to go through them, and it's public information anyway.'

I was impressed. He'd put some thought into what I'd need and made sure it was available. I thanked him, put the two piles to one side, and waited for what was coming next.

'The rest I'll work through with you.' He stopped and stared as I produced a ringed notebook and a pen.

If he was this sensitive a tape-recorder wouldn't have gone down well. But a lot of people feel the same, which is why I don't use one. Carefully censored chat is a waste of air.

'I'm just going to jot down any points I might want to check later.'

'Okay, you can take notes. These papers stay.' He waved at the remainder and leaned his elbows on the table. 'You can have access to them any time you want. Whether I'm here or not. I've arranged it with Aileen.'

He couldn't be fairer. So what was the catch? I spent nearly two hours with him and still didn't find it. But that didn't mean it wasn't there.

Two pots of coffee and the sandwiches were consumed in passing. I was given a run down of personnel, their duties, and his opinion of their capabilities; off the record. I scribbled it down anyway, despite a basilisk stare every time I lifted my pen.

The avoidable accidents he'd spoken of had not all taken place on the rigs. Those that had involved a variety of falling objects, and a spell in sick-bay for three men. Yukon had covered the expenses and sick leave for those cases.

The other two had been workers crashing their cars on their way home on leave, and fortunately neither had been seriously hurt. Since these accidents were not considered work-related, their own insurances had picked up the tab.

But I was glad Tomlinson had included them. It showed he wasn't taking things at their face value.

He said he'd had a list prepared giving details of each incident. He passed it across. 'Dr Grant's accident can't be related to any of this,' he said quietly. 'He'd only been on the rigs a matter of months. These other men have been employees for upwards of a year. Some as many as three, when we first started up. We've no reason to think he was caught up in whatever's going on there.'

So much for what he knows, I thought bitterly. But I wasn't prepared to enlighten him. 'What about him being forced to take sick leave?'

He seemed surprised that I knew about that. 'The way I hear it the man was seriously overtired. And an oil rig's no place for anyone who's not on their toes.' He looked at me thoughtfully. 'I also heard he did a good job, and was well liked by the men.' That didn't surprise me, but it was nice of him to say so.

'Who did Dr Grant report to?'

'Me. Through Joe Sawers.'

'Never directly?'

'No. Joe's the man on the spot.'

'And Mr Sawers provided the accident details?'

'Of course.' He looked as if he was wondering why I was wasting time on the obvious. 'That's routine. Although I did ask him to include any off-the-job incidents that he knew about.'

I nodded and moved on. Since there might not be a right

time to raise the next point, this was as good as any. But for the moment, I was going in sideways.

'Three minor accidents off-shore over a period of four months isn't a bad safety record,' I said. 'Couldn't calling in an independent investigator be seen as overkill?'

He leaned back, his eyes careful. 'I believe I already explained that any suspicions of sabotage had to be cleared up before the board would feel confident that they were dealing with a policy problem.' I nodded, he had.

He produced another angle. 'And where safety is a priority, the accident record is taken to reflect a company's efforts.' He gestured to the papers between us. 'Although these are minor, they make bad statistics and could affect our future activities in the area.'

All very reasonable, but it wasn't what I was looking for. Somebody had pushed for an independent investigation. And I wanted to know who, because then I might be nearer knowing why.

I looked across. The shutters had come down. It was clear that he had no intention of saying any more on that particular topic. I stuck a mental memo on it for the future.

'We have stringent safety and operating procedures on the rigs,' Tomlinson said. 'I haven't gone into these in any detail, because Joe Sawers is most closely involved in the day-to-day management and he'll be able to tell you everything you need to know.' He added casually, 'I presume you've arranged to see him?'

I half smiled. He was checking up on me already. 'I'll be seeing him.' I started to tidy the papers together. 'What about this training course? Who set that up?'

'Art Haldane, our Training Manager. I'll find out when he'll be over here next. You'll need to meet him.'

I wasn't in any hurry; there was plenty to be getting on with. I sat back and closed my notebook and capped my pen. I'd probably got as far as I could for the time being.

Tomlinson loosened his tie and sank into the leather upholstery. He'd done a lot of talking. He looked at his watch, and said, 'No questions?' He smiled suddenly, the first real smile I'd seen on his face. 'Or should I say, no more questions? I have a feeling I've just been given the once over.'

Was this meant to be a compliment? I decided to take it as one, and grinned. I didn't feel too bad about this morning's work myself.

I slipped the first two bundles in my briefcase. It was time to go. We shook hands amiably and I said I'd be in touch. He saw me to the door.

Now for the hard part. Donald's parents.

With my visit to the Grants in mind, I had taken care dressing that morning; I wore a pale grey woollen suit, sort of casual but not quite. Nothing depresses me more than the black-clothed visitors who zoom in after a death.

Donald's parents live in a bungalow near Eaglesham. I crossed the river in a swirl of cars on the conglomeration of the Kingston Bridge and headed south. Once off the motorway I had something to look at.

The backdrop kept changing. The road, hustling with small businesses, narrowed and opened up again, tree-lined and airy. Bleak, narrow multi-storey blocks appeared, with balconies stretched around like grey sticking plaster. Then partially hidden large old villas, which gave way to small stone bungalows built between the wars.

I drove automatically. South of the river isn't my patch, I just point the car and hope I'll end up where I'm supposed to be going.

I'd already decided that I had to find out what Donald's parents knew about his work and movements over the last few months. I just wasn't sure how to go about it.

I tried out a few angles in my head, and decided to play it by ear.

I turned on to a narrow country road and a view over farmland, straddled by pylons, that pointed towards East Kilbride. A mile further on I reached the Grants' red-roofed bungalow, extended by twice its size since it was built in the 1930s.

I drew into the drive, took a deep breath, and got out of the car. The rose bushes on either side of the path carried unseasonal red and yellow blooms. The tips had been frosted brown. It was an unwelcome reminder.

I shivered, and rang the bell.

Donald's father, Arthur, answered. He must be in his seventies now, but he's still the ramrod straight ex-Army officer. He was an older version of Donald, the same big frame with less flesh and timeworn eyes, and wore his authority easily.

'Come in, my dear. It's good of you to visit us.'

I hadn't meant it to happen, but my eyes filled with tears. 'I'm so sorry, Arthur.'

'There, there, Cat,' he said gruffly, patting me on the back. I felt a fool. I was the one supposed to be doing the consoling. 'In you come,' he murmured. 'Margaret's expecting you.' As he closed the door, he looked a little unsteady on his feet. 'She's bearing up well. But it's a hard thing for a mother to lose her son.' His grey eyes grew moist. 'Very hard.'

It was now or never.

'Arthur. Before we go in, there's something I wanted to ask you. If you didn't mind.' He stopped and looked at me. 'Well, a couple of things, actually,' I confessed, feeling like a skunk.

His gaze went down the hall. 'In private?' he asked quietly. I nodded. He pushed the door nearest us open. 'We can talk here.'

We each took a chair by the fire. And I wondered where to start.

He gave me a keen look. 'Is it about what happened to Donald?'

'It could be,' I said cautiously. I took a deep breath. 'You know the sort of work I do Arthur?' He nodded. 'Well, I have to follow up leads that may or may not be connected.' It was the best I could come up with, and I pushed on quickly. 'I was wondering if Donald had told you anything about his work at Yukon Discovery?'

Arthur studied me carefully, and his eyes registered that he had sussed me out. I hoped he wasn't going to push it. He leaned forward, his hands on his knees. 'Donald was worried about something that was happening up there. But he wouldn't discuss it.'

'Did he say how long it had been going on?'

Arthur sighed heavily. 'The first I knew was three months ago, when he was home for the weekend. There was a phone call.'

'A phone call?'

'Yes. An American.' I looked at him questioningly. 'I answered,' he explained. 'Donald wasn't too happy about it. He didn't stay long after that. Said he had to meet somebody.'

'Nothing else?'

Arthur shook his head. 'No.' I sagged back, disappointed. He shot me a quick look. 'But we've had the police around. Asking the same questions.'

I sat up. 'When? Who?'

'Yesterday. A Detective Inspector Thompson.' I might have known. But that was quick off the mark. I wondered why. 'I want you to promise me something, Cat.'

I looked at him. 'Of course.'

'If you find out anything about Donald's death, I want to know about it. And I want you to tell me everything.'

Everything? The very thought made me feel even sadder. But he had the right. 'I'll do that, Arthur.'

He nodded, satisfied. 'Perhaps it's best not to worry Margaret with any of this at the moment.' I agreed. He walked in front of me down the hall. We looked at each other and went in.

The room looked as if it had been redecorated recently, the white paint and emulsioned embossed paper were pristine. There again I couldn't visualise things being otherwise. I recognised the heavy gilt framed Scottish landscapes, and the furniture; mahogany framed winged armchairs, a rosewood escritoire, and an oak roll-top desk.

Donald's mother stood up. She's a proud and determined woman; always has been. And it wasn't letting her down. Immaculately groomed, she still had that look about her that could pin a fly to the wall.

She wore a floral silk dress, a modest string of pearls, and her grey hair was softly curled around her face. Her bone structure was fine, giving her a delicate air, but as an army wife I knew she'd kept everyone on the hop. And rumour has it she does the same locally.

She held out her hands, 'So good of you to come, Caithlin.' She proferred her cheek. I kissed it. She indicated which chair I should sit on. I sat.

While Arthur poured the sherry, I had my first sight of the extent of her pain. A life of self discipline and obligation had been stripped bare. And it showed.

She said, 'Arthur and I were hoping you could stay for lunch, Caithlin. Nothing special. But it would be nice to talk about the old days, and Donald.'

It was a plea I couldn't refuse. I just prayed I'd have the strength to see it through. Donald and I had been like Siamese twins for three years. There were a lot of memories.

I swallowed the lump in my throat as they started flooding back. 'I'd be pleased to, Mrs Grant.'

Saying Margaret would've burned my mouth off. And as far as I was concerned she could call me Caithlin till doomsday.

It wasn't as bad as I'd expected. We talked about Donald, finished our sherry, and meandered through to lunch and talked some more. I wasn't hungry. I just chased the food round the plate and excused myself by saying I'd had a large breakfast.

After lunch, the photograph albums were dragged out and we pored over them. There were pictures of me that made us all laugh. A spot of explosive in that beehive hairstyle and I could've been a guided missile.

And Donald. There was a photograph of him sitting on his motor bike. With that mass of sleekly greased hair, coiffed at the front and DA'd at the back, he hadn't needed a crash helmet. Would have ricocheted off concrete.

I giggled. What a pair, so pleased with ourselves. My throat went dry. And with each other.

It was three o'clock before I left. I didn't feel guilty about staying so long; it had done us all good. I went straight home and tried to work. I pulled out the folders and stared at them. It was useless. There was a block somewhere. I gave up.

Something had struck a chord. It was just that my subconscious wasn't ready to release it yet. But it would, in its own good time.

I spent a couple of hours catching up with my mail, most of them bills and circulars. Clemency's letter sat glaring at me. I ignored it, tidied the outgoing mail, filed away the necessary then, feeling pleased with myself, went through to make a mug of Earl Grey.

When I wandered back in, I eyed the pink envelope warily. I was going to have to open it. It could be important. Worse than that, it could be serious. She might be planning on paying me a visit.

I picked it up and threw myself disgruntedly on to the settee, and tore it open. I sat up, shaken.

Clemency had heard of Donald's death, she knew how upset I'd be, and they were coming up for the funeral. I shook my head in disbelief. She must have shot this off the minute she'd heard. That was Clemency all over, a nose for disaster and the size tens to make it worse.

I read on. I hadn't to worry about putting them up, they'd book in at an hotel. A postscript informed me tartly that she'd given up trying to telephone, because I was never in.

Like all bad news, this took some digesting.

I tried again. They. My heart reached my feet. The only thing that depressed me more than Clemency was stiff-upper-lip Raymond wafting about doing his devoted husband routine.

He doesn't like me either. I think it's something to do with me being single, and happy. Apparently this is selfish. I should be going round in sackcloth and ashes, wailing and tearing my hair out.

Our other bone of contention is Clemency and her flirting. Clemency flirts like other people breathe. And probably for the same reason. What aggravates me is that when we're together, I'm the one that gets the blame.

In a burst of temper, I ripped the letter up and chucked it

in the bin. I wasn't going to let them upset me. And if Clemency started any of her nonsense, she'd be sorry.

I crawled into bed and mercifully fell asleep. I wakened in the middle of the night, made tea, and stood at the window staring over my beloved city lights.

I was there a long time. When it got colder than I could bear, I went back to bed, and listened to the silence.

From the Ashes

Martin insisted he come to Donald's funeral. And since he'd arranged the car and placed my order with the florist, when he arrived on the doorstep I could hardly turn him away. He inspected the black wool suit I was wearing, and picked up the clothes brush and started to run it over me.

'I can do that myself!' I grabbed the brush, made a few vague passes over the cloth and put it down.

I could tell that he was itching to have another go, I'd probably missed a speck of dust, and sent an eye message that he'd better not try it.

He smiled and backed off. 'Okay.' He shrugged himself into his coat, and turned serious. 'Time we were on our way.'

I nodded numbly and picked up my bag. I hoped he was going to have the sense to let me alone. We went out, I locked up, and we walked downstairs in silence and out to the car.

The sun shone coldly through the skeleton trees and glinted on the garden railings. The cloudless blue sky promised a clear dry spell and hard frost. I took a deep breath. There was something in the air that said there could be snow on the way.

I got in and sat back. The car purred slowly along the wide and grassy centred boulevard. It eased to a halt at the lights. We'd be turning off soon.

I sneaked a look at Martin. He's every bit the successful, city lawyer, with the bland composure shot through with complacency that clients find so reassuring. The greying at his temples merely adds distinction.

He is also a kind and generous man. But I was beginning to feel like a steer that had been landed and branded, and I wasn't liking it much. And I couldn't work out how I'd ever got involved with him.

I turned and gazed out the window. Come to that, I didn't know what he saw in me. I'm hardly a prize package. I don't like the sort of civilised drinks parties and social business meetings that make up his life, and usually show it. Although I had to admit I'd behaved quite well at the few I'd allowed him to parade me at.

I sighed. The only thing I was certain of at that moment was that I wished Martin was a thousand miles away. When I felt tears running down my face, I swore under my breath. I'd promised myself this wouldn't happen.

'You all right?' Martin said softly. He put his arm around me. I snuffled and irritably shook him off. He took his arm back and looked at me with hurt eyes. He handed over a large white handkerchief. 'Here. Take this.'

I took it and mopped up. I thought of Donald's parents. What did I have to whine about? I blew my nose and put the soggy white bundle in my bag. What can't be changed has to be borne.

Martin was staring woodenly ahead. I turned back to the window. I wasn't up to making amends.

The car turned left on to the sweeping approach to the crematorium, crept up the drive and stopped. Car after car purred to a halt behind us, emptied, and crept away. A lot of people were turning up.

Martin and I made our way to one side. Neither of us spoke. I recognised some people and exchanged nods.

— 69 —

Floral tributes were spread all around the low building. I was about to walk over to them, when a flurry of perfume invaded my nostrils and I was engulfed in fur, right up my nose.

Clemency released me and I started breathing again. 'Darling,' she cooed. 'This is too awful. You must be feeling simply dreadful.' She was a bundle of candy floss, make-up from Paris, hair from Dallas.

She looked inquiringly at Martin, and started one of her slow, interested smiles. The one where the glossy lips peel back to reveal sharp white teeth, centimetre by centimetre: oral strip-tease.

This always makes me nervous: gives me a tight feeling in my throat, and a sudden desire to clutch a bunch of garlic, and a crucifix. But men seem to like it. Martin was slavering. I introduced them.

Raymond loomed up wearing his long face. He has one for every occasion. I suffered a passing kiss on the cheek, and introduced him as well. Martin shook his hand and returned to admiring Clemency.

She fluttered her lashes. 'So this is your new boyfriend, darling. How sweet.' I sighed, I could see it coming. She tapped Martin roguishly on the chest with a beautifully gloved hand. 'Why have you been hiding him from us, darling?'

My nerves cringed as if a nail had been drawn over glass. Martin looked pleased. I said nothing. I'd seen the childish venom peeping through her lashes. What did she have planned for her next trick?

'Raymond and I were just saying, darling, how awfully sad this is for you.' She smiled sadly at me, then at Martin. 'After all, we've been expecting to hear wedding bells for you and Donald for years.' She turned, and said mournfully, 'Haven't we, Raymond?'

Raymond agreed, looking stricken. I shot him a foul look – the old fart. Martin stopped smiling. I decided I'd had enough. Clemency could do her viper routine if she liked, I didn't have to listen.

I walked over to the flowers and strolled along, reading

the cards. I'd chosen simple white daisies in remembrance of a summer a lifetime ago. When I found them, I stood and stared.

A beam of cold sun lit up the dark corner, and the stark white blooms with their bright orange-yellow centre stood out like cacti in an oasis. A great sadness swept over me. In a few days, even their beauty would crumble and disappear.

Dust in the wind.

Martin appeared at my side and attached himself like a vice. I walked along looking at the tributes, he walked along looking at me. 'Donald must have been well liked,' he said thoughtfully.

I agreed and walked off. I'd enough on my mind without wondering what else Clemency had been saying to him. But I had a feeling that if I stayed there I was going to hear it; like it or not.

I caught sight of Tomlinson. He was standing chatting to two men whose faces worked outdoors a lot: big, brawny and macho. Did I need this? I must've done, because I kept on in their direction. He saw me, said something to his companions, and all three made moves to narrow the gap.

Tomlinson shook my hand briefly and gave Martin a nod. He looked back to me. 'Not the best time, Cat. But I'd like you to meet Joe Sawers and Mike Brown. They work between the Aberdeen office and the rigs.'

I was glad that he'd taken the trouble. Those two were at the top of my list. I studied them carefully, big silent types, with white collars, black ties and heavy overcoats. Confidence seeped from their masculine pores, and they wore it like a very thick skin.

Tomlinson briefly explained to Sawers and Brown who I was, and that I'd been hired to carry out an investigation. They looked me over, said the right things, and looked unimpressed. Martin drifted off.

The blond, Joe Sawers, stared at me openly, from top to toe, and smiled secretively. It was written all over his smarmy face that he knew where women belonged and what they should be investigating. And the oil business didn't come into either category.

I decided I was going to have to introduce this man to Clemency. They were made for each other.

'Ms O'Connell will be in touch, Joe,' Tomlinson said. 'She'll want to look around, meet people. Help her out as much as you can.' He turned his steely gaze on Brown. 'You too, Mike.'

Brown nodded. 'Will do.'

'Sure thing, boss,' Sawers agreed lazily, reissuing the stare.

I pretended not to notice, and kept my smile going until I was looking at their backs pushing through the crowd. Those two spelled macho trouble, and I was going to have to find a way of dealing with it.

I went back to join the others. Clemency was deep in conversation with Martin, and he still had that daft infatuated look on his face. Raymond was hovering anxiously, trying to earwig what they were saying.

Doreen and Stanley joined us, looking chilled. Just then the wooden doors opened and people started to come out. I quickly introduced Martin. They knew Clemency and Raymond.

Doreen gave Clemency a cold one-two with her eyes, and said a brisk hello. She doesn't like Clemency and doesn't mind showing it. She stuck her hand firmly on Stanley's arm, This is my property, hands-off. If it'd been me I wouldn't have bothered.

Clemency is wary of Doreen, because they've had a number of spats in the past and she hasn't come out the winner. She stopped wrapping herself around Martin and took a grip of her own spouse. I didn't know what she was hanging on for either. Couldn't give him away at a jumble sale.

Stanley studied Martin closely, and sidled over to buttonhole him for a whispered exchange of pleasantries. Didn't surprise me. Martin is a prosperous and upstanding member of the community; right up Stanley's alley.

Doreen and I smiled bleakly at each other. We had nothing to say.

The men I'd identified as our funereal team made sombrely for the doorway. It was our turn. The Grants made the first move and the rest of us huddled into a rough line behind them.

'Family or friend?' was the hushed inquiry.

'Friend,' I said, getting narky. Did it matter?

'To the left, any row after the front.' I was told. I bristled.

Martin nudged me on and pushed me to the left. 'Cool it, Cat,' he murmured. 'This isn't your private funeral.' He hustled me along and I stared at him in astonishment. Who did he think he was? 'Cut it out,' he whispered. 'Just get in there, and sit down.'

I couldn't think of anything else to do, so I did as I was told.

A hushed organ started up. Everyone got to their feet. A minister walked to the front and stood at the dais and cleared his throat. We sat down. The unctuous voice started to speak about somebody I didn't know.

My eyes fixed on the long box in front of us, tastefully covered by a embroidered cloth. Donald was in there. The minister droned on and the box slid along the rollers towards the roar of fire.

My head started to buzz and I felt myself slipping down.

When I came to, I was outside sitting on a bench, supported by Martin. His overcoat was wrapped round my shoulders. Doreen was bending over me, looking anxious, telling Martin that I probably hadn't been eating properly and that what I needed was a good meal, and straight to bed. There were a few people still milling about. Another cortège was drawing up.

'Come on, Cat. Let's get you home,' Martin said gently. He helped me to my feet. 'The car's over here.'

'Quite right, Martin,' Stanley puffed self-importantly. 'That's the best thing for her. Something to eat and straight to bed.'

'I'll come with you,' Doreen said, looking worried.

'Caithlin's in good hands, Doreen,' Stanley said firmly, ushering her away. He called back over his shoulder, 'Ring us later, Martin. Tell us how she is.'

I grinned weakly. Stanley had given Martin his seal of

approval. If I wasn't careful I was going to be rising in his estimation. Might even reach the dizzy heights of normality.

I leaned against Martin and got inside the car. I couldn't have coped with the post-funeral drinks. Doreen had hit the nail on the head. Apart from a couple of sandwiches and a lettuce leaf or two, I hadn't eaten anything for over twenty-four hours.

Martin directed me upstairs, pushed me into the bathroom with a robe, and told me to get undressed. I heard him on the phone before I turned on the shower.

I stood under the hot water, my skin turning pink, and gave up thinking. I dried myself slowly and gently. Folding the towel carefully, I hung it over the rail and pulled on the robe.

When I went back into the sitting-room, he was prising the lids off cartons and a delicious smell was wafting around the room. Chicken Jalfraisy, my favourite, and there was nan bread and fried rice.

Martin pushed me gently on to the settee, and handed over a plateful of food and a fork. He ripped a lump from the bread and held it out. 'Take this. Eat.'

I gripped everything he gave me as if my life depended on it, and ate. And enjoyed it. Another lump of nan swept up the remnants of sauce. Full up, I put the plate on the side table and collapsed back against the cushions.

'That better?'

'Yes,' I murmured. 'Much better.' I watched sleepily as Martin walked over to the wireless and tuned in to Radio 3. A piano concerto. He came back and sat down beside me.

I lay back, listening. Then I remembered Clemency. How could I forget? 'Where did my sister and her husband go?'

'They went to the Grants,' he said absently. 'Says she'll be round tomorrow.' He half turned and looked at me. 'Those two men you were introduced to at the funeral?'

I perked up. 'What about them?'

'I think I came across one of them in an assault case. Must be about two years ago now.' I held my breath. 'Yes, that's right,' he reflected. 'A man was badly beaten up, nearly killed, in an alley behind a pub in Aberdeen.'

I had a sinking feeling that I knew the answer, but had to ask. 'Which one?'

'The blond one, Sawers. But he produced an alibi a foot long.' I listened in chilled silence. 'Funny business,' Martin mused. 'The prosecution witnesses disappeared like snow in summer. Verdict was Not Proven.'

That appeared to be the end of Martin's recollections. He smiled at me as if he had other things on his mind. 'Come on,' he whispered. 'Time for bed.'

'Yes, I am tired,' I yawned. 'Thanks for looking after me, Martin. I'll phone you.'

'Fine.' He had me up and moving in the direction of the bedroom, his arm tight around my waist.

I balked in the doorway. 'I'll manage this myself,' I said irritably. I looked pointedly at the narrow space between me and the bed. 'All I need to do is walk over there.'

He dug his chin into my neck and held me so tight I thought I'd expire. He breathed hotly on my skin: 'Let's go to bed.'

I gave him a swift push. 'Leave me alone.'

'What is this?' He looked injured, and took a firmer grip of my arms. 'What are you playing at, Cat?'

'I am not,' I tried to shake myself free, 'playing at anything. I just want to go to bed. Alone.'

He stood still for a moment, then let me go. 'Clemency said . . . I didn't believe her.' A wordly expression took over his face. 'So he was special to you, this Donald.'

I could've wept. Such insight is hard to bear. I was at a loss for words, and the few I managed to dredge up I had to discard as obscene.

I compromised. 'Bugger off, Martin.'

'You were lovers.' He grabbed me, his mouth clenched tight with jealousy. 'That's why you're so upset, isn't it?' His eyes looked to be in danger of popping out of his head. 'You told me he was just a friend. But you were sleeping with him, weren't you?'

His hands gripped tighter. I couldn't believe it was happening. I could've broken his grip, but thought we both deserved a more dignified exit than a brawl.

I tried to keep my voice from shaking. 'It's been a difficult day. Let's not make it any worse.'

Martin hesitated, looking hurt. I felt like crying.

He kissed me hungrily. I tried to work up some enthusiasm. When I managed to get free I showed him the door, and heard him say he would contact me.

I stood shivering and rubbing my arms. Here was me thinking that my problem with Martin was over. It looked as if it was just beginning.

First Things First

I looked in the mirror. A ravaged white face stared back, wan eyes set in dark circles, a malnourished panda. The hair surrounding it stood out in a fearful frizz. I wondered if I could afford a visit to the hairdresser.

I became aware that my arms hurt. I examined the purpling bruises dolefully. I spend weeks considering Martin's feelings, and I end up getting shoved around.

I decided to go jogging. When you feel this bad, the only way is up. Anyway, a spot of steady running is the best way I know of concentrating the mind. I pounded round, the blood started circulating, and I came back feeling marginally more alive.

I showered and dressed, and munched a slice of wholemeal bread spread thickly with home-made raspberry jam – HAG's contribution to my welfare – and enjoyed every crumb. Now I had work to do.

My first stop was to be a small garage on Clydeside. It was 8.15 in the morning, early by my standards, but I wasn't taking any chances of being at home if Clemency called round.

I wore jeans tucked into a pair of furry lined knee-high

boots, a heavy sweater on top of a fine wool top, and a sheepskin jacket. This ensemble was topped by a long red scarf, wound round twice, and furry lined leather gloves. My woollen hat was in a jacket pocket.

I could hardly move.

I needed every layer. Even looking at the frost made my flesh clench tight in self-defence. What it would be like in Aberdeen, where the icy east wind can trim the bottom off a stalagmite, didn't bear thinking about.

And that was where I was heading. Later.

I parked the car outside the entrance to Bert's place, a dank hole in the wall that shook every time a train rumbled overhead. I took a last look at the bright blue sky and stepped smartly into the gloom of the workshop, and went on the search for Bert.

There were two mechanics working under a car hoisted inelegantly into the air. He wasn't likely to be one of them, but I checked anyway. Both men turned. The older man wiped his hands on a dirty rag and gave me a blank stare.

I looked past him, across the oily rubble of car pieces, and raised my eyes to the boxed-in office at the top of rickety stairs. There was a light on and the windows were steamed up. Bert was in. No doubt trying to work out even more ingenious ways of avoiding tax.

I nodded vaguely in the direction of the two under the car, since they'd paid me the compliment of stopping work to see what I was up to, and wound my way through the heaps of tyres and metal to the stairs.

I clambered up the Heath Robinson construction knowing that I was taking my life in my hands. One of these days the stairs were going to collapse. I hoped I wouldn't be on them when they did.

When I reached the shaky wooden platform at the top, I banged on the door and shoved my way in without waiting for an answer.

The inside didn't look any safer. The walls were covered with knocked-together shelving, stacked loosely with heavy metal objects that were ready to make a break for it.

And filthy? I'll say. Health and safety isn't Bert's bag.

A large desk, covered with papers and cigarette ash took up the tiny floor space. Two chairs had been squeezed in, one at either side of the desk. The one I could see had a sagging torn leather seat. The sort you sit on very carefully and have a helluva job getting out of. I speak from experience.

Bert was sitting on the other chair, hunched over his papers like a latter-day Scrooge. He looked pretty much the same. A bright gnomish-face that advertised a daily battle with adversity, and a clothing disaster area.

He wore several layers of green, a grimy red-checked shirt and a dark blue scruffy anorak. If his tie was anything to go by, he'd eaten tomato soup in the last week or two. A lavish scattering of ash down his front completed the picture.

He lowered his glasses, squinted over the taped join, and favoured me with a gleam of welcome. 'Well, well, well. Look what the wind's blown in. Top o' the mornin' to ye, Caithlin, top o' the mornin'.' He got up and battered the window. 'Two coffees up here,' he roared, and sat back down. 'Caithlin O'Connell,' his face twisted into a smile, 'it's a stranger you are, to be sure.'

I grinned. Bert had never been any nearer Ireland than Dunoon, but he liked to make out Galway was his mother turf. When he was a young lad he'd worked for my father, and I suspect that was when he picked up the accent. He is one of the few people allowed to call me by my given name.

'Hi, Bert. How's life treating you?'

'No complaints.' His protruding front teeth showed foxily. 'And what would ye be after, Caithlin, my dear?'

Since getting anything out of Bert demands certain formalities and an inordinate amount of time, I unwound my scarf, slipped off my gloves and struggled out of my jacket. I panted in the heat. He had three portable radiators going full blast.

'I'm looking for a car,' I said. For some reason, this seemed to surprise him. Maybe the garage is only a front, and he's really into squeaky toys.

'A car?' he said thoughtfully. 'But why would ye be looking for a car?' He leaned forward and eyed me soulfully.

'Would yer own be off the road for some reason, Caithlin lass? An accident maybe?' The old goat.

'Not exactly, Bert. But I could do with a nippier number for a day or two. On loan.'

'On loan,' he pondered. 'Not a hire by any chance?'

'Well, maybe a bit of both,' I conceded, as usual.

The door crashed open, and the young mechanic bombed in with steaming mugs and panicky eyes. 'Here y'are, Mr Sullivan.'

'Right. Put them down, son. Surely ye don't expect us to drink it from yer hands.' Coffee splashed on to the paper-littered desk and Bert glowered. The lad paled as if he was about to faint. 'Very good, son. Off ye go.' The door crashed shut and Bert pushed a mug across to me with a sly grin; he likes to inflict a bit of terror. 'There ye are Caithlin, my dear. Nothing like a coffee te get ye going in the morning.'

I took it and gulped the hot liquid. It never gets any better. 'Lovely,' I lied, and got down to business. 'I need a zippy number for a few days, Bert. One with power under the bonnet, but looks as if it can't lift its feet.'

He stared at me in silence. I knew that he knew exactly what was required. I also know he gets a lot of requests like this. It's even been suggested that he's a supplier of get-away cars. If he is, I don't want to know about it.

Bert's other talent is that he keeps an ear very close to the ground. He collects information like a squirrel storing up nuts for a hard winter. And parts with it about as willingly. But everything is negotiable. First, the car.

'You know what I'm looking for, Bert.'

He shook his head sorrowfully. 'Business is bad. A load of rubbish about these days.' He raised sad eyes, 'Very difficult te get anything dacent. Could be expensive, lass.' He looked pained at the very thought.

'That's a pity. Can't run to much. Money's a bit tight.' I started to rewind the scarf around my neck.

'That's not te say I might not be able te lay my hands on something,' he said grudgingly. 'Maybe not exactly what ye're lookin' for though.' I stood up and started to pull on the sheepskin. He considered the matter. 'How does a souped up Scirocco strike ye? Pretty old, I'll admit. But lively.'

'How lively?' I shot back.

A wicked smile slithered out. 'Enough te give the polis a problem?'

'Well, it might do,' I said, trying to act doubtful. 'Usual rates?'

'Aw, come on lass. A man's got te live.'

I calculated quickly. 'Three per cent up?' Not that I'm stingy or anything.

He took his time thinking, and stretched out a blackened hand. 'It's a deal.' We shook on it and I counted out the cash.

When I saw the car I had serious doubts. The number plates were tied on with string, and it had so many dents on the body that it threatened to collapse if somebody breathed on it. If this bodywork had passed the MOT somebody must've been looking the other way.

I looked inside. It had been gutted, carelessly. Behind the two front seats was a vacuum of neglect. Maybe I should ask for my money back.

I got in anyway and started it up. The engine roared sweet and pure. Great. Now for that other little matter. I got out and walked up close, real close.

'There was something else, Bert,' I murmured, trying to look shifty. 'I need some information.'

His eyes lit up like a dog seeing the rabbit. Conspiracy is Bert's life force. Make him think something was afoot and you had his full attention. He huddled even closer, and tried to speak without moving his lips.

'And what would that be concerning, Caithlin me dear?'

The mechanics had their backs to us and were steadily working away. They could have waved a placard saying 'We've gone deaf', but it really wasn't necessary.

'Aberdeen,' I said. 'Two men.'

He nodded, listening hard. 'Names?'

'Joe Sawers and Mike Brown. Know them?'

Bert stared at me incredulously. 'Know them?' He sent a

cautious look around the workshop, in case he was being raided, and sidled even closer. If he kept this up we'd soon be inseparable. 'Put it this way, Caithlin, me dear. I've heard things. And what I've heard isn't good news. Stay well clear.'

I wasn't in the mood for mysteries. 'What have you heard, Bert?'

'Those two are trouble, Caithlin.' He was about to say something else, when his mouth clamped shut as if he didn't intend to open it again – ever.

I followed his eyes. He was gazing through the doorway to the road, where the tail end of a black Jag was cruising silently out of sight. 'The less ye know about them the better, lass,' he whispered agitatedly.

He moved away, and started bellowing so that they could hear him at the end of the street. 'There ye are then, me dear. Glad te've been able te help ye out with a motor.'

I just had time to throw him the keys of the mini before he shot off towards the safety of his office. I drove out. The car was purring, I was flummoxed.

I thought about it. Bert had given as good a version of a scared man as I'd seen for a while. But he was a play-actor, well practised and of long-standing. What was I to make of it?

Going via High Street was the shorter route, it was also, at this time in the morning, likely to take twice as long. So I cut back, along the expressway and on to the M8.

I decided to forget Bert. I'd get on to him again later. And maybe if I dug up a few bargaining counters of my own, I'd have more success next time.

Anyway, there was no point letting him put the fear of God in me before I'd even started. I could do that on my own. Without any help.

I had a rough idea what I wanted from my day. But no clear plans. I rarely do at the beginning. I like to meet people, get my bearings and see what turns up. It's surprising how often something does.

The car was running well. I tested the acceleration on the uphill drag between Dunblane and Perth. There was an instant power surge and I rocketed past lorries and cars at an illegal eighty-five.

Satisfied with the sweet roar, and pleased that I wasn't leaving a trail of bodywork, I checked the mirror for flashing blue lights. I didn't see any but slowed down anyway. Why push my luck?

I reached the Perth roundabout, turned North, and checked my watch; 10 a.m., under an hour from Glasgow. I could get to like this car. I settled back, feeling the tingle that comes with each new case.

But this time it had a sharper edge. This time I had a score to settle.

Eastern
Connection

———

Aberdeen was every bit as cold and windy as I'd anticipated. I parked in a side road off Union Street, and had to fight the gale to get the car door shut.

I rewrapped the scarf to stop me tripping over it, and tied it in a knot under my chin, loose enough to stick my face in when I felt frost-bite coming on. Which would be any minute now. I was chilled to the bone. Bert had forgotten to mention that the heater wasn't working.

I leaned forward at the forty-five degree angle that progress dictated, struggled on to Union Street and fell into the first coffee shop. Too early for lunch, but I needed something hot. I'd learned my lesson. I wasn't going to forget to eat again. I managed to get a toasted sandwich and a mug of weak coffee and began to feel better.

I checked my notebook. Yukon Discovery had a small office here. That was my first port of call. My second was to be the hospital. Hopefully I'd get a lead from one of them.

I marched past several grey granite buildings checking the numbers. The sunlight sparkled against shiny particles of stone on the stark puritanical façades, bringing a visual iciness to the chill that was already permeating my body.

I was blown up slippery smooth granite stairs and through swing doors. I checked the board. Yukon Discovery was on the third floor. There was no lift.

When I reached the landing I was panting. At least I wasn't leaning against the wall sucking in air. The state I would've been in if I'd still been smoking.

The same bright emblem was slashed across the glass. This time I didn't even wince. It must be growing on me. I shoved in.

The room was large and dingy; the decor, furniture and carpet looking as if they'd all seen more of life than they had a right to. I couldn't imagine Tomlinson spending any time here.

The receptionist was younger than the others, and had the disinterested air of a visitor. She wore a grimy white blouse and a black micro skirt. The way she was sitting I got the full benefit of her thin legs, and then some.

One way and another, the impression I was getting of the efficiency of the Aberdeen office was not a good one.

She put down her nail file and said cheerily, 'Can I help you?'

I explained who I was and who I wanted to see, Mr Brown or Mr Sawers. I hoped they'd both be out. I wanted a word with her first.

'They aren't here today,' she chirruped, looking at me as if I didn't know a lot. 'They work on the rigs. Only come here once or twice a week. For letters and that.' She took pity on me. 'They were here yesterday, and I don't expect them back until next Friday.'

I tried a winning smile. 'Have you worked here long?'

She shrugged. 'Nearly a year. I'm really a temp, but they keep asking me to stay on.'

'In that case, maybe you can help me,' I said brightly.

She looked doubtful, so I brought out the letter that Tomlinson had prepared. She took it and read it. 'You're an investigator, and I've to give you any help you need,' she paraphrased, more or less accurately. She handed it back. 'What do you want to know then?'

I'd come prepared with a list of names, including the accident prone. I wanted to know if, and when, any of these employees showed up in this office. Who they were. And whether they made a habit of it.

I ran it past her. She'd only seen five of them. And them fairly regularly. That left thirty who never showed face. I asked her why.

From her expression she was wondering who'd been daft enough to hire me. 'Because they don't need to,' she said. 'They work two weeks on and two weeks off. Mr Brown pays them on the rigs, and when they're due back they go straight to the pick-up point.'

'Why did those men come in?'

'To see Mr Sawers.' She shrugged again. 'I don't know why.'

And didn't care by the look of it. But I wanted to know more about these visits. A lot more. Of the five in question, three were on Tomlinson's accident list.

'When did they come to the office? On their way out to the rig or on the way back?'

She gazed at me, transfixed. Had nobody asked her questions before. 'I don't know.' She thought. 'On the way back, maybe.' She thought again. 'No, both I think. Oh, I'm not sure.'

I realised I was pressing her too hard. If I kept this up, she'd settle for any answer, just to get me off her back, and stick to it.

'That's all right, you can think about it and let me know later. One last question,' I gave her a reassuring smile, 'I was wondering if you'd met a Dr Donald Grant?'

'Dr Grant? Sure. He's in and out here all the time. I haven't seen him for a while though.' She felt secure enough to go back to filing her nails. 'But he's getting awful thin.' She interrupted the attack on her thumbnail to look up. 'You'd think his girlfriend would look after him better,' she said disapprovingly. 'Her being a nurse and that.'

My insides tightened when I realised that she didn't know Donald was dead. Didn't this company communicate with its staff? Didn't she pay any attention to the news? My nerves settled into overdrive, when she mentioned his girl-friend.

I took a calming breath and kept smiling. 'His girlfriend might be able to help me, Miss . . .' I searched the desk, '. . . MacInlay. How can I contact her?'

'She works at the hospital.' Again the pitying look, as if I was tuppence short of a shilling. That was where nurses worked, wasn't it?

'Can you tell me her name?' I asked patiently

She stopped filing, looking surprised. 'Helen MacPherson.'

I understood. I should have known that. Along with the current price of coffee in Brazil, and whether the UN was going to do anything about people getting murdered in what used to be Yugoslavia.

'Thanks.'

I was turning to go when the door swung open and a man barged in. He stopped walking when he saw me. Sawers. I wished myself somewhere else. I wasn't ready to tangle with him yet.

He was wearing a pair of well-worn jeans, a checked shirt, and a short sheepskin jacket, and needed a shave. His eyes were red-rimmed, but still brazen. He must've been working all night on the rigs. Shame it didn't make me like him any better.

Sawers' lips pulled back to reveal a perfect set of teeth. 'Why, Miss O'Connell. This is a surprise. How can we help you?' He shot a look at the receptionist, as if trying to work out what she might have said.

I decided to help her out; I might need her again. 'I've just arrived, Mr Sawers.' I reached out a hand and kept smiling when he grabbed it in a bone crusher. 'I was about to make an appointment to see you.'

'Fine.' He darted another glance at the receptionist. She was watching us with calm disinterest. It seemed to reassure him. 'Well met then, Miss O'Connell. But I'm a bit busy at the moment.'

I was relieved to hear it. 'I'm here for the day. Perhaps you could fit me in later on in the afternoon?'

He looked at me keenly. 'Won't that mean you hanging about, Miss O'Connell. Wasting time?'

He was fishing. And I wasn't telling.

'I have plenty of work to do.'

He stared. I gazed back sphinx-like. There was a flash of annoyance in the blue eyes, then they ranged over me dismissively. He'd got my number at the funeral and didn't see any reason to change it: a nuisance female.

'Give Miss O'Connell an appointment around four o'clock, Betty,' he instructed, nodded curtly and marched past.

Betty pulled a book over and made a careful entry on a blank page. 'Right you are, four o'clock,' she said cheerfully. She smiled happily and raised a manicured hand in a twiddle of farewell.

I made a stab at returning the twiddle on my way out.

This time I was being blown towards the car so it was quicker getting back. I scrabbled in the glove compartment and pulled out the map folder which, with surprising foresight, I had transferred over.

I found the one marked Aberdeen and unravelled the spread over the steering wheel. Large span is a nuisance but I can't use a map that comes in book form. Even if I'm able to read the small print, which isn't often, I fall off the end of the page and get lost.

I got my bearings and laboriously traced a route to the hospital. Not too far. I checked my watch. Should manage there and back with plenty of time to spare. For there was someone else I wanted to speak to before seeing Sawers.

The hospital was an old building with added on car parking, a corner here, a corner there, and all of them full. I found a space outside the boiler rooms, and walked half a mile to the main entrance.

Hospitals give me the heebie-jeebies. I think it's a form of precognition. Knowing that I'm going to end up in one of them one of these days, and not being overjoyed at the prospect.

I swung through the door and found myself facing a female dragon ensconced behind a large crescent-shaped desk. Her white dress was so stiff I expected it to creak. She stared at me as if I was making the place untidy.

I walked over and said my piece.

'Miss MacPherson?' The lilting voice told all. This lady was from the islands. She'd brought the voice across, unfortunately she'd left the humanity behind. She gave me the stony eye. 'We don't have any Miss MacPherson here.'

I'm a patient woman. Because I know this, I was able to stay cool. 'Helen MacPherson?' I said pleasantly.

She stared at me as if I'd committed a crime. 'We have a Mrs,' she underlined the Mrs in deathly tones, 'a Mrs Helen MacPherson. Our hospital administrator.'

I went for it. 'That's her,' I announced. 'Could I see her please?' The look I got you would've thought I was wearing a stocking stretched over my head. 'Tell her it concerns a Dr Donald Grant,' I said between clenched teeth. 'I'll wait here.' I walked over and plonked myself on a chair.

I must have acted as if I was taking up residence, because she picked up the phone and started to talk into it, keeping the cold eyes firmly focused on my person.

I took hold of an out-of-date magazine and turned the pages. I didn't know what was coming next, or how I'd cope with it. The only thing I did know was that I had to keep going.

'Cat O'Connell? I'm Helen MacPherson. I'm so pleased to meet you, at last.'

Helen MacPherson was tall, quietly spoken and exuded an air of calm. She wore a plain but elegantly tailored blue dress. Her only jewellery was a Pictish shield inset with agate, and a pair of stud earrings.

I was looking at my double. They say everyone has one. I'd never believed it. But here it was: the same drawn face and bruised eyes that I'd seen in the mirror this morning, and the same dark hair, only hers was tidier. And if she'd been sleeping any better than me recently, she was hiding it well.

There was one obvious difference. She had an air of refinement about her, that even when I'm on my best behaviour I'm willing to admit I lack.

I was too surprised to do more than shake her hand and mutter that I appreciated her seeing me. She led me along the corridor to a door that bore her name and title in large functional letters, at eye level. Even I could've found it.

'Come in, Cat. Have a seat.' She picked up a phone and was answered instantly, and ordered tea.

I took the opportunity to peer about. The hospital severity of the room was softened by several large watercolours, and growths of greenery landscaping each corner. When I looked back, she was sitting with her hands resting on the desk.

'I saw you at the funeral, Cat,' Helen said quietly, 'but I didn't think that was the best time for us to meet. I'm glad you've come. Donald said you would help.'

That nearly destroyed me. Donald was dead, for God's sake. A lot of help I'd been. I had to take a couple of deep breaths.

Fortunately, there was a knock at the door and a tea trolley was swished in. Choosing the perfect chocolate biscuit to go with my thick china cup of weak hospital tea gave me a chance to calm down.

But I wasn't in the mood for beating about the bush.

'Donald stayed over with me the night before he died.' The minute I said it, I could've cut out my tongue. 'After what he told me,' I added quickly, 'we thought it would be safer.'

She nodded, 'I know. He phoned me before he left to let me know he was on his way back.'

'Did you . . .?'

'No, I didn't see him again.' Her eyes shadowed. 'And that was the last time I spoke to him.'

I stopped myself from asking if he'd said why he was zooming back to Aberdeen. I had to be careful here or I was going to get us both confused. Start at the beginning, Cat, I told myself, And keep your own feelings out of it.

'All I know,' I leaned forward, 'is that he'd run into trouble at Yukon Discovery, and that he'd been doing some freelance investigating. I'm hoping you can tell me a bit more.'

'I'll try. But I'm not quite sure where to start.'

'I'll help you.' I took out my notebook and settled back. 'What I want you to do, Helen—' When her name slipped out, she smiled. I grinned back. We were going to get on fine, Helen and me. 'What I want you to do is to start by telling me how you met Donald, and the sort of work he was doing at the time. We'll take it from there. Don't edit, just talk. Let me worry about what's relevant.'

Helen gave me a measured look, picked up the phone and told somebody she wasn't to be disturbed. And started talking.

How she'd met Donald wasn't a surprise, that had happened when he first started working for Yukon Discovery and was based in the hospital. They'd hit it off right away and taken it from there.

They had lived together through the bitter last two months, and had been happy. But he'd got more and more worried, and more and more close-mouthed. She thought he was trying to protect her. I thought she was right.

'Did he tell you anything about what was going on?'

She thought about it, and said, 'About three months ago he said he'd expressed concern to the safety manager about accidents on one of the rigs, and was told to concentrate on his own work.' She blinked as if she'd just remembered something. 'The only other thing I can tell you was that he got a phone call, about a month ago. He wouldn't say who it was from, but' – she stared hard at me – 'he took it very seriously.'

If it was anything like the one I'd picked up, well he might. I sighed, thanked her, and said I'd be in touch. I didn't understand why Donald hadn't mentioned any of this sooner. That time he phoned, he'd talked about being overworked, but said everything was fine.

An unpleasant thought pushed forward. We had only spoken for a couple of minutes. What if he had intended to tell me, and had tried, but I'd been too busy to listen? I wandered out, torturing myself, and made the marathon trip back to the car.

I drove round the grounds and out the gate, still thinking.

Helen had done her best to help, but this wasn't much to go on. Even his last phone call left a lot unanswered. He'd told her that he'd been in touch with an informer, someone on the inside willing to speak, and that he had to see him right away.

Him. That wasn't much of a step forward, considering that so far everybody who looked to be in the thick of things was a him. I gave a bitter grin. Maybe it was the culture, or the way the wind was blowing.

Like up your shufty.

Ditch-water

I drove sombrely away from the hospital towards my next port of call and parked the car three streets away from where I'd started that morning. I got out and tried to push coins into the meter. It refused to take them. I stuffed them back in my pocket. Suit yourself.

I was looking for Jack Baker. Jack works in Peterhead but lives in Aberdeen. He has a fifth share in a fishing boat, and when he isn't out on a trip he makes the deals and handles the paperwork. Since he starts work early, he often pops into his gym when he's finished. I'd figured that could be about now.

Jack gets around. He knows a lot of people locally, on the ships, and among the helicopter pilots doing the ferrying to the rigs. He is also a member of a tight social community that takes a strong interest in what everybody else is up to. If he didn't know what was going on, chances were he could find out.

And he owes me one.

Three years ago I helped defend his young brother, who'd fought back when he was jumped by a couple of

Glasgow tearaways. The state he left them in, he was the one who'd ended up in court charged with assault. But we got him off.

Jack had been very grateful, and told me to call if there was ever anything he could do for me. I was calling.

I reached the gym and tried for entry by saying I'd arranged to meet Jack Baker. This didn't cause anyone to leap forward and open the door. But after a moment's deep thought, the Neanderthal bouncer moved his bulk to one side and allowed me to sidle pass.

I stood in the steamy heat and loosened the layers. From the look of things, man mountain wasn't there to stop people getting in. He was making sure they didn't get out.

It was enough to bring tears to your eyes. I was surrounded by bodies in torment, some pounding on moving catwalks, others straining with weights. The sweat was pouring off the lot of them, and none of them fitted my image of Jack.

I shrugged. I hadn't chosen the right time. I'd just have to catch up with him later.

I was turning to go, when a six-foot-two under-thirty bronzed body materialised in front of my eyes, health and energy radiating from every pore. A broad smile was spread all over the handsome face.

Jack. Women must faint as he walks by. One day I must ask him how he copes.

'Hey, Cat,' Jack bellowed happily. He grabbed my hand and shook it, 'Great to see you. How's it going, kid?'

Kid, he calls me, at my age. I fought a maternal urge to sock him on the jaw. Restraint won. 'Good to see you, Jack. Can you can spare me a minute? I'd like a word.'

'Sure,' he breezed. 'No problem.' He seemed to pick up on my atmosphere. 'Something wrong?'

He picked up a towel and rubbed it over his muscles. I watched unashamedly. Jack is my answer to anybody that says it's either brawn or brains. He has both.

'I've only got a couple of minutes, Jack.'

'Sure. Let me put this stuff out of the way and I'll be right with you.'

I chose a table as far away from the action as I could, I can't bear the sight of pain. The Inquisition would've run out of ideas for these people. For extra insurance I turned my back.

Jack reappeared. I wondered if I'd ever bounced like that. I didn't think so, and it was too late now. I refused his offer of coffee, tea, Lucozade – I was awash with liquid – and waited while he gulped down some water.

'I need some information, Jack.'

He didn't even blink. 'Whatever you need, Cat. Just ask.'

I'm a truthful person by nature, because a life based on lies doesn't strike me as worth anything. But when I'm working on a case, I'm usually tighter than a pair of home-shrunk jeans, and small lies come easy. When I found myself being blatantly honest, I was mildly surprised.

'A friend of mine was killed recently,' I said. 'He worked for Yukon Discovery. And I think the two are connected.'

I mean, how bald can you get?

Jack took a while to think things over. 'Yukon Discovery? I don't know much about them, except that they pay well and they've laid some people off recently.' He looked up. 'Who was your friend?' I told him. 'Wasn't that the car that was fished out of the harbour?' I nodded. 'Bad news,' he said sombrely.

He was telling me? I kept my mouth shut. He took another swig of water. I wished I had his clean living habits. Maybe in the next life.

'Only rumours,' Jack said quietly, 'but from what I hear the word was out on your friend. He'd been pushing his nose in where it wasn't wanted.'

This didn't exactly come as news, but hearing it from Jack was a brutal confirmation. Donald must've been well marked for his name to reach the grape-vine. Like advertising for an assassin at the local employment exchange.

'Sounds a heavy scene,' I said, trying to work out what to say next.

'Yup.'

I thought some more. How far does a debt stretch? Donald's death had brought a chilling reality. The players in this game weren't playing games. So how much had I a right to ask of Jack? I hesitated.

'What do you want to know, Cat?'

That decided me. 'I need to know if what's happening up here has anything to do with Yukon Discovery. And if so, who's involved.'

'I did hear a mention about drugs.' Jack shook his head. 'But I think it was grudge talk. One of the men who'd been fired was mouthing off. I guess he wasn't very happy.'

I probably wouldn't have been very happy either. But I was relieved to hear that Jack was writing off drugs, because I'd no intention of messing around with that sort of trouble. Any hint of a connection, and I'd be hollering for the boys in blue as if my life depended on it, which it might well do.

I sighed. All the signs were that Donald had blitzed out under the strain of too much work and not enough sleep. But even if my instincts were right, and there was something fishy about his accident, it was beginning to look as if he had drawn the wrong conclusions. And ended up upsetting the wrong people.

Either way, what a waste.

'Will you put out feelers for me anyway, Jack? See what you can come up with?'

'Sure. No problem.'

I took a quick look at my watch. Time for me to go, I had to meet Sawers in a few minutes. More importantly, I was becoming aware that faces were turning in our direction, and the last thing I wanted was to cause Jack problems. I wasn't forgetting that I might be carrying my own version of the black spot.

I started flirting around, smiling bug-eyed, to make it look as if this was a romantic interlude. One-sided, of course, and nobody should have a problem believing that.

Jack caught on quickly, he's a smart guy, and he grinned mischievously. I got up to go.

He whispered, 'Take care.' A phone number followed. I sashayed off, trying to memorise it.

I was wrapping the layers back on when I passed the

bouncer on my way out. His knuckles were still scraping the floor. If he'd started jumping up and down and beating his chest, I wouldn't have been at all surprised.

The way I was feeling I might have joined him.

I left the car where it was and walked along to Yukon's office to meet Sawers. He kept me waiting ten minutes. And when he finally deigned to have me ushered in, he spent another ten minutes roaring orders into the telephone.

I think I was supposed to be impressed. Think he was a hotshot or something.

He'd shaved and changed into a suit, and his hair was spruced back. But he was still a roustabout. He splayed all over his chair, tanned and bulging, his tie carelessly pulled down and to one side.

The buttons of his shirt strained all the way down the front and the collar gaped open. I could see the hairs on his chest. I looked for the medallion, there'd be one in there somewhere, then sighed and studied the dreary wallpaper.

When he finally decided to give me his attention, he gave it all. All over. His eyes roamed like a pair of hands, his mouth smiling the secretive smile he'd been brandishing at the funeral.

It wasn't a compliment. And it wasn't intended to be. I had seen enough summers to know that much. Just the old macho aggro raising its hairy head.

If I'd been a member of a mind-reading club I'd have resigned on the spot, in case I accidentally tuned into his. What a downer.

'Good of you to see me, Mr Sawers,' I said, primly, wishing I'd had a bucket of cold water handy.

'It's very good to see you, Miss O'Connell,' he leered. 'Anything I can do to help, you just have to ask.' His eyes fixed on mine like a pair of limpets.

I felt like saying, Aw gie's peace. Instead, I took out Tomlinson's letter and slapped it on the desk.

Sawers took his eyes off me long enough to read it. He

passed it back slowly, managing to draw his hand over mine in the process, and his eyes went back to where they'd left off.

The people I have to mix with. I should give some thought to finding another way of not managing to make a living.

I took out my notebook and gave him a dead fish stare. Time to throw a little weight around. 'This investigation has been requested by your board, Mr Sawers. Top level,' I said, voice clipped to the marrow. 'And as you can see from the letter, it's a matter of some priority.'

I stared coolly at him, wondering if he was getting the message. The way he sat up and switched off the ranging eyes, it seemed he was. To make sure, and make my back feel less prone to a knife appearing in it, I went on.

'I will be submitting regular reports on my findings. This, of course, will include comments on the cooperation and assistance I receive from staff.' Well, it was half true. That was what I was supposed to be doing.

He was sitting to attention, a sycophantic smile spread over his face. The contempt was unveiled now, and shone through. I didn't mind. Having it out in the open was a change for the better.

'Miss O'Connell, you can depend on the fullest cooperation from me. And I'll personally see to it, that you get every assistance all the way down the line.'

'I appreciate that, Mr Sawers.' I held the pen over the paper. 'Perhaps we could start by you telling me about these three accidents.' He looked at me attentively. 'And what action you took in each case.'

'The three accidents on the rigs?' he asked. I nodded. 'Certainly.' His face grew serious. 'Accidents happen, Miss O'Connell. Even with the best will in the world and the most stringent precautions.' I nodded again, can't argue with that. 'I had each case thoroughly investigated and found it came down to human error.' He leaned back. 'Since we can't carry incompetent or careless workers on rigs, I had to get rid of the people involved.'

I chilled. Was this a Freudian slip of the tongue? 'You mean you sacked them, Mr Sawers?'

'I'm afraid I had to. And with the high unemployment in this area, it was a very difficult decision to make. But I had no choice.'

I would have liked to ask how many other people he'd sacked, and why. But that was outwith my remit. As, no doubt, he would've pointed out.

'Other than that, did you decide to change any safety routines?'

'I thought about it, Miss O'Connell, but it wasn't necessary. The routines checked out fine.' He shot me a sharp look. 'The problems have been dealt with.'

I felt my heart had been stabbed. Maybe one of the problems that had been dealt with had been Donald. I broke out in a sweat. Get a grip, Cat. Get a grip.

I got a grip, and decided to put the sort of question that is ridiculed when it comes from a woman. I wanted to hear how he'd deal with it.

'Could you give me a brief run-through of your safety set-up on the rigs?'

'A brief run-through . . .?' he gasped and stared. You'd have thought a troupe of pink elephants had started to dance the can-can around my chair. 'Miss O'Connell,' he spluttered, 'we run a great many complicated procedures and systems. In the time we've got left, I couldn't even begin to cover them.'

It's not so much the constant pats on the head that aggravate the hell out of me. It's the civilised way I put up with them. I smiled. There I go, doing it again.

'Just an outline of the safety provisions, Mr Sawers.'

Sawers looked disgusted, and sank back into his chair, clawing at his collar. He was going to have that shirt off his back in a minute. He gave me another foul look and started speed talking to the wall.

'We have continuous computer monitoring and good weather physical checks of the structure. There is situational monitoring by flame, smoke, gas and in certain areas heat detectors, which can set off deluge systems and, if necessary, go for shut down.'

He stopped to draw breath, and checked that I was still

hanging on in there. When he saw that I was, his mouth tightened and he started up again.

'There are strict operating procedures for work crews and evacuation routines for rig personnel, and a stand-by vessel is constantly in the field. The safety courses we run range from the specific to the general, everybody has to take those that are appropriate to their work or unit and attend repeat courses when asked.'

I felt as if I'd just been read a PR circular. 'Fine. Now if you could just let me have a copy of the check you ran on safety routines. And a transcript of your interviews with the men concerned.'

'That'll be no trouble, Miss O'Connell,' he said, gritting his teeth. 'I'll have them looked out.'

'And if you could have the transcript sent to this address, special delivery.' When it comes to pushing my luck, there are times when I feel I have no equal. I laid down my card. 'I'd be very grateful.'

His jaw clenched white. 'Is there anything else?'

'Not at the moment.' I looked him straight in the eye. 'But I may want to speak to some of the men in the next day or two.'

'Tell me how many and when, and I'll get it set up.'

Everybody likes to be a gatekeeper.

I smiled, 'That's very kind of you, but there's no need. I'll catch up with them when I'm ready.'

For an instant he reminded me of Stanley, the self-control fighting a battle with an urge to reach across the desk and grab me by the throat.

'The rigs are a man's world, Miss O'Connell. And it's a working world,' he said tightly. 'The men might not take kindly to having that work interrupted by a woman.'

Rigs? Who said anything about rigs?

There's a lot of very deep, very cold water out there, and as far as I'm concerned he could keep it. If I had any choice in the matter, the nearest I was going to get to a rig would be the helipad at the airport. No, what I had in mind was securely land-based.

I drummed up an enchanting smile. 'If I decide a visit to

a rig is necessary, Mr Sawers, I'll let you know.'

I left after that, hoping that I wasn't going to be the next problem that was going to be dealt with. But I decided that if he called me Miss once more, I'd forget any pretensions I might have of being a lady.

I'd biff him in the mush.

Blood and Wine
are Red

———

Time was pressing. I was aware of this fact when I left Sawers and hit the gale. I just wasn't sure what to do about it.

I turned indecisively in the direction of the car, then had a rethink. I was starving, and the only eatery in that direction was the café I'd popped into when I arrived. I faced the other way and leaned forward.

I found a trattoria tucked between a bookies and a newsagent. Red gingham checked curtains, and a cheapo menu stuck in the window alongside a sign Open All Day, said this was for me.

Tomlinson had given me a cheque for expenses but I hadn't had a chance to pay it in yet. And I was getting fed up going to cash lines and getting the Not Authorised brush off. One of these days Stanley.

The place was deserted. This could be bad news, but I was here and I was staying. I started to take off the garb and felt the sheepskin being lifted from my shoulders. A young Italian waiter beamed happily and whizzed me to a table. Hoping for the best, I ordered *Pesto alla Genovese* and allowed myself a glass of house wine.

I swanned out feeling I'd just won the pools. I ran my tongue round my mouth to pick up the last of the flavour, and allowed the wind on my back to blow me towards the car.

I made good time back to Glasgow. And since the heater had got up it's flumfy and decided to work, the journey was bearable.

I parked and set up the stairs. It was after eight, the end of a twelve hour stint, and I was looking forward to putting my feet up. I had the key in the lock before I noticed the chipped woodwork.

I froze and checked it out. The lock still held. Whoever had been here had tampered, but they hadn't managed to get in.

Footsteps were on their way up. My first instinct was to pin myself against the door and prepare to fight for my life. When it dawned on me they were cloddingly familiar, I relaxed, slightly. Sanderson. God Almighty.

He rounded the corner and stood on the landing below, puffing even more than usual. I glared at him. This I needed like a hole in the head.

Sanderson glared back, and straightened up self-importantly. He obviously had something to say. I hoped it wasn't going to be something I'd heard before. And that whatever it was it wouldn't take long.

'Ms O'Connell,' he said heavily. 'We had an incident here a few hours ago. And our neighbour, Miss Green, has been taken to hospital.'

'What sort of incident?' I said sharply. 'And what's wrong with Miss Green?'

'Apparently she disturbed an intruder. Someone who was trying to break into your flat.'

His eyes said that nothing that went on in or around my flat would come as a surprise to anyone. That my neighbours were the poor unfortunates who had to put up with it. And now see what's happened.

I repeated between clenched teeth. 'What's wrong with Miss Green?'

'She has a head injury. I called an ambulance.'

If he hadn't looked so smug I would have been grateful. 'Which hospital was she taken to?' I snapped, starting downstairs.

He told me. Unfortunately, I was almost face to face with him at the time. I reeled back from his breath and raced on down, my heart beating like a drum.

It was all coming back to me now. HAG had mentioned a man at my door. He must've been sussing it out. And I hadn't paid any attention.

Some investigator me. Wouldn't see a wall in front of my nose unless it got up and hit me.

I screeched into the hospital grounds, dumped the car and set off at a run. When I found admissions, I jigged about impatiently until the couple in front of me finished their spiel and walked away.

'Miss Green. Miss Hilda Green,' I said urgently. 'She was admitted a few hours ago. Can you tell me which ward she's in?'

The receptionist looked kindly at me. 'Are you family?'

Not again. What was this?

'No. A friend,' I snapped. I stared her straight in the eye, ready to create a scene. 'A close friend.'

She gave me a wary glance and started to check through some papers. Running her fingers along the lines of writing, she found what she was searching for, and looked up.

'It's very late, but you can see her for a few moments. Ward 17.' Her eyes grew stern. 'Miss Green is not to be upset. She's an old lady and she's had a bad shock.'

I promised I wouldn't upset Miss Green.

She directed me to take the lift to the second floor, and to turn right when I got out. I did as I was told and approached the nurse on duty. She pointed me to the bed in the corner. I walked the length of the ward in fear and trepidation.

HAG lay prone in the bed, her eyes closed, a tiny figurine in an expanse of bedclothes. Her frail head had a massive bandage wrapped around it. Thin tendrils of white hair peeked through the edges, below a large red stain.

I could've wept.

Her eyes flickered open and shut again. 'Cat,' she breathed.

'Oh, HAG.' She shouldn't have found out I called her that but it was too late now. 'What happened? Are you all right?'

Is she all right? What a question.

A skeletal hand eased from the covers and patted mine gently. 'Don't worry. I'm fine, Cat,' she whispered. 'I'm fine.'

Lying there looking as if she had both feet in the grave, and she tells me she's fine. I stroked her hand. 'How d'you feel?'

'Better,' she murmured. Her eyes shot open and she tried to sit up. 'Someone was at your door, Cat.' She relaxed back and closed her eyes. 'But I gave them what for.'

I bet you did, HAG. I just bet you did.

I felt a tap on the shoulder and looked up.

A fresh-faced nurse stood at my side. 'I think you'd better go now. Miss Green's very tired.' She smiled. 'You can visit tomorrow.'

I thanked her and walked away. The chill of the last few days was turning into a determined core of ice. They'd taken Donald. And now they'd hurt HAG.

I might not know yet who 'they' were, or what they were up to. But, by Christ, it was time somebody marked their cards.

I was no sooner in the door when the phone rang. It was Doreen. She sounded panicky.

'I've been trying to get you for two hours, Cat. Is everything okay?' When I said it was, she rattled on, 'Your neighbour, a Mr Sanderson, called earlier looking for you. Said something about an attempted break-in, and that the old woman downstairs had been hurt.'

How had Sanderson got hold of Doreen's number? Then I realised, HAG. I said nothing.

She started up again, her voice growing sharper. 'If this has anything to do with Donald you've got to go to the police.' Her voice rose. 'Cat. If you don't, I will.'

— 105 —

I was sorry to hear that. Very sorry. I felt the blood rush to my head. Putting up with Stanley treating me like an idiot was one thing. Taking it from Doreen was another kettle of fish altogether.

This was my business. I'd decide when it was time to go to the police. And I'd do it on my own.

'What the hell are you playing at, Doreen?' I said furiously. 'What makes you think you can tell me how to do my job?'

There was a long silence.

'I'm sorry, Cat,' Doreen said quietly. 'It's just that I'm scared you'll get hurt too.'

That should have been enough for me. It wasn't. I gave the bone another chew. 'I don't interfere in your business, Doreen, so keep out of mine.' I slammed the phone down before I said anything else I was going to regret.

The doorbell went. I steamed through and yanked the door open. Clemency, the walking fox fur, stood on the doorstep, smiling sweetly. My cup runneth over.

But you've got to hand it to her. The woman's got guts. Most people have given up wearing real fur, in case somebody rips it off their back, or puts another bullet it in.

She gave me an even bigger smile, pushed forward a bunch of orange lilies, and chanted, 'And Cowslips, and Kingcups, and loved Lilies.' Spencer. Father used to read his work to us when we were children.

I found myself grinning and opening the door wider. Clemency can make me as mad as a hornet, but when she turns on the soft soap I'm as big a mug as the next one.

At times like this, I tell myself that underneath it all she's good-hearted and well meaning. And I try to forget that she has a waspish tongue, and is congenitally incapable of minding her own business.

I peered out. No Raymond. And them usually attached at the hip too. They must have had the operation. Being grateful for the smallest of mercies, I was instantly cheered.

'You'd better come in now you're here,' I said ungraciously. She swanned past me in a breeze of Poison. I crinkled my nose.

'I've come to take you to supper, darling.'

Clemency's eyes went on a tour, checking to see if things had improved since the last time she'd been here. From the look on her face, they hadn't. The bright smile faltered, and picked up.

'Raymond's waiting for us,' she gushed, 'with a perfectly charming couple he knows through business.'

'Clem,' I said patiently. 'I've had a hard day. I'm going nowhere.'

'Nonsense, darling.' She turned from her assessment of my meagre belongings. 'Phone your handsome new boyfriend . . .' she clicked her fingers as if she had a problem remembering the name, '. . . ah yes, Martin. Tell him to join us.'

I looked at her sourly. Clemency never forgets a man's name. And to hear her tell it they are always handsome. I snorted. Often wish I shared that viewpoint.

'Sorry. Not tonight.' I hardened my heart against the disappointed look in the melting blue eyes. 'No, Clem,' I said firmly, beginning to feel as if I was up against the wall with a knife at my throat.

I was making a noise in deaf ears. She zoomed in to inspect the kitchen, calling back gaily that I had to hurry up. I tried to change the subject.

'How's mother?' I called through. A muffled voice informed me she was simply splendid and sent her love.

Clemency reappeared. It hadn't taken her long to look over the dishes and inspect the fridge. I supposed the bathroom would come next.

'And when's the happy day, darling?' she cooed.

That did it. A one-track mind has nothing on this madam.

'Read my lips, Clem,' I spat, looking daggers. 'One, there isn't going to be any happy day. Two, I am not joining you for supper.'

She looked me over sniffily. 'I'm very sorry to have to say this, darling. But unless you change your attitude, you're going to end up an old maid in a garret.'

The ultimate put-down. We glared evilly at each other.

This was ridiculous. 'Too late,' I said charitably, 'I already am.' To drive the point home, I indicated our surroundings with a graceful sweeping gesture.

'Am what?'

'An old maid in a garret.'

'Don't be silly,' she snapped. 'You just happen to live in an upper flat.' I smirked. So that's what they call it nowadays. 'And you know perfectly well what I mean.' She unpursed her lips and put on a concerned face. 'If you keep chasing people away, Cat, they'll stop visiting,' the voice dropped dramatically, 'and then you'll be all alone.'

All alone. Her idea of the gloomiest of gloomy fates. My idea of heaven.

'Can I count on that?' I snarled.

Clemency gave an unladylike snort, and huffily pulled the fox remains up around her chin. 'There's no point talking to you when you're in one of your moods, darling. I'll phone you tomorrow.' She flounced off, pulling the door shut behind her.

I padded around in the silence like a caged tiger, wishing I had something to kick that wouldn't collapse on impact. How long were she and Raymond staying up here, for God's sake?

I tidied up, roughly. Having seen the place through her eyes, I had to do something. When I still couldn't settle, I stormed out for a brisk walk. I came back half an hour later, drank a mug of hot milk, and collapsed into bed.

A Time
For Reflection

I got up feeling depressed. I hadn't a lot to be proud about.
Correction, I had nothing to be proud about. Doreen had
been concerned about me, and I'd behaved like a bear with
a sore head.

I should've been grateful somebody bothered.

Falling out with Clemency didn't worry me. That was
just a re-run of a very old and very bad movie. Father used
to laugh at our squabbles, but mother was forever lecturing.
She said that I had to be taught to get along with people.
Well, no one could say she hadn't tried.

As for my investigating skills. So far, there wasn't any sign
of either incisive thinking or well-honed deductive powers.
One way and another, I was about as useful as a bikini in a
snowstorm.

Feeling sorry for myself, I washed and dressed, and
phoned the hospital. HAG was doing fine. She'd eaten her
breakfast and was sitting up checking that the nurses were
doing their work properly. She'd given instructions that I was
to come and see her at two o'clock. I said I would and rung
off smiling.

I slipped on my jogging gear: skin-tight cycling shorts, heat-retaining top, stirrup trousers, sports socks and heel-sprung running shoes. And it isn't even colour coordinated. But when I put it on I'm raring to go, and that's fine by me.

I took the car up to Botanic Gardens. I needed open space. I pounded round the gardens and along the Kelvin walkway, and allowed myself a breather on the bridge. I leaned on the parapet and stared down at the sludgy water.

Mallards swirled along the river and under the bridge as if they had urgent appointments. There was ice on the river-bank and frost on the grass. A scattering of hardy dog walkers paraded along the opposite path, stopping from time to time to accommodate poochy sniffing and doggy needs.

I looked up at a nearly bald horse-chestnut. A grey squir-rel was flitting along a branch. It stopped and turned its brown orbs in my direction. It looked sorry for me. That made two of us.

When I got back I threw myself into an orgy of washing. The clothes needed it, but I did it because it's my way of preparing for some serious thinking.

In my line of work, anyone who hires me is buying my time and discretion. The money it costs them is often grudged, by them, and it can prove small consolation to me. Especially when I'm getting done over as the piggy in the middle.

I handle it by working hard, keeping my head down, and accepting everything I'm told. Then I triple check. Whatever the outcome, my mouth stays shut on who said what.

I tell myself I get job satisfaction.

Most of the work I do is internal: moving into a company, following people around, listening, and attending meetings. The only exceptions had been two minor cases of industrial sabotage, where employees had been in the pay of the com-petition.

With the external connections I'd already uncovered in this case, it looked as if I could be in for an extension of the sabotage experience. Or some another variation of company based self-enrichment.

I hoped not. The wider the web, the harder it is to

unravel. And while I have a nose that doesn't know how to stay out of trouble, I prefer to restrict the potential damage to myself to manageable limits.

I poured a coffee, spread papers over the table, and sat down to work. I'd got my first impressions. Now to make sure I had everything recorded, and in some sort of order.

First, I jotted down what Tomlinson had told me: staff dissatisfaction, poor training results and accidents. Then I added what I knew: Donald's death; violence in Aberdeen that Sawers, according to Martin, had been implicated in and, if Bert's attitude was anything to go by, had reached Glasgow; an attempted break-in; and HAG being hurt.

I had details of company organisation and access to information on recent and current business activities. I started to make up a table relating these to the dates of the accidents. When I finished I put it to one side to mull over later, and turned to the current state of play.

Tomlinson, after a bad start, was beginning to look as if he would help. I wasn't sure I could trust him – I still didn't know what part he played, if any – but there were signs of cooperation. And that was useful.

Sawers I believed was suspect, but I had to watch myself here. Because he was the Safety Manager, there was bound to be a question mark over him. There again, there was such a thing as innocent until proved guilty. Just because he made my flesh crawl, and Martin had remembered his name from an old case, wasn't enough to condemn him.

Bert. Now, he knew something. What I had to do was work out how to encourage him to part with it. In the past, being part of the action had done the trick, but it looked as if he intended giving this particular action a very wide berth.

Helen didn't know what Donald had actually been doing, but she'd promised to go through his papers with a fine toothcomb. She'd get in touch if she came up with anything.

Jack. I smiled. Jack would help, and I trusted him. But I'd have to be careful there. He could be dragged into the thick of things. And I didn't want him hurt.

So where did all this leave me?

I got up and wandered about aimlessly for a while, then

made another coffee and sat down at the computer. When the brain doesn't work there is always routine. I opened a file, named and dated it, and transferred my scribbles into type.

Once this was saved and copied on both back-up disks and I'd popped one into my pocket, I got up and wandered about some more. One of the puzzles was the training programme. What its apparent failure had to do with anything was, for the moment, beyond me.

I looked at my watch. I'd think about it later. It was time to obey the summons and visit HAG. Apart from looking forward to seeing her on the mend, I was keen to hear exactly what had happened.

I stopped off for flowers, and came out clutching a bunch of Freesias. Where they'd come from at this time of the year, God only knew, but they looked healthy and smelled nice. I made my way to the hospital.

I smiled brightly at the same receptionist. She gave me a firm look, reminding me to behave, and smiled. Into the lift, second floor, and merrily along the ward, keeping the flowers behind my back. Wouldn't do HAG any harm to think I hadn't brought her anything.

There was a fluster of nurses around her bed. For a second my heart nearly stopped. Then I realised they were giggling. She was probably telling them to have nothing to do with men, and issuing orders on how she liked her tea – two sugars and no milk.

I reached the bed and beamed happily. She was sitting up looking bossy. Things were getting back to normal. I fumbled with the flowers and hoped that she'd been too dazed to notice I'd called her HAG – a vain hope.

The femininely pretty crocheted bed jacket was a front. The munchy little face stuck up from its folds like the head of a hydra. Even looking at it, made my hair curl.

'What's this "hag" business then?' she fired, the mouth turning into a steel trap. Not another word was going to get out until she got an answer, and it had better be good.

'A term of affection,' I mumbled.

'How's that?' she snapped.

'Your initials, Hilda Agnes Green.' I spelled it out. 'H.A.G.' If I got any more sheepish I'd be bleating. I produced the bundle from behind my back, and hoped I was doing something right. 'Brought you flowers.'

She took them, and looked the blooms over judiciously. 'Very kind of you, Ms O'Connell.' That was me put in my place. I grinned. She waved the flowers in the air, and a nurse materialised with a brilliant smile and took them off, promising to find a vase.

Satisfied, HAG sat back and crossed her hands in front of her. 'You'll be wanting to know what happened?'

This was true. I took a chair.

She checked that I was paying attention, and started to talk. 'I was putting out the rubbish, when I heard someone coming in. It was that man that had been there before.' She looked disapprovingly at me. 'The day your Dr Grant came round.'

I nodded. She did remember his name.

'Well, I didn't think too much of it, except when I came out with another bin-bag, and heard noises from upstairs. Cracking noises, as if something was getting broken.' She glared at me as if I'd done it. 'So I went up to see what was going on.'

'And?'

HAG leaned forward indignantly. 'That man was at your door. Trying to break in. I told him I'd phone the police.' She pursed her lips and leaned back looking pleased with herself. She wasn't going to have any nonsense in her flats; she'd shown him.

I couldn't bear the suspense. 'What happened?'

She gave me a pitying look, shame I wasn't very bright. 'He ran away. It's just that my balance isn't so good these days, and I fell down a couple of stairs.' She put her hand up and patted the bandage happily. 'That's how I hurt my head.'

I leaned back and breathed a sigh of relief. At least HAG hadn't been attacked. It was small consolation, but it was one I was ready to hang on to. Whoever 'they' were, they hadn't sunk to the level of beating up eighty-year-old women. Yet.

'What'd he look like?' I asked sharply. She looked at me with eyes of stone. When messages are drummed home even I catch on. I rephrased it. 'Can you describe him to me, Miss G? What he looked like, what he was wearing, that sort of thing?'

Mollified, she deigned to answer, the voice like a frail machine gun. 'A big man, not fat, wearing a Balaclava. He had one of these jackets,' she waved her hand, 'you know, soft. With a zip up the front. Dark blue.' She leaned back, smiling smugly. 'I told that nice young policeman all this this morning.'

My spirits sank. If the police thought that this was anything other than a casual break-in, my wings were going to be severely clipped, rapid like.

'Why was that? I mean, what were the police doing here?'

'Mr Sanderson phoned them.' She looked surprised that I even needed to ask. 'About the break-in, and my accident.'

I wondered when people were going to stop treating me as if I had part of my brain missing. It also crossed my mind that there was a distinct possibility I was next in line for a visit from that nice young policeman.

'Anything else you can remember?'

She thought about it. 'Not really. Except that he smelt funny.'

Being tuned into smells, I grabbed at it. 'What sort of smell? Can you describe it?'

She wrinkled her nostrils. 'Well, he smoked. But it was sort of . . .' she looked disapprovingly at me, again, 'sort of that stuff you cook with.'

That could be a number of things. I searched my mind, trying to dredge up possibilities. Something that HAG had disliked even more than usual? It was difficult.

I had a brain-wave. 'Garlic?'

'Is that that smelly stuff you put in everything?' I nodded. 'That's it, then. Garlic.' She leaned back again, looking tired.

I felt guilty, and said I'd better go. I promised to come the next day, not to forget to put food out for the pigeons, and gave her a kiss on the cheek. I walked off thinking that knowing the intruder was a garlic eater was about as much use as knowing that he was a man who wore trousers.

When I heard myself laughing I knew I had another problem. My sanity.

I phoned Doreen the minute I got in, to make amends. I apologised. She said it was all right, she'd been out of line, but would I please be very careful. I said I would, that I hadn't behaved very well myself, and that I'd get back to her.

I'd just put the phone down when it rang. I debated not answering. I picked it up anyway, in case it was important. It was Martin. My spirits quailed. He asked how I was. I said fine.

'I'm sorry about the other night, Cat. That was stupid. I'd no right to behave like that.'

I felt like asking him what would make him think he had a right, and how he would behave if he did. But what was the point. 'That's okay Martin. Let's forget it.'

'I thought we might take in a meal. I could call round for you in' – there was a pause as if he was checking his watch – 'an hour?'

The arm bruises winced. To my mind, anyone who tries violence once is capable of getting to like it, and apologising can become part of the buzz. And that's one scene I want no part of.

'No, I don't think so, Martin. It's been a heavy week. I'm having an early night.'

'Right.' The silence lengthened. I wished he would hang up. 'We'll make it tomorrow night, then. I'll pick you up at eight.' The phone went dead.

This is what I like, being allowed to make my own decisions. I replaced the receiver. What I really wanted to do was kick it around the floor, but I'd probably need to use it again.

I got up and prowled the kitchen, looking into cupboards that would've been better left unopened. I came up with one carrot, two onions, one sprout of celery, a bulb of garlic, and a screwed up packet of frozen prawns. With my stand-by herbs, tomato paste and spaghetti, I was home and dry. Elizabeth David eat your heart out.

I was out of fresh Parmesan, but I found a bottle of Cabernet rolling about under the laundry bag. What more could I ask? Wine is an essential ingredient in my cooking. The fact that most of it goes inside me is just as it should be. Sign of a good cook.

Sated, I laid back and watched the news. And fell asleep.

I stumbled up at two in the morning and automatically tottered through to bed, my eyes still glued shut and my brain in limbo.

In Deep Water

I wasn't as lucky as HAG. I didn't get the nice young policeman. I got Detective Inspector 'Rambo' Thompson and his
foggy side-kick Detective Constable Miller.

The beating on the door wakened me. I looked at the
clock: 9.30. I'd overslept. I wrapped up and stumbled
through. My eyelids hung on to each other, terrified they
were going to be parted.

When I bleared out and saw who it was, I checked that the
door was still in one piece. It's common knowledge that
Detective Inspector Thompson can cause more damage
with his fists than the average burglar with a jemmy.

Thompson and Miller watched in silence, top heavy book-
ends keeping out the light. Both wore dark overcoats,
unbuttoned. Each had the granite face of a man doing what
a man had to do.

Thompson fixed me a cop stare, and pushed his badge
under my nose. 'Ms O'Connell,' he said officiously, 'can
we have a word?' You'd have thought we'd never met
before.

I looked down. One very large black boot was already on

the way in, I couldn't close the door now even if I wanted to. I kept my mouth shut, opened the door wider and staggered back through. I knew he would take it as an invitation.

Thompson and I go back a long way. In my days as a lawyer I used to come across him depressingly often. His manner towards me at that time had been one of respectful disdain. The only thing that's changed is that nowadays he leaves out the respect.

I think it's something to do with me setting up on my own. I understand he's against private enterprise. I haven't worked out yet how he thinks lawyers make a living.

Thompson is good at his job because he's crafty, tenacious, and tough. At some stage, his blood must've been exchanged for molten steel. The scar down the side of his jaw is an old one. It's been a long time since anybody messed with DI Thompson.

The curious thing is that he has a peculiar appeal for women. They line up, each turned on by the belief that there is a human being inside the hard-bitten shell. And each convinced that she is the only one who can release him from his macho chains.

Masochism gone mad.

I'm ashamed to say that I nearly fell for his hidden charms myself once. Fortunately, I had more sense. But any woman daft enough to take him on has my sympathy.

Now he was at my back in the tiny kitchen, deliberately crowding me. At six one and bristling with pectorals, he took up space like a tanker in a fishing harbour. When he leaned closer, I was nearly pinned to the cooker.

I fumbled with the kettle. 'What can I do for you, Inspector?' As far as I know Thompson is immune to flattery, but there's no harm in trying.

'Just a few questions.' He nodded in the direction of the kettle. 'One sugar, by the way.'

One sugar the man wanted. I was tempted to ask how he'd like it, in a spoon, or just thrown all over him. A look at the hatchet face sent me reaching for the mugs.

He zoomed his eyes around the kitchen; taking in the remnants of the night before, the dirty dishes in the sink and the empty wine bottle. He nodded as if satisfied and turned his attention back to me.

A wolfish grin spread over his face: 'I hear you had an attempted break-in.'

There are times when it's better to get the inevitable over and done with. This appeared to be one of them. I poured three mugs of tea. No point asking Miller if he wanted one. He doesn't use his mouth to speak, only to put things in.

I handed the mugs over and eased myself into a chair. The upstanding representatives of the keepers of the law deposited themselves on the settee, an oversized Bill and Ben.

The official front back in place, Thompson eyeballed me like James Cagney in a bad mood. 'About this attempted break-in. That makes three times,' he flipped open a note-book, 'in two years. Rather a lot, wouldn't you say?'

The way he ran his eyes around the sitting-room, he was suggesting that it wasn't my possessions that anyone was after. I should have been offended, but I happen to agree with him.

I said that these were shocking times we lived in. That the poor police force was shamefully under-manned, but that they did their best in very difficult circumstances. And that I was as surprised as him that anyone should want to break into my humble abode.

I had a feeling it wouldn't be good enough. It wasn't.

A neon warning sign flashed up in the over worldly eyes, and he prodded a finger in my direction. 'Don't waste my time, Ms O'Connell. You know and I both know, that the last two occasions were directly related to work you were involved with.' The way he said 'work' it sounded like a dirty word.

'That doesn't mean that this is,' I pointed out politely.

'What it does mean is that you've been knee deep in shit twice before,' he snarled. 'And I'm right out of patience.'

I thought this was a bit strong, especially with Miller sitting there, ears flapping. 'I don't care for your attitude, Inspector,' I said stiffly. 'Perhaps I should call in a witness.'

He stared hard at me. I had a notion that if I'd been a man I'd have been up against the wall at this point, struggling for air. 'What are you working on at the moment, Ms O'Connell?'

'That could be claimed to be privileged information,' I said. I studied the rim of my mug and wondered if I'd finally taken leave of my senses.

Thompson looked as if his leash had been slipped, and he was enjoying the freedom. 'Could be.' The wolfish grin crept back. 'But it'd better not be.'

I didn't even hesitate. 'I'm contracted with an American company, Yukon Discovery, on an investigation of company routines and practices.'

Thompson sent an icy glance to Miller, who started scribbling furiously. He turned back to me. 'Since when?'

'A few days ago.'

'And you're claiming that the two aren't connected?'

Well, I hadn't as yet. Not in so many words. But I was going to. Lord Save Me. I gazed steadily back at him. 'I've no reason to believe that they are.'

Thompson looked thoughtful. I tried to act innocent. He stood up, and Miller leapt up at his side.

'I just hope you know what you're doing,' Thompson growled, towering over me. 'And that you're not interfering in things that don't concern you. Because I wouldn't like that.' He moved his head slowly from side to side. 'I wouldn't like that one little bit.'

He didn't need to say the rest. It hung in the air as if it had been verbalised. If you do. And if there's anything left of you when the dust settles. We'll sort you out. Good and proper.

The killer stare is built-in, it just varies in strength. I got a mega burst. 'Thank you for your cooperation, Ms O'Connell. We'll see ourselves out.'

I heard the door slam shut and leaned back. Thompson and I had our problems, that was for sure. But this was the first time he'd come across so heavy.

So what did he know that I didn't?

I was in the shower, my head still struggling to face the day, when the insistent ringing of the telephone became too much to bear. I wrapped a towel around me and padded through, leaving a trail of wet footprints.

I picked it up. 'Hello.' I wasn't in the mood for small talk.

'Ms O'Connell? Ms Jordan of Yukon Discovery here. I've been trying your number for some time. I'm glad to have caught you.' I closed my eyes, wishing I could say the same. 'Mr Tomlinson asked me to arrange flight tickets and overnight accommodation for you,' she sparkled on. 'The flight leaves at twelve o'clock. You can pick up your tickets at check-in. A car will meet you, take you to the hotel, and your meeting starts at 4 p.m. Plenty of time,' she ended reassuringly.

There was a buzz of silence on the line. I had a feeling I was expected to say something. 'What meeting?'

'Your meeting in London with Mr Tomlinson and Mr Haldane, the Training Manager,' she said brightly. At a loss for words, I leaned against the table and breathed heavily into the mouthpiece. 'Ms O'Connell? Are you still there?'

I said I was, and asked whether this journey was really necessary. She said it was, gave me the details and rang off.

I picked up the phone again and left a message for HAG that I couldn't visit today after all, and remembered I hadn't fed the damned birds. I patted the last of the water off and got dressed, choosing a sombre brown wool outfit that suited my mood to a T.

Unearthing HAG's key, I nipped down to her flat. The bird food was on the kitchen table and the window-ledge was packed with disgruntled pigeons. One kept strutting up to the glass, battering it with his beak and glaring at me with vicious little pink eyes: boss-man bird. He'd better not be there when I opened this window.

Fortunately for him he wasn't. I spread the food, locked up, and dashed back for my briefcase and overnight bag. I was taking the bag, but I didn't plan on staying over.

One of the benefits of living in Glasgow is that the airport, if one has to use it, isn't too far away. I parked in the short-stay car-park, walked over to the terminal, checked in and settled down to wait. To take my mind off the terror to come when I left the ground in a jet-propelled tin can, I gave some thought to this last minute summons.

Unless the Training Manager was unlikely to be in this country again over the next month, dragging me down to London at a moment's notice didn't make an awful lot of sense.

There again, it could be that Tomlinson was trying to run me. Which would be a pity, because I'd be very hard pushed to avoid a showdown. And I didn't want to lose this contract. Not now. Retaining the access to Yukon Discovery was important, if I wanted to find out what had happened to Donald.

When I heard the flight being called, I got up and headed for the boarding-gate. Fatalism descended on me like a shroud.

Smoother
Than Oil

When I walked out of arrivals I saw my name being waved
on a placard. I went over. The efficient-looking young
woman holding the card stuck it in the air again, her eyes
searching the crowd.

Medium height, blonde hair, she wore a neat jacket and
trouser suit, with a snappy little hat, and looked as if she
enjoyed her work. I introduced myself and got a wide smile
in return.

I followed her out to the car, a Scorpio, and piled in. She
drove smoothly and competently through the jumble of traffic and I was able to relax. And that doesn't happen often.

We got to chatting. I was interested in hearing how she'd
landed the job and why she liked it. She said she'd given
them the hard sell. And what she liked was not knowing
where she was going to end up from one day to the next. I
could understand that.

The next thing, we were drawing up in front of the hotel.
It was in central London, one of an international group,
and expensive. I used to enjoy going to places like this; a
long time ago.

Having sussed out that tipping was perfectly accept-able, I eased out, passed across a few notes and wished her well.

I went in. Inside was quiet, spacious and blandly plush. Large settees upholstered in a pale blue and pink material were grouped beside low glass tables. The carpet was off-white, without a mark on it; the flowers looked real.

When I said who I was looking for I was fussed along a corridor to a pair of double doors. They were opened with a flourish, and I wandered in.

Tomlinson and another man were seated in armchairs at the far end of the room. They both stood up. When I finally reached them I was introduced to Haldane, and we all shook hands and passed comment on the weather.

Good for the time of year, I agreed. And yes, I'd had a pleasant flight. The things I say to try to earn a living.

Haldane was taller than Tomlinson, straight-backed, and looked as if he liked to keep in trim. Around fifty I guessed, and smartly turned out in a light-weight grey suit. It could've been an Armani, but I'm no expert.

He had a deep tan and a permanent smile, and thick grey hair that drifted over his forehead. His attitude was brisk with underlying impatience, and his tawny eyes were expres-sionless.

Compared to him, Tomlinson with his no-nonsense stare looked the honest broker. I knew this was as accurate a gauge as pissing in the wind. On the other hand.

'Sorry about the late notice, Cat,' Tomlinson said. 'Art, here, has a stop-over on his way to Bahrain. Seemed a good chance to get you two together.'

We did the routine. 'It's good of you to see me, Mr Haldane.'

'My pleasure, Ms O'Connell.'

Tomlinson smiled. 'I've got some business to attend to. I'll catch up with you later.' He slid off, and Haldane and I sat down.

Haldane's sten-gun word delivery and Texas accent threat-ened to set my ears into overdrive. I poured a glass of water, using the time to psyche myself out of my aural blinkers, and sat back to listen carefully.

By the time the preliminaries were over, it turned out we were speaking the same language. We just had different ideas on how to go about it.

His description of the thinking behind the training scheme was succinct and presented evenly. He was used to making presentations. Everything was categorised, lined up and shot out.

He explained that after the horrific accidents in the North Sea industry in the recent years, efforts were being made all the way along the line to reduce the risks to personnel. In a high-risk business, this wasn't easy but it was being given high priority.

As well as overhauling safety procedures, a more thorough training scheme had been introduced to try to ensure that men were completely familiar with all the equipment on the rigs, whether they used it or not. The idea being that as well as instilling caution in the use of that equipment or of being around it, it could help in an emergency to cut down the blunders created by panic and ignorance.

The reason this scheme had been introduced in the Scottish rigs was not, Haldane took pains to point out, because the men there were not good at their work. But because the North Sea was an unforgiving environment.

'You see, Cat. Say, you don't mind me calling you Cat?' I smiled and said I didn't. 'You see, Cat,' he rattled on. 'A rig's going to blow in Texas? You get the hell out of there. A rig going in the middle of the North Sea? Where are you going to go? Over the side, sure. But if the fall don't kill you, and the waves don't batter you to a pulp against the rig, you're sure as hell going to freeze to death.'

He stared hard at me. 'They say you have fifteen minutes. I say five. That's why we carry extra space in lifeboats and rafts, and have a stand-by vessel on hand constantly.'

I sat in silence. Five minutes was a sobering thought.

'Ed tells me that you've been called in to carry out a review. And that you might come up with something on why the training scheme isn't working. I'm sure glad to hear it. That's my baby, and I want it right.'

I lifted my mind from the thought of men freezing to death in icy water, and concentrated on the matter in hand. Training wasn't part of my remit. And I didn't want to get caught up in a detailed break-down of the relative merits of different approaches. But I was interested in the general set-up.

'What makes you think the scheme isn't working?' I asked.

Haldane's eyebrows nearly shot out of sight. 'Because we've had a number of accidents on the rigs, Cat. Accidents that shouldn't have happened.'

I didn't follow his logic. I phrased it politely. 'I don't follow your logic, Art.'

This seemed to put him out of sorts. His jaw jutted in a manner that suggested he was trying to get himself under control. Looking at the size of him, I hoped he was going to make it.

He picked up the telephone at his side, said a few words and slammed it down, and got up and marched over to the window. I watched him, saying nothing.

Tomlinson reappeared and took in the scene. He gave an amused smile and prowled past. I sat where I was and tried to talk myself into a philosophical frame of mind.

A waiter arrived, a sparkling white linen napkin draped over his left arm, looking as if nothing would be too much trouble.

'What're we all having,' Haldane bawled, from the other end of the room. He didn't seem any happier.

I checked my watch, 6 o'clock, and decided I could reasonably call it an aperitif. I shouted out for a malt. Tomlinson chose the same.

Haldane ordered rye on the rocks. 'And bring the bottles.'

My heart sank. My tolerance for the hard stuff has deteriorated over the years. Since this is probably my body's way of saying it wants to live out its allotted span, I don't fight it. They could get pie-eyed if they liked. One would do me.

The drink arrived on two silver trays, one holding the bottles and an ice barrel, the other bowls of finger-sized pastries and dips. Haldane waved away the waiter and dolloped out man-sized helpings.

I stretched out my hand for my glass. While I was at it I grabbed a plateful of pastries, I'd need them to fight the alcohol. Both men sat down and took large gulps. A peaceful silence descended for all of three seconds.

'If accidents are still happening, the training scheme isn't working,' Haldane announced. He'd brightened up. Probably the booze. He took another monstrous swallow. 'And if something isn't working you fix it.'

He was a dog worrying a bone. Could be he was putting up a shout for his corner and trying to move me in that direction. After all, resources are squabbled over routinely, and when it came down to it that's all I was. Or he could be serious about training.

I decided to give him the benefit of the doubt. 'Is the structure, content or timing of this course any different from the others that you've run?'

Haldane hesitated. 'It's a structure we've used before and much the same timing, but obviously the content's different.' He shrugged and looked at Tomlinson – we've got a right one here – and turned back to me. 'You see we're covering different topics.'

I refused to be drawn. 'Has the attendance held up?'

'They've got to attend,' he said, ultra patient. 'It's part of their job. Anyway they get paid extra, to discourage them taking a day's sick leave when they feel like it.'

'Are they?'

'Are they what?'

'Taking more sick leave than normal?'

Haldane stared. 'Some,' he said flatly.

I thought about it. So the only thing different about this course was a higher than average sick rate. I don't like snap judgements, but I was going to have to say something. And be diplomatic.

'It may not be the training scheme at fault,' I said. 'There could be other factors.'

'These are good men up North,' Haldane fired back. 'I'm proud to have them working for the company.'

'I wasn't referring to the workforce,' I said quietly. Haldane bristled.

Tomlinson decided to speak. 'What Cat is suggesting is that factors other than the scheme itself or the capabilities of the men could be causing the problem.'

This was the second time Tomlinson had acted as my interpreter, and his help wasn't required. We weren't dealing with any heavy concepts here. I glowered and took a swig of whisky. It hit my stomach and spread a hot glow.

Haldane smiled forbearingly. 'What other factors?'

To stop my lip from curling, I opened and shut my eyes to check that they were still operating. They were, just a bit misty round the edges. This whisky must've come straight from the vat.

'The equipment or procedures?' I suggested finally. Neither of them seemed to like that. No skin off my nose. I hid the irritation behind a bland stare. 'Well, something is putting them off. Or somebody.'

I poured the last of my whisky down my throat. This was kindergarten stuff. Haldane was either very concerned about this course, or he was acting it. The question was which, and why. As I studied the empty glass, another hefty shot was splashed in.

'Putting them off,' Tomlinson said thoughtfully. 'What do you have in mind, Cat?'

It must be his turn to play funny buggers.

I had to stay patient, and watch my back. 'If the course follows the usual format, the equipment and procedures are up to scratch and it's a good workforce,' I said calmly, 'it could be you've got a motivation problem.'

'How will you check that out?' Haldane demanded. He sent another suffering man-to-man look at Tomlinson. 'After all, that's something you can't see, can't add up.' He focused on me, talk your way out of that, smart ass.

I decided I was sick of it. Nobody is expected to walk into the middle of a complicated industrial set-up and a couple of days later come up with all the answers. If they do, it's time to get worried.

I ignored Haldane and turned to Tomlinson. 'I'm

contracted for a month. I'll get as much done as I can in the time available.'

'Extendable, Cat, extendable,' Tomlinson murmured, suavely brushing aside my dig.

'Anyway, what do you mean that we've got a motivation problem?' Haldane broke in, going for the kill. 'They're getting paid extra, aren't they? Isn't that enough?'

Tomlinson's eyes flickered over the pair of us and he looked away. No help there. The effort it took to control my tongue made my jaw hurt.

'I didn't say that you had a motivation problem, Art,' I said evenly. 'I merely pointed out it was a possibility. And you're right, checking that sort of thing isn't easy, since it can cover anything from disinterest to fear.'

'Which do you think it is?' Tomlinson shot out. There must've been a wild look in my eyes, because he added quickly, 'From what you know so far.'

Attractive bonuses were involved, I remembered that from my quick look at company papers. If men were bucking off, there had to be good reason.

'At this stage, I've nothing to go on,' I said. 'If you're asking me for a general comment, I can only say that if good money and sound working conditions aren't getting reasonable results, you're nearer the fear end of the spectrum.'

'Are we talking about the course here?' Haldane snapped. 'Or the rigs?'

As far as I was concerned we were talking nonsense.

But it was interesting that he tied training problems with the more serious unidentified troubles on the rigs. Was there something I wasn't being told?

'Looks as if this is the tip of a large and highly unstable iceberg,' I said cheerfully, watching them like a hawk. They exchanged glances.

'We happen to be of that opinion too,' Tomlinson said quietly. 'Any idea what it could be?'

In for a penny in for a pound, and maybe I'd get something back this time. 'Intimidation?'

Haldane shot Tomlinson another look. 'We're very interested to hear you say that, Cat. Very interested, indeed.' He turned aggressive eyes on me. 'But what grounds have you? Heard something on your travels? Seen something?'

Was he worried? Or just naturally obnoxious?

'I'm only tossing around ideas. There's no reason to think it's anything that serious.' I smiled brightly at the pair of them. 'Is there?'

Nobody said anything.

I hadn't touched the last whisky. Even the smell was making my eyes water. Food was required. Solid, satisfying, fattening food. Fast.

Tomlinson must've read my mind. He picked up the phone and called room service. 'Dinner for three.' He looked across at me. 'Would you like to see a menu?' I shook my head. 'What do you want? Fish, meat, or chicken?'

I said fish, and that I didn't care how it came as long as there was a lot of it. Haldane said steak, large and rare. Tomlinson placed the order, going for chicken himself, and we picked up the silence where we'd left off.

Bad Vibes

Within minutes two white-jacketed staff arrived, speedily set out a table heavy with silver and asked about wine. Nobody wanted any. Next thing a fancy trolley was wheeled in, laden with lidded platters.

I made it to the table and told the waiter to tip everything on to my plate. An hour and an empty plate later, the prognosis was better. I was going to live.

Haldane turned out to be a trencherman. He wolfed his way through a huge steak and managed half of another nearly as big, plus two lots of trimmings. He washed it all down with several large glasses of whisky, anointed with water.

I couldn't work out where he put it, his spare tyre was modest and the rest of him looked well enough stuck together. He didn't speak much. Just the odd pleasantry between mouthfuls. England's a great country, a great country. The workforce is terrific.

I listened politely, trying my best to look open-minded. Far be it for me to point out that the rigs were in Scotland. That nearly half his workforce was Scottish and the other half would best be labelled international. And that by the law of averages they couldn't all be as terrific as he was making out.

Tomlinson had retired behind a three metre high fence awash with Do Not Disturb signs, and topped with barbed wire. He ate slowly and said nothing. Not even, 'How's your fish?' or 'Pass the salt'. He seemed to have forgotten that there was such a thing as good manners.

Haldane paused from his munching occasionally to throw him a searching glance. Water off a duck's back.

I reached for the jug of iced water and filled a glass.

I gave Tomlinson another going over. He was dedicated to the task in hand. I'd never seen anybody put as much concentration into stripping a chicken bone before. I finally dragged my eyes away.

This was just a business meeting that hadn't gone very well. So why did I feel uneasy? Were there deeper seated worries around here that nobody was willing to share? Or was I back in the front line of self-interested warfare?

Tomlinson and Haldane had different remits, and one was European based and the other ranged company wide. But from their manner, they were equal in the pecking order.

That could mean one of two things. They were either in collusion or rivals. If the former, I was going to need to work out what was going on while I was ducking the flack. If the latter, I could get duffed up in the bun fight whether I ducked or not.

I considered the first: that Haldane had been briefed by Tomlinson to lead me on, some sort of test. I threw it out. There were easier ways, and I was sure Tomlinson could've come up with one of them.

As far as the second went, no obvious reason sprang to mind. But there was a lot I didn't know about the internal politics of Yukon Discovery. In particular, Haldane and Tomlinson's relative aspirations, and their current position in the rat race.

I went over my impression of Haldane. He was sharp, overbearing and smooth. The type that would make sure his bread fell butter side up. It would be a mistake to underrate him. And that was one mistake I didn't intend to make.

My final thoughts had the attraction of brevity. I decided it was time I chucked it and went home.

I excused myself from the table and walked over to the chair I'd been sitting on earlier. I found both handbag and briefcase nestling under the frill of the loose-cover.

Bending over activated the incipient headache. As the first hammer blow fell, I knew that the journey back was going to be even worse than the journey down.

'Where do you think you're going?' Tomlinson demanded, staring glacially at me over his pile of bones.

I tried it out to see how he'd like it. 'Home.'

He didn't seem to like it much. 'Surely you mean your room?' he said sharply. I shook my head. No, I didn't mean my room. 'You're not in any fit state to fly back to Glasgow tonight,' he snapped. I wondered whose fault he thought that was. 'Anyway, you're booked in here.'

He turned away to allow Haldane to light his cigar. I'd been told what was what. The matter was closed. I started walking, making for the door.

'I'll see you tomorrow at eleven o'clock, Ms O'Connell,' Tomlinson shouted after me. He sounded mad. 'Be here. Prompt.'

I shoved the door open and made it along to the lift. Eleven o'clock, prompt? Here? I should toto. I'd get back to Tomlinson when I was ready. Until then, he could whistle.

The lift went down as if the cable had snapped, and the G-force repositioned my full stomach upwards, somewhere in the region of my gullet. Apart from the general discomfort, it made speaking difficult. Because I wasn't quite sure what was going to come out when I opened my mouth.

I persevered, however, and succeeded in persuading a retainer to retrieve my overnight bag from a room I had no intention of occupying. And to summon up a car to whisk me back to the airport.

Collapsing gratefully in a corner of the leather-seated luxury, I promised myself that I would never take another mouthful of alcohol as long as I lived.

I gazed at my watch. After I'd shoved my face at it a

couple more times and still got nowhere, I gave it up as hopeless. I had no idea what time it was. Didn't want to know. And was glad there was nobody there to tell me.

I felt as if I'd drunk a Mickey Finn. Lousy.

Planes, like buses, either come in droves or give the impression the service has been withdrawn. I was spoilt for choice.

I could take the first flight and change at Birmingham, wait ten minutes for the second and fly direct, or, and I still haven't worked out how they managed this, wait another five minutes for the third flight, and get there before the other two.

Out of curiosity, I chose the third option and filled myself up with coffee while I was waiting. When the call came I steamed aboard and deposited myself in a window seat.

I took time to check out the distance between me and the nearest exit. I clocked it to the nearest centimetre, working out how many people I'd be competing with to get out when we crashed. And promptly fell asleep.

If anyone had tried to waken me during the flight, they hadn't succeeded. When I came to we were diving straight down, the engines giving that peculiar scream that suggests the pilot has changed his mind about landing; and left it too late.

My tongue was stuck to the roof of my mouth. I felt worse now than when I'd fallen asleep. I swallowed and looked at my watch. This time I saw the numbers: 11.30. Not too bad, I should be cosily tucked up in bed just after twelve. God willing.

We landed. I got off, trundled along to Baggage, finally recognised my bag, retrieved it, and made my way to the exit. Driving was out of the question. I'd get a taxi.

I'd just stepped outside, when I was overcome by a feeling of deepest melancholy. The dull pain spread through me, making me gasp. It was all I could do not to burst into tears.

I breathed in fresh air furiously.

I was bitter about Donald's death. And deeply sad. But why this pain, here and now. It had been years since he and I had been at the airport together.

I liked the answer even less than the question. This feeling would come again and again, out of the blue. And I was going to have to learn to live with it.

A taxi drew up, I crawled in and gave my address, and sat back numbly.

I'd paid the driver and was searching blindly for my keys, when I saw a man standing in the doorway. I froze.

I was in two minds. Should I beat it, sharpish, or hope that my judo skills weren't as impaired as the rest of me, and brazen it out? My eyes cleared and I smiled, the devil you know.

'Martin. What're you doin' here?'

He picked up my bag and briefcase, and stared stonily at me. 'How about we had a dinner date? Several hours ago.'

It came back to me like a knife running through butter. I should've phoned him and cancelled. For a minute my head popped with the effort of trying to think of an excuse. Nothing came to mind.

His face twisted as if a bad smell had materialised under his nose. 'You've been drinking.' He took another whiff. 'For God's sake, Cat. You're drunk. Where the hell have you been?'

For some reason this struck me as funny and I giggled. 'I've been in London on business; a meeting with Tomlinson and Haldane.'

Martin studied me as if I'd acquired two heads. And from the look on his face, he wasn't about to believe a word either of them said.

'Since when did you mix business and booze?'

'I only had one whisky,' I protested. This was strictly accurate, even though there had probably been three measures in the one glass.

'One! You smell as if you've been rolling in it.'

I could have pointed out that one whisky does not a drunk make, it just makes you smell like one; but I couldn't be bothered.

I looked at him. There was a smile lurking round his mouth, despite the po face. Were we talking peace here, or not? Did I care? I decided I had no way of telling.

I positioned myself more securely against him, acting like I needed holding up. There are times when I think my sense of humour needs its head examined.

'Come on.' Martin took the keys, grabbed my shoulders and propelled me upstairs. He leaned me against the wall while he opened the door, and hustled me in.

I was feeling nice and loose. Even his sour face didn't put me off. Frog-marched along to the bedroom door, I heard his voice from a distance.

'You can sort yourself out this time. I'll see you tomorrow.'

I floated in and collapsed on to the bed, giggling at a terrific witticism I thought somebody had just said. I dragged the duvet over me as darkness descended.

The next thing I knew I wakened with a start. I felt as if I had been dropped from a great height. My eyes were staring with fright, my mouth was filled with sawdust and my body was shaking all over. I struggled up and pawed my way to the kitchen and forced down a few pints of water.

Never again, echoed like a dirge in my brain. Never again.

I tottered back and lay and shivered some more, until the light searing through the window assured me that this was the beginning of another wonderful day.

What fun.

On the Rack

———

I had another headache. Time I gave them up. I dragged on a robe and shuffled to the bathroom, a mole hitting the sun. I caught sight of myself in the mirror. The hair was standing out from my head as if it was in the middle of a nightmare. And by the look of things, it didn't want to be interrupted.

I averted my eyes, washed my hands and cleaned my teeth. The only other water that was getting near me for the time being was going down my throat.

I went to the kitchen with a head that threatened to become disconnected every time I moved. I held a wet flannel to my temple with one hand, and left the tap running so I could scoop water up in a glass to my mouth with the other. When I heard the hammering on the door, I groaned and clutched the sink. This wasn't happening. Another frenzied attack said that it was. And that it wasn't going to stop until I answered.

I pulled the robe tighter and aimed for the door. I opened it. As advertised, Detective Inspector Thompson and Detective Constable Miller, the local SWAT team.

They stared. I stared back, my lips clamped like a vice.

Thompson looked as if he couldn't believe his good fortune. The corners of his mouth lifted. 'Ms O'Connell. May we . . .?'

I didn't wait to hear the rest. Turning on my heels and staggering back in, I sat myself on the sofa with what dignity I could muster, and waited for what was coming. They looked down, faces dead-pan.

Thompson sat beside me, still having difficulty with his face. He pushed it pugnaciously close. 'Ms O'Connell, we have to have a word, you and me.'

'Anytime, Inspector.'

'Why didn't you tell me you knew a Dr Grant?' he shouted. I nearly shot off the sofa. 'A Dr Donald Grant!' There was a ringing in my ears. Jesus. 'Well?'

My mouth opened and shut noiselessly, and I sank back, temporarily defeated. His face lit up like a man realising a long-held fantasy.

'You didn't ask,' I croaked. This was true, but the wrong thing to say.

'What d'you mean I didn't ask?' he bawled, centimetres from my lobe. I prayed for deliverance. His voice switched to an ominously low purr. 'Are you trying to get smart with me, Ms O'Connell?'

Would I ever.

'N-no,' I stuttered. 'I didn't know . . . what I mean is . . .' I sank deeper into the sofa, my head screaming for mercy. I knew for whom the bell was tolling all right. Me.

He stared. 'You look as if you need a strong black coffee,' he said, evenly. 'Get Ms O'Connell a coffee, Constable. We'll have one as well.' Miller shot to the kitchen.

I glowered after him, Make yourself at home, why don't you. 'I don't need a coffee,' I mumbled.

Thompson leaned forward, the wolfish grin securely in place. 'I know exactly what you need, Ms O'Connell.' His voice was barely above a breath. 'And one of these days you're gonna get it.'

I glared – you and whose army. A hot mug was shoved into my hand. I studied the mug carefully, and closed the other hand around it as well, just in case, and drank.

Thompson reached over and removed the empty mug from my hands. 'That better?' I nodded, counting his teeth. 'Right. Let's get down to business. Tell me about Dr Grant.'

I told him everything. Well, nearly everything. The only thing I missed out was Donald's troubles with Yukon Discovery, and my suspicions about his accident.

'We've had the report on that incident,' Thompson said, looking grim, his dark eyes fixed on me unblinkingly. I stared into them, mesmerised. 'That's why we're here.' I felt chillier by the second. 'There are signs that the brakes may have been tampered with.'

The blood left my face, and everything started to spin. The next thing I knew my head was being pressed between my knees and I couldn't move. After a minute or two I heard his voice coming from a distance, asking if I was all right.

I squirmed to show that I was, and he lifted his massive paw from the back of my neck and sat me up. I was crying now, and I hated him for it.

He stuck a handkerchief in my face and told Miller to make me another coffee. When it was delivered in the same ungainly fashion as before, Thompson leaned over.

'You don't look well, Ms O'Connell. Shall we get a doctor?'

I stopped snuffling and glared. I could do without the bad guy good guy routine. 'I'm all right.' I pushed my hair back wearily, and tried to think straight. 'That means you're treating this as a suspicious death, not an accident?'

'Let's say, we are pursuing our inquiries.' Thompson gave Miller a look that made him leap to his feet, and turned back to me. 'I'm sorry about your friend,' he said quietly, looking as if he meant it.

I latched on to the glimmer of sympathy. 'Do you have any idea why this happened? Was Donald in some sort of trouble?'

His face lost all expression. 'You should know better than expect me to answer that, Ms O'Connell. But I'll tell you something for nothing. It's out of your league. So stay well

— 139 —

clear.' He stood up and fastened up his coat. 'And don't think we won't know what you're up to. The tabs will be super-glued.' He fixed me with a cold stare. 'I suggest you wise up and start thinking if there's anything you haven't told me.'

They slammed the outside door as they went out. Thompson always has to have the last word.

I drank the coffee slowly. As far as I was concerned, this was merely confirmation that Donald had been murdered. But it forced me to take the fear out of the cupboard and look it straight in the eye.

I gave it time to sink in. Then I thought back over Thompson's attitude.

Underneath the calculating exterior, there had been a hint of the professional brutality that signalled he meant business. And when he was in that frame of mind, anyone who interfered was likely to get trampled.

I had no intention of allowing him to frighten me off. But he had the weight of the law behind him, and was just the man to use it. What I had to figure out was how to continue my investigation, without him stamping on my neck – hard.

Remembering his crack about the super-glue, I went to the window and peered through the side of the curtain. There were three cars parked outside, and a gas van. I recognised two of the cars. I took a note of the number of the third. I'd check up on it and the van, later.

I showered and dressed quickly. I'd earned myself some favours over the last few years. It was time I started collecting. My head was still acting as if it was inflamed, so I took two pain-killers and hoped that the brain wouldn't seize up. I looked out again. Nothing had changed.

Although I have the greatest faith in the freedom of our democracy, I had no intention of putting it to the test. I sorted out some loose change for a call-box, and braced myself for hitting the air.

I walked quickly to the one on the corner, beside the off-sales. The glass panels were clean, and the interior hadn't been ripped out, but I decided to give it a miss. Too near home.

I walked two blocks further on to the next. I prised the door open, reached for the phone, clanked a pile of coins in and dialled. It was picked up and the number was repeated back to me, cautiously.

'Bert,' I said. 'It's Cat.'

'Caithlin, my dear,' he whispered. I could imagine him looking round to see if anyone was creeping up on him. 'What can I do for ye, Caithlin lass? No trouble with the car I hope?'

I told him what I wanted, and when. There was a squawk at the other end of the line. The silence went on so long, I began to wonder if he'd had a heart attack.

'Bert.' I glanced round to see if anyone was creeping up on me. It must be infectious. 'Bert,' I hissed. 'Are you still there?'

'For Gawd's sake, Caithlin. Ye don't want to go looking for trouble. It'll find ye soon enough without inviting it in.'

'It has.'

'Has what?'

'Found me,' I said bleakly.

There was a long silence. I thought it was time to remind him how I'd been able to help him out in several of his frequent disputes with the law. And that maybe he was due me a few favours. He didn't sound too happy about this, and I heard all about his old Aunt Nellie and her bad leg.

We bickered some more before we settled on a place to meet. A disreputable bar on the other side of the river, with a passing trade that kept itself to itself, and a number of useful exits.

I phoned Helen. Mrs MacPherson was at a meeting, I was informed snootily, and could not be disturbed. I left a message to tell her I'd call back.

Finally, I called the number Jack had given me. He wasn't there either. This time the message I left was please not to ring me, I would get in touch with him. The rest were bona fide business calls. I could make them in the comfort of my own home.

I came out and wandered back, picking up some shopping on the way. Apart from the fact that I was now ravenously hungry, it gave me a reason for being out and about in the first place.

Bread upon
the Waters

I made myself a vegetable curry with brown rice and wolfed
it down. Delicious; I felt like Popeye after spinach. I tidied
up, clearing the decks for action. The whole performance
took about two hours, time well spent. My head had settled
down and I'd had time to think.

The first thing I had to do was cast bread on the waters.
Tomlinson had to be sweetened up somehow because I
wanted to keep this contract. It wasn't a money earner any
more. It was a personal vendetta.

I reached for the phone and pressed the receiver to my
ear. Not a sound. I gave it a shake, replaced it, and tried
again. Still nothing. I followed the line and found it had
been pulled out of the wall. Had I done that? I tried to
remember. The state I'd been in the night before anything
was possible. I shrugged, plugged it back in and started
again.

'Yukon Discovery. Ms Jordan here. Who's speaking
please?'

'Cat O'Connell, Ms Jordan. Is Mr Tomlinson available?'

'He's still in London, at a meeting. He was expecting to

see you at eleven this morning.' She sounded puzzled. 'I did try to contact you, but the number was unobtainable.'

'I'll get in touch with him later,' I said shortly. 'If possible I'd like to arrange to meet with you.'

'Me?'

'Please.' There was a long pause. I waited.

'Well, I am travelling through to Glasgow tonight,' she said doubtfully. 'Aileen's off ill and I'll be working there tomorrow. Maybe sometime in the afternoon?'

'How about tonight? When will you get here?' Another silence. 'We both need to eat, Ms Jordan, and we could talk while we're eating.' I turned up the persuasion control. 'It would save a lot of time.'

We agreed on a small restaurant near the station, eight o'clock. I was meeting Bert at seven, so that fitted in nicely. One down, two to go. I tried the hospital, calls were queuing, I hung up.

I phoned Aberdeen. I hadn't received the copy of Sawers' check on the safety routines or the transcript of the interviews, and I wanted to know why. I got through to Betty. Sawers was out, and no, she hadn't been asked to send me any papers.

'Betty, tell Mr Sawers that I need those papers urgently. I can get them from Mr Tomlinson, of course, but it seems a pity to trouble him unless I have to.' The way she drew in her breath suggested she'd got the idea. I hoped she'd pass it on to Sawers.

'I want you to do something for me,' I went on. I told her what it was. I was guessing, but it'd do to be going on with.

She sounded surprised. 'All transatlantic telephone calls made from . . .'

'And to.'

'. . . and to this office, between July and September?'

'Yes. List them, with dates, and send it with these other papers. And Betty, keep this to yourself. Understand?' When she said she did, she sounded more like her old self. I hoped this was a good sign.

I rang off. I intended going back up to Aberdeen as soon as possible, I wanted to see Mike Brown among others, but

— 144 —

there was no point arranging anything until I got those records and had time to go through them.

The phone shrilled in my ear. I picked it up. It was Martin. I tried to be cheerful. 'Hello, Martin. How are you?'

'So you're back in the land of the living,' he said icily. 'How's your head?'

'Fine.'

'Are you ready to explain why you didn't keep our dinner date?' I thought that I had, and said so. 'Oh, come on, Cat. Do you expect me to believe that you got roaring drunk at a business meeting in London?' His voice got tighter. 'And who the hell are Tomlinson and Haldane?'

I wondered why he was so suspicious, and whether it was in-built or learned. I shrugged. My sympathy was with any honest clients that came his way. He must give them a hard time.

'Cat. Are you going to answer me?'

'I already have.'

'Don't be ridiculous,' he snapped. 'The last time I saw you, you could hardly stand, never mind speak. And at your age, you should know better.' I frowned, now he was getting personal. 'We've got to talk. Get this sorted out.' I didn't think there was anything to sort out, but controlled the urge to say so. 'I'll come round after work,' he announced. 'About seven. Be there.'

Another man issuing orders. I must be mug of the year.

It was satisfying to be able to say, 'Can't, Martin, sorry. I'll be out. Working.'

After a deathly silence, I heard, 'Who's the lucky man tonight, Cat? Or is it another threesome?'

I hung up, there was no answer to that. I went over to the calendar. 1993, what a relief. For a minute there, I thought I'd been transported backwards in time, around a century or so.

I picked up the phone again and tried the hospital. This time I got through, and was transferred to the ward.

'Staff Nurse Simpson here, Ms O'Connell. I tried to contact you this morning but the number was unobtainable.'

My heart gave a lurch. 'Is anything wrong?'

'No, no,' she laughed. 'It's just that Miss Green can go home tomorrow and we wondered if you would be able to pick her up around eleven.' She paused and said gently, 'We understand she has no family to help her. But if it's not convenient for you, we'll make other arrangements.'

I smiled. Convenient? When had HAG ever been convenient? I explained the position and managed to get Staff Nurse Simpson to agree to keep her locked up until lunchtime, around one o'clock. Any change to that plan I'd let them know about it.

I'd no sooner sat down at the computer when the phone rang again. I debated: will I, won't I? I did. It was Tomlinson, calling from Heathrow.

'I'll be catching a flight north in a few minutes,' he said, in iceberg tones. 'I believe I requested a meeting with you. Perhaps you can spare the time this evening,' he added sarcastically, 'before you meet Ms Jordan?'

Ms Jordan had been quick off the mark, but a good secretary always keeps her boss informed. And from the sound of things, this was not a happy boss. Maybe it was time I brushed up on my social skills.

'I have an earlier meeting,' I said, briskly. 'So tonight's out. Where will you be tomorrow, Dundee or Glasgow?'

'Glasgow.'

We agreed on eleven o'clock, and I was given the strong impression that I'd better turn up, on time. I went back to work. First I wrote up my diary, where I'd been and who I'd seen. And made a note of anything that I might want to check later.

I opened a file on Haldane and updated my files on Tomlinson and Haldane. No detail, just the main points, under four columns. In the first, facts and verified information, in the second what they'd told me, in the third what other people had told me about them. In the fourth column I added my own comments.

I printed out, put it in a folder and shoved it in a drawer, and switched off feeling satisfied. I might not know yet what was going on, but I sure as hell was going to find out.

This stage I like. It's a walk towards the unknown with

only one guarantee, that it's not going to be dull. In a funny sort of a way, it reminds me of the start of a love affair, all that excitement and not knowing how things will turn out.

It's just as well that I can get this sort of thrill from my work.

The clock had moved on, it was nearly time to meet Bert. Bearing in mind the ambience of the bar and Bert's burgeoning paranoia, I decided that the skin-tight red trews and floppy purple sweater weren't quite the thing.

Anyway, this image didn't suit the sharp-eyed professional investigator that Ms Jordan and me would both like to believe in.

I opted for a deep-blue trouser suit, dark enough to merge into the gloomy background of the bar, neat enough to look smart in the more normal lighting of the restaurant.

With flat pumps it satisfied a third criterion, an essential consideration when visiting the dark streets surrounding Bert's chosen rendezvous. If necessary, I could hoof it. At speed.

I didn't want to be hampered by a coat, but although the freeze had lifted it was pretty cold. So I popped on thermal undies, a sweater, then the suit. It was a tight squeeze.

I went out, furtively casting my eyes up and down the street. The van had gone, but that didn't prove anything one way or the other. Could be waiting around the corner, bulging at the seams with the boys and girls in blue.

If I'd felt draughty round the gills before, now I felt stripped bare in a force ten gale. And I didn't intend taking any chances. I took a taxi to a spot I had in mind nearer the river, paid it off and made my way through the back-alleys.

I walked quickly down the first narrow dirty street, paint scrawls all over the closed metal shutters of the loading bays, and squeezed past a row of bin-bags. The squeaks and scurryings didn't bother me. Any rat that took me on would have a fight on its hands.

The heavy aroma of exotic spices wafted from an air vent high on the corner wall of a dilapidated restaurant front. I turned left, shimmied down the side of parked cars, then right and right again.

The Broomielaw was quiet, only three or four cars at a time coming through the lights and drifting steadily along. At the other side of the road, the yellow-red lights of the bridge shone down on the black, oily stillness of the Clyde.

That was one place I wouldn't care to end up in.

There were taxis cruising. I hailed one, jumped in and gave the street. The name of the bar would probably have left me watching rear lights. I paid over the money and thanked him before getting out.

He took the money and seemed to like the tip. His head twisted round, 'Yu all right, hen. S'no a very good area this. Want me te wait?'

I only wished I could afford it. 'No, thanks. I'll be about three quarters of an hour.'

'Quartur te eight?' I nodded. 'Well, Ah might be passing by here aboot then. If Ah do, Ah'll wait furr'a couple of minits. Okay by yu?'

Okay by me? I'll say it was. I beamed him a best smile and scrabbled out feeling almost light-hearted. The thought of my unexpected Sir Galahad kept me going past the high dank brick wall, with its sprayed-on abuse and peeling posters, across the corner where the street lights were out of action, and towards my rendezvous.

The bar lurked like a sleazy shadow beneath the block of neglected masonry. I stepped into the tight front entrance and swung the door open. As I stepped inside, I sent up a prayer that I wasn't about to come face to face with a bottle winging its way out.

A Meeting
of Minds

The pub was a hang over from the good old days. When men were men and women stayed at home, and the sawdust got spat on between gasping draws to prove it.

Time had moved on. There was no sawdust.

The walls were lined in a sooty dark wood that intensified the gloom. A pervasive musky smell suggested that the small windows weren't the only things that would've benefited from a good going over with soap and water.

The low ceiling held the bulk of the smoke at just the right height for asphyxia. I peered through the smog. From the look of some of the clientele, standing upright was just a phase they were going through.

Eyes slid over me and did a re-run.

I'd increased the female contingency by a third. At first glance, the only thing we had in common was our sex. But, as Stanley might have said, appearances can be deceptive.

One was a bag-lady who followed the winos around the city. Wrapped in several layers of dirty woollens and a washed out headscarf, she was clutching a half-pint glass filled with a dark red liquid. She looked happy.

The other was a young blonde with worried eyes, wearing a suede jacket longer than her skirt, black tights and white stilettos, who was hanging determinedly on the arm of an older man decked out in sharp suit. She didn't.

I recognised him. Jimmy Roston, a flat-eyed bookie whose thoughts concentrated on money, and whose reputation for shady dealing was well deserved. I clocked the weaselly figure by his side. His gofer. And with an extra scar on his cheek unless I was much mistaken.

But where was Bert?

Then I saw him. He was stuck in a corner, baring his teeth in an ingenuous, undirected smile. He wore a flat bonnet over his grey, thinning locks, and a dull green anorak that made him look as if he was wearing a flak jacket.

I eased my way through the mob. 'Hello, Bert.'

He struggled out from behind the table and stood up. 'Caithlin, me dear. Good te see you. What'll ye have?'

I answered automatically, 'Whisky, Bert. With water.' As soon as I said it, my stomach heaved. I took a deep breath. How I was going to drink it was problem number two. Problem number one was to get Bert talking.

He arrived back with the drinks and squashed himself between the fixed table and the wooden bench seat. The only thing that wasn't screwed down in this pub was the booze, and the people drinking it. He propped himself up in the corner and returned to his close study of every movement.

We each took a sip, smiled vaguely and settled back. I looked at him. A nervous twitch had started up in the corner of his eye. If this had been just another case, I think I'd have let him off the hook there and then.

I thought about Donald and hardened my heart. 'I want to know what's going on, Bert.'

'Caithlin,' he said, shaking his head, 'I don't know what ye mean, lass.' He gave me the benefit of a pair of honest eyes. I wondered where he'd picked them up.

'Forget the nonsense, Bert. You bloody do know what I mean. And it's about time you started talking.'

We tried to stare each other out. He threw his beer and

chaser down his throat as if he'd heard them calling time, then took a couple of minutes to savour the after-effects.

'The two ye were asking about?' he said finally. I nodded. 'They're a couple of toughs. The type ye leave well alone, Caithlin.' His eyes shot round the room. 'Well alone.'

I was disgusted, absolutely fed up with the histrionics. What a patter merchant. I fixed him with a nose-to-nose stare.

'When did you start being scared of a couple of toughs?' I said ill-temperedly. 'Some of the people you mix with eat toughs for breakfast, and still have room for their bacon and eggs.'

It was the first time I'd let slip that I knew the sort of company he kept. His brows drew down like a pair of irritated caterpillars, and he looked at me askance.

'Will ye listen,' he snapped. 'It's not me I'm worried about. It's you. And I'm trying te give ye some good advice. Leave well alone.'

He took time out to breathe deeply and eyeball the clientele. When he turned back he'd readjusted his face, the friendly gremlin was back up front.

'Caithlin, me dear,' he said persuasively. 'These people've been linked to some very nasty situations.' He jogged my arm and signalled the direction with his eyes. 'See Shug boy there,' he muttered, speaking into his collar. I looked, the gofer, and quickly looked away. 'He should've crossed the road and walked by with his eyes shut. But he didn't. And see what's happened.' He gave a disgusted snort. 'Somebody tried te give him another breathing hole.'

I clenched my teeth. 'What's going on, Bert?'

'Drugs. Some new boys.'

A chill settled over me and my stomach started churning as if tomorrow was a tale only a fool would believe in. The talk of drugs was cropping up far too often for my liking. I should take my head out of the sand.

But there was something about this news item that didn't ring true. I worked out what it was, and started to get annoyed all over again. Did he think I was daft?

'Don't try and tell me that your friends are just sitting

back,' I snarled, 'and letting some new faces push in on their patch and walk all over them.'

He looked at me pityingly. 'These new boys aren't operating here. Their action is up north. And as long as they keep it that way they'll be left te get on with it.'

'But you just said they did Shug over. And he's part of here.'

'Shug's a silly boy. Always has been,' he said indifferently. 'Brings it on himself.' He got up, ready to do a runner. 'I'll try te find out more for ye. But fer Christ's sake, take care. And keep me out of it.'

I watched him zoom through the mass like quicksilver. A nod here, a nod there, and he was gone. I was left gazing sadly at my almost untouched glass. I'd never thought it would ever come to this, but I knew that if I took as much as another swallow I was going to be sick.

'Cat O'Connell. Haven't seen you round these parts for a while.'

I looked up. It was the ambitious bookie himself, oily and chancing his arm. The girlfriend stood deserted at the bar, looking forlorn.

I nodded, 'Jimmy.' If I had a pound for every Jimmy I meet in Glasgow, I'd be a millionaire.

When I stared hard at him he looked uncomfortable, but not as much as I'd have liked. The broad-jawed face and squat nose reminded me of a hyena. As I watched the nostrils twitch, I tried to dig up what I could remember of my old legal manner.

'Jimmy Roston,' I said briskly. 'Last conviction a year ago, still on probation. Not good news for a bookie.'

He looked at me sourly. 'Mistaken identity that was, Ms O'Connell. Water under the bridge.' He was cool enough to notice I was still listening, and smiled ingratiatingly. 'I hear you've left the practice. Out on your own now.'

'Old news, Jimmy.'

He grunted, selected a cigarette, lit it, and added some more smoke to the atmosphere. 'You looking for information?'

'Why? You got some to offer?'

He took a long swallow of beer and put the glass down, and thoughtfully licked the froth from his lips. 'Could be.' Another puff of smoke. 'For a price.'

I shrugged. I knew Jimmy's prices, and my ear wasn't as close to the legal ground as it used to be. But he must have worked that out for himself. If he was still sniffing round there must be something in it for him.

I wondered what it was, and how to find out. Silence seemed the best policy. It lengthened. Jimmy took another swig and several puffs. I stared into the fug and waited.

'Put it this way,' he said eventually. 'I might have a score to settle. Just might, you understand.'

I understood. 'What's your price, Jimmy?'

'That you see that the bastards get theirs,' he said viciously. 'And that I'm kept well out of it.'

'Why not tell the police?'

He turned a pair of injured eyes in my direction. 'Ms O'Connell, I have my reputation to consider.'

I knew for a fact that Jimmy boy was not averse to the odd tip-off when it suited him. Clearly, on this occasion it didn't. I wondered whether his gofer's new facial adornment had anything to do with it.

'What have you got?'

He lowered his voice. 'Names and dates on certain accidents. Interested?'

'Might be.' I can play cool too.

He gave me a look that said I should give up trying to act smart, because I wasn't any good at it. 'I'll get that to you then, Ms O'Connell.' As he stood up, his eyes flashed the vacant sign, The light's on, but nobody's in. 'Just remember. I know nuthin',' he muttered.

He walked over to his girlfriend and stood with his back to me. She smiled up at him, pitiably grateful. I studied the glass, and had to admit that the flesh was too weak.

I left it lying, scraped myself out from behind the table and made for the door. My eyes were out on stalks, looking for the quiet nod or casual move that could suggest company, unwelcome company, outside.

I hoped that taxi driver had remembered his role of Sir

Galahad. If not, I had a hundred and fifty metres to get to a main road. I could manage that much at speed if necessary, but not much more.

There it was, a taxi burning light. I dived in, gave the address and sank into the seat. He was going to get an even bigger tip this time round. Stanley or no Stanley.

The taxi drew up outside the restaurant. He seemed to like the tip. 'Take ma number, hen.' He poked a hand through the grill, pointing at the gold figures. 'If ye're phoning, ask for me.' I smiled, and said I would.

He gave me a cheery wave and drove off, and I stepped indoors. I was ten minutes early but glad to have the time on my own. I felt as if I'd just stepped on to a roller-coaster and was waiting until it slowed down at a corner.

So that I could jump off.

I looked round. The place was busy, mainly couples. The neat tables were covered with crisp white linen. I'd been shown to a wall table, midway between the entrance and the kitchen.

Women on their own learn to notice such things. All too often you get dumped in a draughty seat or one next to the kitchen, and have to create a scene to be treated like a paying customer.

I went back to tossing things around in my mind. Jimmy Roston would deliver, there was no doubt about that. It was just a matter of where and when. But he'd been pretty quick to pick up on me.

There were only two possibilities. Either I'd already been linked with Donald and his investigations, or I was marked by my questioning of Sawers.

What frightened me was that I didn't know which of these possibilities was the most likely, or the more dangerous.

I shook my head. Whatever the reason, I had to accept that the link had been made because Jimmy Roston's contacts didn't miss much. And although I knew he just wanted to use me to get his own back, I had no complaints. I'd be returning the compliment.

What worried me more was that I might be causing

problems for Bert. He had survived this long by keeping in with the right people, and knowing when to look the other way when they were going about their business.

He was a pacifist living in a war zone. And I was pushing him.

I ordered a Perrier. When it came I took a long swallow, and gave some thought to the forces that were likely to enhance my life in the near future.

I totted things up. I had Detective Inspector Thompson breathing down my neck; and he didn't issue casual threats. Not that I would ever suggest it publicly, but there are rumours that when he stitches somebody up, they stay stitched.

I had another opponent in Sawers. So far he was dragging his heels, just messing me about as long as he thought he could get off with it. What he might progress to when the chips were down, I could only guess at.

As for Mike Brown, he was an unknown quantity. But he and Sawers were firmly linked, and they made a bad combination.

The most frightening unknown was the mysterious new boys, who were being allowed to operate as long as they stayed in their own patch. They apparently worked on a short fuse, and didn't issue two warnings.

I could only hope to Christ they still believed in giving one, because I was ready to take it.

I went back to Thompson. After what I'd heard tonight, if I had any sense I should be beating on his door, pleading with him to listen to me. The drawback was that that would be the end of me trying to find out what Donald had got mixed up in. If I stuck my nose in after that, a couple of hefty hands would be feeling my collar.

I took another sip of water. I also have to earn a living. Yukon Discovery had hired me for a confidential company investigation. If I got them unwelcome publicity, I might as well sign on the dole, permanently.

I sighed. All this thinking wasn't improving things any. Maybe I should just wash my hands of the matter.

I told myself to get it together. Like it or not, I didn't have the luxury of a choice. My name had been broadcast where it mattered. Jimmy Roston had brought that unpalatable fact to my notice. And anybody who'd made up their mind to find me wouldn't have to go to the expense of buying a street map.

I decided I was not a happy lady. And I wasn't silly enough to mix it with a drug ring. So was this it? Time to turn and run? Donald hadn't.

But look what had happened to him.

I brooded some more. Somebody at Yukon Discovery end must have set Donald up. I just wanted to find out who it was. With the access this contract offered, there'd never be a better opportunity.

Once I found out? Well, there's more than one way of skinning a cat.

Still Waters

———

I glanced up and saw Ms Jordan walking towards me. I put
out a bright smile, and watched as the waiter fussed around
her, falling over himself to be suave and charming. He
hadn't taken that trouble with me.

Her make-up was a work of art, and the hair swung dark
and glossy to the shoulder. A wide-eyed Bambi look, which
I have to admit I find incongruous on a woman, was flashed
modestly by the big hazel eyes.

I told myself to stop being crabby, and noted that the pat-
terned full-length skirt and short jacket of pillar-box red
was chic, and expensive.

She slid elegantly into the seat opposite and apologised
for keeping me waiting, the train was a few minutes late. I
said that was all right, handed her the menu, and kept
looking.

She studied the menu, perfectly composed. I wondered
how much she earned, and took a memo to look it up. The
last time I'd seen clothes that good was in Paris, carrying
price tags out of the reach of most working women. But she
could have a private income, or something.

We ate our way chattily through a dull, but reasonably tasty, starter of parma ham and melon, tarted up with fancily-cut fruit to justify the price. That cheque had better be cleared by now, or I'd be washing the dishes.

We had nearly finished our main course before we touched on the matter in hand. I thanked her for meeting me at such short notice.

'I'm not sure how I can help you, Ms O'Connell.' She smiled. 'You'll have to keep me right.'

I smiled back. It makes a change not to be treated like the village idiot. 'I'm looking for information on certain individuals, Ms Jordan.' I quickly ran through how I worked, and assured her that anything she said would be treated as confidential.

'Yes, Mr Tomlinson has explained all that. What do you want to know?'

I gave her a quick look. If I'd miscalculated here I was in more trouble. 'I'd like your opinion on a number of people.' I ticked them off: 'Sawers, Brown, Haldane, and a Dr Donald Grant.' I was drawing the line at Tomlinson for the time being.

She looked coolly at me. The waiter arrived to whip away our plates and asked about the sweet course. We said we would have a break. When he'd gone, she settled back.

'Mr Sawers seems very proficient,' she said evenly. 'But I see very little of him, most of our communication is by telephone or letter.'

'Do you like him?'

Her eyes opened even wider. 'I didn't expect you to be interested in my personal likes and dislikes.'

'But I am. Very much so.'

She assessed me for a moment, then said, 'Since you ask, I can't say that I do like him. I'm not very keen on his colleague, Mr Brown, either.' She reached for her bag. 'Do you mind if I smoke?'

I said I didn't mind. She lit up and took a draw, releasing a long spiral of smoke. I hoped that some of it would waft in my direction.

'What don't you like about them?' I asked.

She puffed some more, looking set to get up and go. I wondered why she didn't, I wasn't tying her down. I waited patiently while the grey clouds reeked past my nose.

She frowned. 'It's difficult to explain.'

'Why don't you try?'

She looked at me nervously, and stubbed out the cigarette, half-smoked. She must have a private income after all. 'Are you recording this?'

I spread my hands wide and looked pointedly around the table. Glasses, cutlery and a single-stemmed rose in a vase. Where did she think I had a tape-recorder, stuffed up my armpit?

'No,' I said.

She still looked uncertain. 'Just how confidential is this conversation?'

'Between you and me,' I said quietly.

'But you have to report back to Mr Tomlinson and the board.'

'Only the outcome of my investigations, not the details. And certainly not the names of my sources.'

She considered this while she lit a second cigarette, gazing steadily at me all the time. 'All right, Ms O'Connell, I'll tell you what I know.' That suited me fine and I gave a smile that said so.

'Some of the requisitions that have gone through for Aberdeen appear to be falsified.' She looked meaningfully at me. 'Mr Sawers initiates these requisitions, and Mr Brown is involved as well.'

'Have you told Mr Tomlinson this?' I asked.

'I am his secretary, Ms O'Connell,' she said sharply. 'Stock-taking isn't part of my job. But since you ask, yes, I did mention that they didn't seem to tally with previous years.' The manicured eyebrows took a nose dive. 'He didn't appear to be overly concerned.'

Fair enough. But now I wanted these records even more than I wanted a cigarette. 'Can you get me a copy of these transactions?'

She turned doubtful again. 'I suppose so. Would the day after tomorrow do?'

'Fine. Anything else you've noticed?' There must be something else, she wouldn't be this panicky otherwise.

'I get on well with Mr Haldane. And he is very good at his work.' She took a deeper draw and released a bigger cloud of smoke. 'As far as Dr Grant is concerned, I hardly knew him. I saw him only three or four times. But he seemed very nice.'

Nice? She'd stumbled across a light sensitive beam. Donald nice? Now, I'd loved Donald. But, nice? No way. Not good enough, Ms Jordan, not nearly good enough.

'Tell me about it,' I suggested pleasantly.

'About what?' she said.

I homed in. 'The problem with Dr Grant.'

She shakily flicked ash and took another puff. 'As far as I know there wasn't any problem.' I stared hard at her. 'Well, there was some talk that he wasn't up to it, couldn't cope.'

She stubbed out the cigarette, screwing the end into the ashtray as if it had done something to upset her. I smelled the fear. It was an effort to hold myself back, but I didn't want to frighten her off completely.

'Do you think that, Ms Jordan?'

Long minutes passed before she answered. 'No I don't. I think he was set up.' There was another long pause before she spoke again. 'It is very difficult for me to say this about colleagues, Ms O'Connell, but I think Sawers and Brown were responsible.'

Either a brave lady, or I was being played for a sucker.

I pressed for more details. She gave them. A pudding and two coffees later we sat staring at each other, talked out. I had so much to think about my head was bursting.

I had one last question. 'May I ask why you decided to be so open with me, Ms Jordan?'

'Mr Tomlinson said you were to be given every assistance; that it was confidential, and he wouldn't be told what had been said.'

'Nor will he, Ms Jordan.' She nodded, perfectly composed once again. To give myself time to mull it over, I opted for benign mode. Easy, simply a matter of turning the grey cells off and smiling. 'I'm grateful for your help.'

We stood up, she handed me the receipt for my expenses, her business acumen was obviously better than mine, and we were ushered from the table. We waited for a taxi. She was only going three blocks so I'd end up with that bill as well.

A taxi swerved up and we got in. We sat in silence. It stopped, she said goodbye and got out. I gave my address and sat back. Enough's enough in any language. Would I sleep tonight? Between me and me, I doubted it.

When the taxi stopped again, I handed over more money and crawled out. Thinking things over, I walked slowly upstairs and let myself into my flat.

There wasn't any doubt that Sawers and Brown were an unpleasant pair, so maybe they were creaming a little off on the side.

But if they were also moonlighting as heavies for drug dealers, Donald couldn't have known what he'd stumbled on. Otherwise he'd have stayed well clear, or gone to the police. Either way, he would have told me.

One way or another, the accident theory was the only thing that was standing up. The accident of being in the wrong place at the wrong time.

I felt a wave of depression. A bit of curiosity and Donald ends up with his life squashed out like a fly.

Is there any justice in this world? I often wonder.

I slept better than I thought I would, and got up at eight o'clock feeling surprisingly frisky. This was just as well. I had a lot on. I was seeing Tomlinson at eleven and picking up HAG at one, which meant I had to check that her heating was on and think about a bite of lunch.

I flicked through the mail, and my heart gave a flutter. A postcard from Allan, saying he was alive, healthy, and having a great time in Sydney. He was making his way north to the Great Barrier Reef, then would head east to Perth, overland. Humming, I stuck it on the board with all the others.

I ransacked the cupboards and sorted out the makings of a salad – I'd buy some ham when I was out – and went down to HAG's flat. The heating was fine but I turned it up a

— 161 —

little. I tossed food out for the pigeons, and plumped a few cushions.

I was closing her door when I heard Sanderson's voice booming out. I was glad I wasn't the one being talked at, and only gave a passing thought to who was.

I turned the corner. He was standing on my landing with two men, the three of them giving a new meaning to overcrowding. Sanderson moved. My heart dropped to my feet and I took a steadying gulp of air.

I allowed my emotions full rein: deep aggravation in one second flat. When Detective Inspector Thompson decides to give somebody a hard time, he doesn't believe in sparing himself.

Sanderson's little eyes lit up. 'There she is now, Inspector.' He squashed himself against the wall, all set to hang around to see O'Connell get hers.

I stood and stared. I couldn't think of any better way of passing the time. Thompson gave Sanderson a look that suggested it was time he removed himself from the scene, pronto.

Sanderson took the hint, but shot a triumphant leer at me as he squeezed past. I resisted the impulse to help him on his way, and started up, dragging out my key.

Thompson stood with his hands in his pockets. 'You won't need that, Ms O'Connell.' His shoulders expanded. 'You're coming with us. To the station.'

I had a brief surge of panic. Another visit from Thompson, this close on the heels of the last one, boded ill. Being asked to accompany him to the station was worse.

I ran my mind back over where I'd been and what I'd done since I last saw him. Nothing out of order. Getting aggravated all over again, I decided to face him up.

'I have a busy day ahead of me, Inspector.' I looked at my watch, 'And an appointment in an hour and a half. I hope you have a good reason for this.'

His confidence didn't flicker. Does it ever. 'More than enough, Ms O'Connell. Don't you worry.'

He started down towards me. With Miller at his shoulder, a draught couldn't have squeezed past. I was going in their direction, one way or the other. It might as well be upright. I turned and walked ahead.

We got to the car, an official Rover, and I was shoved in the back with Miller. Thompson eased his bulk into the front, gave the driver the nod, and we screamed away from the kerb, siren blaring.

I studied the stony profile. Thompson liked acting the heavy, but he was too smart to overstep the line. This was serious. I sank into the upholstery and shut my eyes, and tried to work out how little I could safely claim to know. I was thrown forward as we jerked to a halt.

'Out.'

I got out. Thompson marched off and Miller hustled me in step behind, hanging on my arm as if I was going to make a run for it.

'Leave Ms O'Connell alone, Miller,' Thompson barked. Eyes in the back of his head, this man. We careered into the station like a familial group, and Thompson peeled off to the right, tossing over his shoulder, 'Interview room three.'

Miller bounced open a door labelled IR3 and herded me in. The room was minute and dark, with one small barred window set high. A sparse wooden table about five-foot long had one hard chair at one side, and two at the other.

Miller retired to stand beside the door, which was now firmly closed. Between the two of us and the scratchy furniture, IR3 was full up. How was Thompson going to fit in?

Time passed and there was no sign of him. I was being left to chew things over for a while. I decided I might as well sit down. And worry in comfort.

Tarnished

I was left sitting there for over half an hour. When I got tired cudgelling my brains trying to work out what Thompson had in mind, I took up studying Miller.

Detective Constable Miller never seems to get any older. Probably in his late thirties, with a broad open face, he still looks wet behind the ears. His mouth must've been fixed with Thompson's super-glue. Any tighter and his teeth would fall out.

He was watching me warily. I couldn't understand why. He was twice my size. We were in the cop shop. What did he think I was going to do? Dematerialise?

The door opened. Miller gave up leaning on the wall and sprang to attention. Thompson strode in. I was so bored I was almost pleased to see him.

Around fifty, black hair going grey, his face looks as if it's been lived in much longer. And if the current expression was anything to go by, it hadn't enjoyed the experience.

He had removed his overcoat and was wearing a neat dark grey suit. Very business-like. I looked up and saw that the eyes matched.

Despite his undoubted appeal, as far as I'm concerned Thompson is a wooden-top. Politically to the right of Attila the Hun, and with as much compassion as a ferret with blood-lust.

Our eyes met. And stuck.

I reminded myself that I was lucky my brief fancy for him hadn't got off the ground. Safer grappling with King Kong. He stared at me as if he knew what I was thinking. I hoped not.

He gave a suggestive half smile, You might be in with a shout here, if you play your cards right. Cheeky bugger. I sent across a prissy look.

Thompson came over bored, turned to Miller and gave a nod. Miller stuck his head out of the door. Silence. Then footsteps drew nearer, and a uniformed policeman came in carrying a tray with three steaming mugs.

Thompson drew up a chair nearer the table. Miller joined him. 'You been read your rights before, Ms O'Connell?' I shook my head. 'Read them, Constable,' he ordered. Miller read them. I agreed that I'd heard and understood.

Thompson narrowed his eyes. 'Bert Sullivan.'

I had to concentrate on keeping my heartbeat running at normal. If they'd picked Bert up, he and I had a relationship problem. For his was not a forgiving nature. And I needed his help on this case, badly.

The definitive glacial stare hardened. 'I understand you met Mr Sullivan last night,' Thompson announced, 'in a certain establishment near the river.'

My mind started racing. How Thompson knew I'd met Bert and where, only took up part of the time, and that part I could fret about later. What I wanted to know was why I'd been dragged in here, and what Bert had to do with it?

I took a pessimistic view. 'Has something happened to Bert?' Stone-face said nothing. I sat up straight, getting bolshy. 'What's this all about?'

Thompson lounged back, his eyes watchful.

Miller piped up as if on cue. 'Mr Sullivan was fished out of the Clyde at approximately . . .' he looked to Thompson for confirmation, and getting the nod continued, '. . . at

— 165 —

approximately 8.30 p.m. yesterday, an hour after he left your company.'

Oh, no. Not Bert as well. I felt the blood drain from my face.

'You all right?' Thompson asked sharply.

'I'm fine,' I snapped. Remembering the last time, I glared, daring him to touch me. How did he fancy a charge of assault?

Thompson shrugged that he wasn't bothered one way or the other. I could believe it. 'You were the last person to be seen with him,' he said smoothly. 'That's why you're here. To help us with our inquiries.' A threatening gleam mingled with the sneer. 'I think you'd better start helping, don't you?'

I was still trying to get a fix on this news about Bert. It must be connected, and I'd dragged him into it. The guilt was like a physical weight. But I had to know.

'Is Bert . . .?'

'He's alive.'

'Alive.' I smiled. 'He's all right then.'

'I didn't say that. I said he's alive.' Thompson leaned over to Miller and hushed in his ear. Miller sprang up and left the room. He came back a few minutes later and replied in kind. Thompson grunted, and looked across. 'According to the hospital, Mr Sullivan is doing fine. He was lucky.'

I sagged back in relief.

'He's told us some of what's going on, Ms O'Connell. We want to know all of it.'

There are times when I wonder how many emotions a body can take. This was one of them. I felt as if my psyche had been rolled out and stretched on the rack.

But I didn't believe that Bert had told them anything. He wouldn't give the police the time of day, in case it was used in evidence against him. That I knew for certain.

I shook my head to get rid of the panicky jumble. What was I going to say? I stared at Thompson, feeling foggier than Miller looked.

I cleared my throat. 'I hired a car from Bert the other day, and I wasn't happy with it.'

'And?'

I waved my hands in the air to signify – end of story.

'Don't give me any of your nonsense, Ms O'Connell,' he said softly. 'You must have had something more important than that to discuss. And I want to know what it was.'

I stared over his shoulder and pointedly closed my mouth, tight. He and Miller helped themselves to mugs of coffee. They didn't offer me one. My tongue felt like sandpaper.

Thompson put his mug on the tray. 'We've been doing some checking up on your Dr Grant. It seems he was trading in drugs. Must have been raking it in.'

I shot upright. 'Donald was a doctor . . .'

'Exactly,' Thompson said caustically. He'd been there, seen it, done it. Surprise was a word that had been removed from his vocabulary, years ago. A prodding finger kept time. 'Your Dr Grant had the access, and the cover, and he used them.'

I shook my head in disbelief. 'Donald was a good doctor. He'd never have anything to do with drugs.'

'Your opinion can't change the facts, Ms O'Connell.'

'What facts?'

He looked casually down at the paperwork in front of him. 'Dr Grant met with several known addicts over a period of four months, and was seen in the company of a known drug dealer on three occasions during this period.' He shifted his elbows on the table, and stuck his face across. 'So don't try and tell me that he had nothing to do with the drug trade.'

'That proves nothing,' I said quickly. But I found myself starting to wonder. And I felt like a traitor.

'It's over half-way there,' Thompson said quietly. He stared lazily up at the ceiling; he had all the time in the world. Then back to me. 'Ms O'Connell, this isn't your line of business. Why not be sensible and tell us what you know?'

The reasonable approach. I gritted my teeth.

If I told Thompson what little I knew, not only would I be breaking my word to the people who had trusted me, but I would be defaulting on my professional agreement with Yukon Discovery.

All right, I was going to have to tell him sometime. But not until I had some hard facts to go on, and could deliver them without revealing my sources. And only after I had reported to Yukon Discovery.

Anyway, that was the plan. Whether I was going to get off with it was another matter. I worked up an honest stare.

'If I find out anything I think the police should hear about, Inspector,' I assured him. 'You'll be the first to know.'

Thompson smiled pleasantly. 'I'll give you two days.' I couldn't believe my ears. What was he up to? He gave a shark-like grin. 'I'll be seeing you.' Not if I see you first, you won't. 'Show Ms O'Connell out, Constable.'

I beat Miller to the door and flagged down a taxi, sick to the pit of my stomach. I felt as if I'd gone three rounds with Muhammad Ali, with my feet nailed to the canvas.

The news about Donald was the worst part. His meetings with addicts and a dealer were difficult to handle. And put an entirely different slant on the matter.

Donald had either been more deeply involved than he'd told me – I winced – had time to tell me, or, he was part of the ring himself. Either way, the accident theory was finally out the window.

And that made my own position even shakier than I'd thought. For a start, it brought my chances of pleading ignorance, to any interested parties that caught up with me, down to precisely nil.

Thompson leaning on me was bad enough. But there were people out there who didn't recognise that there were limits to legally acceptable behaviour.

I brooded some more. I didn't believe Donald would've had anything to do with pushing drugs. Misplaced loyalty? Maybe. But I was ready to swear it wasn't.

I'd known Donald for too many years. I'd seen him do his VSO, two years in Africa, and coming back a physical wreck but still racing around fundraising. And the time he'd spent lobbying for drug centres and controlled detoxification. No, no way would he be any part of drug dealing.

I switched over to poor old Bert. The police would be

interviewing him as to the reason he had to be fished out of the Clyde. He wouldn't like that, but at least he was alive.

The bad news was that somebody had put him there. The question was who, and why. I'd have to visit him to find out, and I wasn't looking forward to it.

The taxi still wasn't moving. I peered out at the traffic. All I could see were buses and they weren't moving either. It started to rain. Umbrellas mushroomed and pedestrians scurried through the traffic, shoulders set in the protective Glasgow hunch.

A few minutes later we started up. I sank back. Thompson had run me ragged, again. Not that it was something he had to work at it. Seeing him was enough.

I checked the time. I was late for Tomlinson. After missing one appointment, being unavoidably detained wouldn't pass muster. I'd have to tell him where I'd been. But should I tell him why?

I puzzled it over. Tomlinson was showing up clean but it was early days yet. I decided to wait and see how the land lay before making up my mind.

An Alliance

I was half an hour late. Tomlinson didn't look too pleased, and I didn't blame him. Smartly dressed, this time the suit was a thin grey stripe on dark charcoal, he walked round the desk and shook hands, his mouth a fixed line.

He'd been to the barber. The tight curls were reduced to a flat frizz, and there was a thin pale band beside each ear. The white shirt was pristine and the regimental tie neatly knotted. I wondered if he had a right to the tie, or just liked the colours.

'Coffee?' he asked coldly. When I said yes, he buzzed through. Then he sat down, ready to hear my good excuse.

I was going to have to tell him.

'I was picked up for questioning, and I've been cooling my heels in a police station for the last hour and a half.' Tomlinson's eyebrows lifted, ever so slightly. Easy for him to be cool. 'The invitation was issued by a Detective Inspector Thompson.' The name didn't seem to mean anything to him.

Ms Jordan came in with a tray. She laid the tray down and placed a plate of biscuits in front of Tomlinson. She smiled at me, I smiled back, she poured the coffee and left. I grabbed my cup like a man reeling out of the desert.

Tomlinson studied me thoughtfully. I waited for the verdict. If he decided that flying shit was bad news for Yukon Discovery, or for him, I might be leaving quicker than I'd come in.

'May I ask why?' he said icily.

I poured myself a second cup. If Tomlinson couldn't take the news, tough. I was on this case. And I was staying on it. Paid or not.

I told him that a friend of mine had been dragged from the Clyde, that he was alive but the police were very interested in knowing how he'd got there. I went on to say that another friend, who had been killed, had been linked by the police to a drug ring.

I watched him as I delivered the punch line – he might as well hear it now as later, if he didn't know already – and I wanted to see his reaction. 'With one, there's a direct link with Yukon Discovery,' I said carefully. 'And the other appears to be connected.'

'How much do the police know?'

It was my turn to look pitying. Made a change. 'The police are not in the habit of confiding in me. If you're asking whether I told them what I'm telling you, the answer is no.'

Sticking his elbows on the chair arms and bringing his hands together in a thoughtful steeple, Tomlinson went back to giving me the once over. I'd have given a lot to know what he was thinking.

'What's your opinion of Haldane?' he asked abruptly.

I hesitated, but sometimes you have to stick your neck out. 'A streetwise, slick negotiator who probably spends more time looking after his own interests than the company's. And,' I stared across the desk, 'I think he's edgy. Could be up to something.' I shrugged. 'But whether it has anything to do with whatever's going on . . .'

There was a flash of surprise in the blue eyes. And I could have sworn a glimmer of respect. A bit late in the day. What did he think I was, an airhead?

'I'd go as far as to say that I'm pretty sure that he is up to something,' he said quietly.

This was news to me. And I wasn't pleased to hear it. I had enough problems without Tomlinson messing me around. 'Why didn't you say so before?' I demanded.

'I had my reasons.' He raised a hand. 'Let's not get het up about it.'

I liked that last remark even less. I don't go in for emotional outbursts when I'm working, I save that sort of thing for my private life. Doesn't do me any good there either. But that's another story.

'Keeping information back from someone you've hired to carry out an investigation', I pointed out, 'is unprofessional. And could be dangerous.'

I was right. And the way he was frowning, he knew it.

He took time out to pour more coffee, and sat back. 'I've been suspicious of Haldane for some time now, but I couldn't make any accusations. One, I'd no proof. Two, he's got powerful friends in the company. And three, he's in the running for a seat on the board. If I said anything without rock-hard evidence, it would look like power play. And that could let him off the hook at the end of the day.' He paused. 'I don't want that to happen. If he's the one causing the trouble, I want him landed, and gutted.'

What he said made sense. But now I wanted it all. And I was ready to push to get it. 'If I'm to continue working for Yukon Discovery, I need to know everything,' I said stiffly.

'Be fair. It worked both ways. I didn't know whether I could rely on you. And you didn't know if you could trust me.'

I got out my notebook. He could cut out the soft soap. 'Tell me about your suspicions of Haldane.'

He smiled. 'Where will I start?'

I handed out a cool look. I still hadn't got to grips with Tomlinson. The winning smile humanised the computer-man image a bit too conveniently for my liking. But we didn't have to be bosom friends. Just work together.

'At the beginning.' If there was any censoring to be done around here, I was going to be the one doing it.

He talked on for close to an hour, uninterrupted. I

listened and scribbled. We had more coffee sent in, and drank it. After a refill, he looked at me questioningly. I finished the coffee and put my cup down.

'Right,' I flicked back several pages, 'let's see what we've got.' I picked out the main points to throw back at him, to confirm I'd got my facts right, and jog his memory if he'd forgotten anything.

We had covered a lot of these points before, but there was no harm going over them again. The rest I knew already – and more – but I had no intention of telling him.

'Haldane has been protecting Sawers. On two occasions when Sawers was had up on charges of assault, he managed to block his dismissal.' I gave the dates, who'd said what, got the nod, and went on. 'You suspect Sawers has been putting through invoices for non-existent goods. The larger items are counter-signed by Haldane, but he could plead misplaced trust.'

I leaned back and turned another page. 'The word is that men are being scared off the training course because they're being pressured into a bit of drug-running. Those who refused outright have met with unfortunate accidents, or been sacked.'

I flicked over another page. I felt the bitterness well up inside and had to force myself to go on. 'When Dr Grant requested an investigation, Haldane argued against him, and got the board to agree that he should be removed from his post, on the grounds of ill-health.'

I summed up. 'The evidence is shaky. Apart from the invoices it's all word of mouth. And even assuming Haldane's involved, if you nail Sawers for fraud he'll carry the can and Haldane'll get off scot-free.' Tomlinson nodded that that had been his problem. I read out three names. 'Would these people provide a signed statement?'

'As a last resort, it would be worth a try. But you know how it is, what people will say in confidence and what they'll say in public are two different things.'

I nodded. I knew, only too well. I looked up. 'Anything else you haven't told me about Haldane?'

'No.' He held my gaze. 'Other than I suspect that he and

— 173 —

Ms Jordan are more than good friends.' I looked at him. He nodded. 'From things Ms Jordan has let slip, I'm pretty sure.'

She'd certainly said that she got on well with Haldane. Sounded as if his job wasn't the only thing he was good at. I started to smile and stopped myself in time. Behave, O'Connell.

I digested this latest news. It could explain the designer outfit. After all, Haldane didn't look short of a bob or two. I shook my head. Why should I assume he was doing the buying?

I had conflicting thoughts on the matter. The first was that it was all very interesting, but none of my business. The second was: is it affecting this case? It was the second one that worried me.

I put it to one side.

I had something else to check out. It wouldn't be the first time an attempt had been made to use me to remove a competitor from the running. And while that wouldn't stop me in this case, I prefer to know about it.

'How secure is your position in the company?'

Tomlinson gave a wry look. 'As secure as anything can be. As long as I don't go out on a limb by talking out of turn.'

'You've talked to me.'

'In confidence. And you came recommended.' He smiled. 'I was led to believe that if you were as tight with your money as you are with your sources, the national debt would be halved overnight.'

Stanley, ever the money man. At least this time he'd done me a favour. I thawed marginally, and grinned. 'It took you a while.'

'I'm a cautious man.'

That was okay by me. I like cautious men, if they're on my side. I packed the notebook away and looked at my watch. Late again. HAG would not be pleased.

'A point of interest,' I said. 'Does Ms Jordan know your views on Haldane, or the Aberdeen situation?'

He gave me a sharp look. 'I've never discussed them with her.'

I nodded. That tallied. Unless they were both leading me

up the garden path. 'There are two things I'd like you to do for me.'

When I told him, he looked surprised but said he would. I hoped so. Otherwise, I'd be up the Swanee without a paddle. I said I had to go, and went.

The rain had stopped. I asked the taxi driver to drop me at the road entrance to the hospital and wait for me at the main door. I'd be dashing around like a headless chicken soon enough. I might as well have a minute or two of peace and quiet while I had the chance.

I walked slowly up the drive, enjoying my first breath of fresh air that day. Raindrops hung from branches like clear pearls, grew fat, and plopped to the ground. A bird chirped. The watery sunlight gleamed and disappeared.

I reached the door, and went in reluctantly, bracing myself.

I did a double take, and stared incredulously at the figures in front of the reception desk. I'd known what was to come. I just hadn't expected it this quickly.

HAG sat in a wheelchair, wrapped in a tartan rug, being fussed over by a young nurse. The look I got from the pair of them as I walked up, you'd have thought I was the one that had put her in hospital in the first place.

'Miss Green was getting worried,' the nurse said, moving the rug another inch nearer the stubborn chin. 'She's been waiting here for over twenty minutes,' she looked at me accusingly, 'and she's an old lady.'

So who asked her to wait here?

I gritted my teeth. It aggravates the hell out of me when people play the martyr. HAG could've stayed in a nice warm ward until I arrived, instead of shivering near the outside door. As for the old lady bit, she was looking a damn sight sprightlier than I felt.

I thanked the nurse with tight lips, took charge of the chair and wheeled it briskly towards the door. Just don't say anything HAG. Let me cool down.

Maybe it was the speed I whisked her down to the taxi, but not a word did she say until the driver shot round to help her out of the wheelchair.

I got nothing, he got a thank you and a plaintive smile. He fussed all the harder, Is everything all right now, Mrs? Are ye quite comfy?

HAG has this effect on people. And it's not just her age. Line her up with a bunch of elderly compatriots, and if there's anybody going to be helped it'll be her.

I plonked myself down and gave her a sour look. She was staring straight ahead, as stubborn as a monkey. I took another look. Her lips were trembling.

My heart expanded so quickly I thought it was going to burst. One of these days I was going to have to take up religion so I could beg forgiveness for all my sins.

I reached out a hand to cover hers. 'I'm sorry,' I whispered. 'It's just that I'm pretty tired.'

The tremble in her mouth increased. 'I don't want to be any trouble.' She stuck her chin in the air and turned to face me. 'I can manage on my own, you know.'

I looked at the proud eyes and shrank into an animated penance. 'Of course you can,' I said huskily. I felt the tears and didn't give a bugger. 'But you're stuck with me, and you'll just have to lump it.'

She gave me a disapproving look. Although the frozen face made it clear she wasn't going to forgive me that easily, I knew then that everything would be all right. A few hours kissing her feet should do it.

I grinned like an idiot, 'Okay?' She unbent far enough to nod. I gave her a kiss and settled back holding her hand. She allowed me to keep it. The world was back on its axis.

I got her indoors with the help of the taxi driver. If he'd stuck around to do any more he'd have been as well moving in. I'd forgotten the ham, but produced a mean omelette to accompany the tossed salad.

When I remembered I had a box of chocolate gingers, I sped upstairs to fetch them. They went down a treat. After we finished eating, we had coffee and munched gingers for a couple of hours, HAG feet up in front of the TV, me stretched out on the settee, and the place pulsing with heat. I dozed off.

I awakened to the clatter of dishes. Jesus Christ! Was this woman never going to give me a break?

She was just out of hospital. She'd been told to rest and go to bed early, and here she was doing the dishes.

I leapt up and went in gnashing my teeth, to be told, in no uncertain terms, that this was her house, that she'd wash the dishes any time she felt like it. And if that didn't suit me I knew what I could do about it.

I shook my head to clear the racket.

Still in full voice, she raved on. Since I'd finally decided to stop lying around as if I was tired, and me only half her age, I could go down to the corner shop and get her some milk – and an evening paper, if there was one left. If there wasn't, it was my fault; I should've bought one earlier.

There was no point arguing.

I pulled on my jacket and slunk off into the cold and dark outdoors, bought the milk and paper and wandered back. When I got to the door, I stuck them under my arm and searched for the key.

I felt a dull thump on my head and was surprised to discover that I was falling. I grabbed for the doorway and started to slide down it. On the way to the pavement, I heard a noise like a shout.

Some instinct made me use the last of my strength to push myself sideways. It wasn't far enough. The next thump brought multi-coloured stars and my knees buckled under me.

And the lights went out.

Rough Water

When I came to, I'd been fitted with a strait-jacket and anchored to the floor. I moved my head. Not one of my better ideas.

I went limp, and waited until the fireworks died down. Where was I?

I peered through half-shut lids. The room was bright and white and smelled of disinfectant. I turned painfully to the source of whispering, and tried to persuade my eyes to open up, all the way.

The mist cleared briefly and I saw HAG's anxious face. She was sitting in a chair, her face level with mine. Her mouth was moving, but I couldn't hear what she was saying. There was someone standing behind her.

I went back to the beginning and started again. This time, when my eyes creaked round my ears started working. I heard her ask how I was. If I'd been up to it I would've laughed.

'I'm fine,' I slurred, blearing out to see who was with her.

'A man attacked you. Oh, it's terrible, terrible,' she fussed. 'Mr Sanderson chased him away. If he hadn't come along there's no telling what would have happened.'

My eyes finally latched on to the figure at her back. Sanderson, pretending to look sympathetic. I felt a relapse coming on. As I faded away, I heard HAG twittering on about how she'd be back, and did I want anything.

I think I smiled.

The next time I surfaced, it was to more voices. My eyes swivelled round. The only part of me that I could move.

Doreen was studying me, her blue eyes wide and anxious, looking more like a mother hen than a death-defying doctor. She wore the smock she uses when she does a bit of painting. Must've dashed out in a hurry.

The worry on her face was battling with indignation. I knew how she felt.

Beside her stood Stanley, muffled in his cashmere coat, acting wealthy. I'd heard of getting people when they're down, but this was ridiculous. I looked again. Even Stanley was pale round the gills.

That was when I knew I was in a bad way. He could be worrying how I was going to clear my overdraft.

Doreen seemed to give up hope of finding signs of life. I must be seeing through my eyelids. She started to speak to Stanley as if I wasn't there, and he had just crawled out from under a stone.

It was all his fault. He'd got me into it. He was the one who'd recommended me for that contract. And now look what's happened. Stanley stood like a whipped dog, taking it.

This was making my day.

I closed my eyes. Atta girl, Doreen, keep on his case. I smiled as more home truths were dredged up and spat out. And hoped I was going to remember them later.

As I started to go under again, I felt smug. At least, when I fall out with somebody, I don't have to go home with them and climb into the same bed.

I snored off contentedly.

I awoke with a start. My subconscious was sending warning signals. There was a dark figure looming over me. I fought to get my head together.

'She mustn't be upset. She has to rest. She's had a bad knock on the head.'

My eyes had re-glued themselves. I struggled to open them.

'Don't worry, nurse,' said the growl. 'I won't upset her.'

The bits of me that were able to move stiffened. Detective Inspector Thompson, in the flesh. If there was ever a time for playing possum, this was it. I felt his breath on my ear. Any closer and there'd be two of us in here. And I didn't think I'd like that.

'Ms O'Connell, I think you're chancing your arm. And if you keep this up, getting upset is going to be the least of your worries.' He breathed heavily, and waited. I kept as still as the tomb.

'I'm leaving a nice policeman outside your door,' he whispered threateningly, the mouth near enough to bite. 'When you decide to wake up, he's going to tell me. And I'll be back.'

There was a waft of air. I chanced a quick look out of one half open eye. His shoulders were hunched so high with aggression that the neck had disappeared. I wondered if he was going to open the door, or walk through it.

He opened it.

I relaxed. Now I knew where I was, in hospital, my least favourite place. I thought back. I'd been clobbered. What was the damage?

I tested. Toes, legs, fingers, arms, I lifted my head off the pillow, everything was working again. Painful, but working. I began to feel better, and hungry.

The door opened again and a nurse whirled in. She stopped and smiled when she realised I was taking notice. 'You're awake. That's good.' She adjusted my pillows. 'Would you like something to eat?'

I nodded gratefully, my stomach felt as if my throat had been cut. But I had another problem. I caught her arm as she was turning away, and tried to sound as if I was on my last legs. It wasn't difficult.

'Nurse,' I croaked. 'That policeman outside. I don't feel able to talk to anyone just yet.'

'Of course not.' Her eyes filled with indignation, she was with me all the way down the line. She wasn't going to have any nasty policeman upsetting her patient. 'I won't say you're awake,' she said reassuringly. She smiled, 'I'll smuggle some food in.'

And she did, under a cloth. I sat up as she wheeled a table over and swung the top across the bed. 'I hope you're not a vegetarian,' she said worriedly. 'This was all I could get.'

I didn't know what was coming, and I didn't care. I could close my eyes while I was eating it. Whatever it was.

She removed the lid, and I was faced with a steaming plateful of steak pudding, creamed carrots and boiled potatoes. She lifted the lid on the other dish. Jam sponge surrounded by custard. I could have kissed her. She went out smiling, leaving me to it.

I wolfed everything in record time, straight down the throat. I lay back and studied the little round paunch pushing up the blankets. Happiness is a full belly. I drifted off with a contented sigh.

When I regained consciousness again, it was dark outside and my co-conspirator was pulling the curtains. I dragged myself into a sitting position and felt my head. It was wrapped in a large bandage.

'How long have I been here, nurse?'

She walked briskly across. 'Don't worry about that.' She smiled and leaned over to give the pillows another battering. 'You just rest.'

'How long?' I insisted.

She checked me out, and decided I could take it. 'This is your second day.'

Two days!

I smiled weakly and leaned back. I was actually feeling pretty much back to normal. But I didn't want her to know that. I had to get out of here, smartish, in case Thompson decided to pay a return visit.

I closed my eyes and pretended to doze off.

She adjusted the blankets, pinning me to the bed. I let it

happen. I was desperate for a pee, but I had a vague recollection of already been sat on a bedpan. And it wasn't an experience I was in a hurry to repeat.

She turned the lights low and left the room. I gave it a few minutes, struggled to sit up, and looked around. There were two doors. One must be a loo. I fought free of the blankets, eased myself out of bed and tottered across.

My luck was in. Not only was there a loo, but when I opened a wall cupboard I found my clothes. I grabbed them and teetered back. By the time I'd dressed I'd found my legs again. They were shaky, but operational.

I unravelled the bandage and felt a large egg-shaped lump on the back of my head, there was another smaller lump to one side. I remembered my mother's advice: if it hurts when you touch it, don't touch it, and took my hand away.

I went to the window and peered out. Good luck isn't the only thing that comes in threes apparently: I had my clothes, I was on the ground floor, and the window wasn't locked.

I went back, wrapped the loops of bandage around the two door knobs, and tied it in a firm knot. That wouldn't keep anyone out for long, but it might give me precious minutes if anyone decided to visit while I was climbing out.

It was a struggle, but I got the window open enough to slide over the sill. I held on to the ledge for a minute, let go, and landed with a jerk that set my head screaming. I didn't stop to feel sorry for myself.

Keeping in the shadows, I skirted the building. Where I was going I hadn't quite worked out yet. I fumbled in my pockets and blessed my casual attitude with money. I had cash; I could get a taxi.

By the time I reached a main road, I was shivering. I flagged a cab. It swerved and screeched to a halt, and I got in. I was settling myself, when I met the cabbie's eyes in the mirror. He looked as if he was having a bad dream.

I smiled to reassure him that I wasn't an escapee from the psychiatric unit, or the victim of a hit-and-run. It didn't seem to work.

I gave the address. That cheered him up. I think the fact

that it was upmarket was irrelevant. It was somewhere he could dump me.

I paid and staggered out, the taxi screeched off. I struggled up the drive as quietly as I could, and made it to the door. I pulled the bell and leaned against the doorframe. There was no answer. I pulled again, feeling my head beginning to swim.

The door opened and I fell in – in a dead faint.

Pit Stop

Doreen told me later that Stanley caught me as I fell in the door, and carried me upstairs. I'm glad I didn't know that at the time.

I woke up to find myself in their guest room. I sat up and took note. Gleaming mahogany furniture, chintz shades, a small hand-basin with soft towels, and a large Chinese rug over a fitted wool carpet; it made me feel pampered.

There was a glass of water, an alarm clock, and some magazines within easy reach on a small side table. It was still dark outside. I checked the time. 6 a.m.

I needed to get up. I went to the bathroom, then slipped along to the palatial kitchen and made a mug of Earl Grey and took it back to bed.

The way I was feeling, a miraculous healing process had taken place overnight. Which was probably just as well, since I might have to face Stanley.

I drank some tea, savoured it, and started to berate myself for coming to Stanley's den. Why look for aggravation? Enough of it about even on a good day. I decided the bop on the head must've done it.

The calculating side of my nature stepped forward. Maybe it wasn't that stupid, after all. Thompson would be looking for me. And I didn't think he would look here. Stanley's sort don't shelter people from the police.

I took another gulp of life-saving tea and faced an unpalatable truth. I'd played it sly without even having to think about it. I sighed. My subconscious is obviously better left untapped.

The door opened and Doreen came sleepily in, hair standing on end. 'I heard you wandering about,' she mumbled. She came and sat on the edge of the bed. 'When did they discharge you?' She rubbed her eyes. 'You looked like death last night, Cat.'

I glanced at her pale face and the dark shadows under her eyes. 'You're not looking so bright yourself.'

She focused on me glacily. 'That is because I was up half the night checking that you hadn't passed away.'

I laughed. 'I'll make you some tea,' I offered, starting to get up.

'Hold it.' She fixed me with her doctor stare and pressed me back. 'You stay there.' Pulling the covers up, she reached for my mug: 'I'll get it.'

When Doreen came in again, she was sparkling clean and had combed her hair. She was carrying a tray which she dumped unceremoniously on my lap.

Pulling her silk dressing-gown around her, she climbed up beside me. 'Breakfast is served.'

We munched companionably through creamy scrambled eggs, then toast, scattering the crumbs all over the bed, and lazed back with mugs of milky coffee. Mine was laced with whisky. I took an appreciative sip and decided I should be an invalid more often.

Doreen removed the tray to the floor. 'Now you can tell me what has happened.' I gave her a look.

There was a tap on the door, it opened, and Stanley's head appeared. 'Can I come in?' He barged in without waiting for an answer. 'Morning, Caithlin. What's this all about?'

Gets straight to the point does Stanley.

But if he expected me to tell him what was going on, he'd

flipped his lid. We picked up glowering at each other where we'd left off. I think we enjoy it really.

Doreen snapped, 'Will you both stop this nonsense.'

Stanley and I looked at each other, then at Doreen. His face started to act injured. He was a reasonable man, asking a reasonable question, in his own home. I sniggered.

Doreen turned to me. 'Cat, you must have had a good reason to come here. But we can't help you if we don't know what's going on.'

Feeling a sneaking guilt at disturbing the serenity of the love nest, I said quickly, 'You have helped me Doreen, and I'm very grateful. But there's nothing to worry about.'

'Nothing to worry about?' she said disbelievingly. 'You were attacked. You obviously don't think it's safe to go home. And we've not to worry?' Her face turned suspicious. 'It's something to do with your work, isn't it?'

'I can't tell you about my work, Doreen. You know that.' She suddenly looked uncharacteristically close to tears. It defeated me. 'It's nothing important,' I muttered. 'It's just that the police are looking for me.'

'Just!' Stanley roared. He took a quick run across the floor and whizzed back, eyes popping. He took a deep breath. 'What for?'

I stared blankly at him and pressed my lips together.

Doreen metamorphosed into the sort of Matron figure I've never wanted to meet: back straight, bust out, mouth grim. 'The police can't be written off as unimportant, Cat,' she said firmly. 'So why are they looking for you?'

I sighed. Doreen is a born worrier, but if Stanley, the perpetual burr under my skin, hadn't stuck his oar in this could have been avoided. 'They've got some questions they think I've got answers to,' I said wearily. 'That's all.'

'Do you?' Stanley asked coldly. He had recovered the bank manager composure. If I hadn't been lying down, I might have thought I was in his office, listening to the big N-O.

I stared mulishly. 'Do I what?'

He fixed me with cash register eyes. 'These questions you're talking about. Could I be expected to know any of the answers?'

'No,' I snapped. Him and his manager speak. And self first as usual. And since he never had anything to do with my work, how could he be expected to know anything about it? God give me strength.

Stanley's mouth opened. I leaned back and shut my eyes, wishing I could do the same with my ears. A proverb was on the way. I could smell it.

'What you don't know can't hurt you,' he pronounced. 'So let's keep it that way.' After a pause, he added grudgingly, 'Of course, you can stay here until you're feeling better.'

When his words registered, my eyes shot open. One of the many problems I have with Stanley is that he is a social tight-arse. This was a new view. But I don't care for being beholden, especially to Stanley.

'Don't worry. I'll be on my way as soon as I'm able to get up and dress.'

He gave me a dirty look, and walked up and hugged Doreen. He told his darling that he'd be back for dinner, and that she was to have a good day.

He didn't bother saying goodbye to me.

I got up, smartened up, and hovered around Doreen while she packed her case. 'I need to make some phone calls, Do. Is that all right.'

'Help yourself.' She looked over. 'I'll be back around three. Will you be here?' I shook my head. 'Do you need a car?' My eyes lit up. 'Here,' she handed me keys, 'you can borrow mine for a couple of days. But I want it back in one piece.' Her eyes turned serious. 'This situation doesn't look good. You'll need to take care, Cat.'

She was telling me?

I said I would, took the keys, thanked her, and waved her off. I gave the keys a jingle and grinned. A respectable Polo. Nobody would expect to see me driving around in that.

I made for the phone.

My luck was in. Or maybe half eight in the morning is the optimum time to get hold of people. In quick succession I got through to Jack, Helen MacPherson and HAG.

Jack was his usual cheerful self. He'd done some checking for me, and produced the interesting information that a friend of a friend of his had been sacked by Sawers. The stated reason was carelessness over safety checks. The friend of a friend said it was because he'd refused to carry a package off the rig.

'Will he talk to me, Jack?'

'He's pretty nervous, but I think I could persuade him.'

'When?' There was a silence as if Jack was thinking it over. 'I'm coming up to Aberdeen today,' I said hurriedly. 'You make the arrangements and I'll check with you later.' He said he would. 'And Jack, I need to know the date this happened, and the dates of any other cases he might have heard about.'

He said he'd do what he could. I rang off.

When I finally got past the hospital guard, she of the lilting voice and endemic ill-nature, Helen MacPherson's calm tones floated over the wire.

'Cat, I've been trying to get in touch. I've found some papers that Donald left. I've put them in an envelope. Shall I post them on?'

'No, don't do that,' I said quickly. 'I'll pick them up later today.' We discussed a suitable time. 'One more thing. Can you try to remember the dates of the incidents Donald complained about, and jot them down for me?' She said she would. 'And Helen, please keep those papers safe.'

There was a pregnant silence.

'I will. Take care, Cat.'

I was beginning to wish everybody would stop saying that. What did they think I was doing, going around looking for trouble? I rang off and tried HAG's number. She picked it up on the second ring. It was five minutes before I could get a word in.

'I'm perfectly all right,' I repeated, for the umpteenth time. 'And don't worry about the police coming round. It's just routine.' She started to twitter again. 'HAG!' I shouted. 'Will you please listen?'

There was a deeply offended silence.

I didn't have time to worry about it. I told her what I

wanted, my mail and the green folder in the top drawer of my desk, and that I'd ask Joy to pick them up. I said I would explain later, and put the phone down.

My ears were buzzing and I was out in a sweat. Excitement must be bad for me. But at least I'd get my notes, those records from Sawers, and maybe even the promised info from Jimmy Roston. If Joy agreed.

A quick phone call established that Joy had been expecting to hear from me for over a week about the research contract; that it was too late now, and that I was pretty low down on her popularity rating.

When she'd finished sniping, she said she would collect the papers and meet me in an hour's time, in Princes Square. It was near her office.

While I was waiting, I decided to do the decent thing and tidy up. The dishes didn't take long and the designer kitchen quickly went back to looking as if nobody ever used it. A quick toss of the duvet saw to the bed. I went to the window and gazed out over the neat garden, and fretted.

The ideas were coming fast and furious, but I'd no way of checking them out until I got my hands on all these papers. I wondered if Tomlinson had done as I'd asked. If so, there might be some developments when I reached Aberdeen.

I checked the time, and went outside.

It was a pleasure to drive the Polo. It was new and everything worked. I cruised along feeling as if I'd acquired a sugar daddy. Pity I'd never got round to getting one. Too late now, O'Connell.

I parked in West Nile Street, fed the meter, and legged it round the corner and into Buchanan Street, a busy pedestrian thoroughfare with concrete planters. I walked down the right-hand side. Opposite the first of the two entrances to Princes Square, I happened to look up.

I stared, transfixed, at the enormous iron peacock perched on the roof edge. It gazed over the precinct like a primeval god, the tail spread the width of the square's frontage, its feather eyes glinting as if they'd had an infusion of mother-of-pearl.

And I'd never even noticed it before.

I was nudged from behind, and asked to buy a magazine for the homeless. I hadn't heard of that either. I handed over money, took a copy, and rushed along the narrow corridor into the square, feeling brainless.

Inside the curved, glass-roofed open space of basement floor area and shapely balconies, I peered around. Princes Square is showy: tasteful ironwork, balcony railings capped with pale ash, engraved glass and gold-topped glass lifts. The basement flooring opens out into a shaped central area, with low wooden step-seating and an inner mosaic. The canned music was bearable.

There is food in the basement, but the terrace and short upper balcony give the view. I gazed upwards, looking for Joy. Nobody was waving, but being pretty sure I'd find her there, I took smooth elevators up the two floors.

I found Joy half-way along, gazing moodily into a coffee, her pert face glum. I hoped she wasn't going to give me a hard time. I'd had enough lectures for one day.

I ordered a coffee, the least I could do, and plonked myself down. 'Did you get them?' She indicated a carrier bag at her feet. I grabbed it and stuck my head in. Good, everything was there. I couldn't wait to get started.

'I presume you'll spare the time to keep me company for a few minutes?' she said sulkily.

'Joy . . .'

'I went out on a limb for you with that research job, and you didn't even take the trouble to phone and let me know whether you wanted it or not.'

Joy is a blasé, sharp-talking career woman, and some people think that means hard-boiled. They don't know her. Inside she's a soft mush, quick to take offence.

Right now she was giving me the full benefit of sad brown eyes. I was her friend, and I'd let her down.

I looked across at the fashionable shop-fronts, new, yet strangely Dickensian. They stock goods I usually can't afford, but I'm always tempted to wander in just to make sure. Be easier if I could convince myself they were selling rubbish.

I turned to face the music. 'I'm sorry, Joy. But I've been snowed under. The contract I'm working on has run into problems.'

'What problems?' I said nothing. She gave me an irritated look. 'It's a waste of time asking you anything, isn't it?'

'Thanks for picking this stuff up. It was a great help,' I gulped down the coffee and gave her a peck, 'but I've got to go now.' She stopped me. I smiled ruefully. 'I'll take care,' I promised.

I raced back to Doreen's – well Stanley's as well, but who's counting? – parked, and carried my valuable cargo indoors. I still felt pretty sure that no one would come looking for me here, but kept an eye out just in case.

Same couple of cars in the lane. And nobody was walking a borrowed dog. You can always tell. It's the only canine that treats the human at the other end of the lead with any respect.

I spread the papers all over the regency dining-table, taking the precaution to slip a newspaper under the sheet I was going to scribble on. One mark on this gleaming mahogany and I'd be as well leaving the country.

I looked at the accident reports from Sawers first, and compared the dates and who was supposed to have been where and when, with my notes. This was a fuller version of the information he'd given Tomlinson. Next, I ran over his check of safety routines. Then the three pages of justifying blurb.

I looked at the blurb again. I didn't have the background to assess the technical detail, but it sounded authentic. The over-use of jargon and the shaky logic of the argument, however, suggested that the writer of this paper didn't know as much about the management of his line of business as he was trying to make out.

I sat back. People get promotion for a number of reasons: for competence, for years worked, or for services rendered. On this evidence, Sawers' route hadn't been the first. And I knew it hadn't been the second.

That left the third.

Okay, it goes on all the time, and it's not necessarily unreasonable. So why did it bother me? A tingle sped over my spine, because I knew the answer. It depended on what service was rendered, why, and for whom.

And from what I'd learned so far, I didn't think it was the goodies who were calling the shots at Yukon Discovery. At least, not in the small part of the company that I knew about.

I turned to the squashed brown envelope with the carefully printed address. This looked like Jimmy Roston's style.

Inside were two sheets of lined paper covered by the same anonymous upright lettering. Documented, detailed and useful. Very useful. I didn't know he had it in him.

I browsed on, getting more and more excited.

Pipe Lines

It was time to check with Tomlinson. One of the things I'd asked him for was the dates of Haldane's visits to the UK over the last year, including stop-overs. The visits he'd know. The stop-overs he would have to check out with Head Office. And I was hoping Haldane would get to hear about it.

Tomlinson was in, and had the information. Haldane had paid four visits to Aberdeen: July, August, September and October. And had four stop-overs in London in March, May, June and November.

'Haldane's usually only in the UK three or four times a year,' Tomlinson said pointedly.

'But he was setting up a training course, and it ran into difficulties.' I paused. 'And we know there is another attraction.'

'The course certainly didn't need that much attention.' He sounded disgruntled. 'Anyway, the dates.'

He read them out slowly and I scrawled them down. I knew it was a long-shot and I still had to prove a connection, but I liked what I was hearing.

'That's the lot,' Tomlinson said. 'By the way, I've tried to contact you several times. Have you been away?'

I felt the irritation coming over the wire and resisted the impulse to bite back. 'I was in hospital.' He didn't say anything, maybe thought it would be indelicate to ask. 'Somebody tried to rearrange my skull,' I added facetiously.

'Somebody what?' When I repeated it, there was another pause. 'I don't think that's funny.'

'I didn't either, believe you me.'

'Anything to do with this investigation?'

'Possibly.'

'Are you all right?' When I said I was, the phone went silent.

I got fed up waiting for him to speak. 'You still there?'

'That was one of the reasons I didn't want a woman on this case,' he said heavily.

My feathers started to ruffle. Don't men get clonked on the head? Or maybe theirs are harder. 'Are you suggesting that because I'm a woman I'm not competent to carry out this work?'

'No, I'm not. But this is a tough business.'

I bristled. 'Let me worry about it.' A thought struck me. I decided it was time to put it to him again. 'You never did tell me who pushed for this investigation.'

'I wanted it,' he grated. Before I could say anything, he changed the subject. 'I had to ask around for this information. That means there's a good chance Haldane'll hear about it.' His voice grew sharper, 'So you'd better have eyes in the back of your head.'

Tomlinson's urbane exterior was cracking. Either he was regretting calling me in, or Haldane was seriously vexing him. Or maybe he'd just decided he didn't have to be polite to me any more.

'I'll see what I can do about getting some,' I snapped, and hung up. Useless advice I can live without.

I had a cup of coffee and tidied myself. I used Doreen's make-up, although it was the wrong colour anything's an improvement on zero, and scribbled a thank you note and stuck it under the coffee pot.

My first stop was at a petrol station to fill the tank. The second was a post office, where I mailed the papers in three large envelopes to myself, care of my lawyer. He doesn't see much of me, and when he does he never looks very happy about it. This should please him.

That done, I was ready for Aberdeen. But first, Bert.

I stopped outside the workshop. There was no sign of life in the rickety power-house, and the same two mechanics were working away. At the speed they were going they must be on a homer. I was glad I wasn't paying them.

The older one swaggered over, rubbing his hands on an oil-black cloth. His eyes dashed behind me looking for my minders. 'Mr Sullivan's no in.'

I waited patiently for more. Nothing. If my ambition in life was to stand around getting nowhere fast, I wouldn't have minded. As it was, my right hand was itching to give him a hefty shove.

'I heard Mr Sullivan had an accident,' I encouraged. The dungareed shoulders rose and fell, the mouth stayed shut. It was like pulling teeth. I persevered, 'Is he still in hospital, or is he at home?'

His eyes looked up and down, and shot behind me again. 'Hame. Got oot yisterday.'

I marvelled. Four words on the trot. I didn't bother to ask after Bert's health. Waiting for an answer would take time I couldn't spare.

'Thanks.'

I drove round. Bert lives in a sprawling beat up housing scheme east of the city. It's been on the social reform agenda for thirty years, and doesn't look any the better for it.

Bert thinks that living here helps to convince the Inland Revenue that his income is as meagre as he makes out. Maybe it does. I think I'd rather pay the taxes.

I toured along checking out the street, trying to avoid patches of broken glass and the odd bit of masonry. I parked in front of a battered row of shops. My theory is that there's less chance of coming back to a car on bricks if one or two people pass by it from time to time.

The graffiti was the only bright thing in sight. Two of the dark grey shops were closed, permanently. The other four just looked it. Their windows were hidden behind the same framed metal bars, but the iron shutters in the doorways had been pulled up to head height, open for business.

I locked up, skulked along the pavement, and dived in the close. Up to the second floor, all quiet. I shook my head; this door could do with a lick of paint. I leaned on the bell.

Bert opened the door. We stared at each other. A large cotton pad held by two plasters sat on the top of his head. He didn't seem too happy with the addition.

'Bert,' I said. 'I've just heard. How are you feeling?'

He pulled the door wider, 'Caithlin, me dear. Come in.'

I went in carefully. If he kept up this looking at me as if I'd done it, we were going to fall out. I wandered through to his sitting-room and flopped into an armchair that was coming apart at the seams. Something like myself.

When he disappeared into the kitchen, I cast an eye around. He'd added to his collection of furniture since I'd been here last. Floor space was at a premium. The walls weren't much better, anything that could hang had been hung. A nightmare.

Bert came back clutching two mugs, handed me one and eased himself into a chair. He spoke as if we'd been having a conversation.

'I was hit when I left the pub. Ended up in the Clyde.' He looked affronted. 'Could've been killed.'

'Where did it happen?'

'On my way back te the car. I thought I heard a noise. Next thing I knew I was hanging on te an old tyre, spitting up water.'

I didn't like the sound of that. 'They kept you in hospital for two days, Bert,' I said worriedly. 'You must've been in bad shape.'

He waved a disclaiming hand, 'I'm not as young as I used te be.' A sly grin appeared. 'But the food was good. Nurses weren't bad either.'

'Who, Bert?'

'I don't know, but I'll be asking around.' The amiable slyness disappeared. 'Be some tearaway looking for hassle.'

If I knew Bert, he'd already done his asking. Phone had probably hit meltdown within minutes of his return. And he must have received some satisfactory answers or he'd be spitting tacks.

I sat back. Bert was spinning a yarn and then trying to wrap it over my eyes. This was the work of outsiders. And we both knew it.

'You said something about a face in the wrong place.' He nodded. 'Any connection with this new team?' He seemed astonished at the very thought. 'Bert,' I said in desperation, 'I'm up to my neck in this. I need to know what's going on.'

He looked accusingly at me. 'I had a visit from yer friend, DI Thompson.' I waved a protesting hand in the air. My friend? Aw wait a minute. 'He said ye were helping them with their inquiries.'

'I wouldn't help him across the road,' I protested.

'Maybe.'

'No maybe about it,' I said hotly. 'Come on, Bert. You know me better than that. All right, Thompson's going to catch up with me one of these days. But that's why I need to get this sorted out first.' He still didn't look convinced. I stared at him. 'I need your help on this one.'

'I'm staying well clear. It's nothing te do with me.'

I stared pointedly at his head. 'Pity you didn't tell them that.'

He touched the pad and glared as if I'd done it. 'That's been sorted.'

I wondered who'd had their wrists slapped, how, and by whom. But this was wasting time. I turned the screw. 'You owe me one, Bert. And I'm calling it in.'

He shot up so quickly he slopped his coffee. 'Ye're ye're father's daughter right enough, Caithlin O'Connell. B'Jasus, that man could remember if he'd put sugar in ye're tea. And ask fer it back.'

The foxy grin showed briefly, so the memory couldn't have been all bad. Whether I was going to benefit from it or not I didn't know yet. We sat eyeball to eyeball. The silence weighed on.

'What sort of help do ye have in mind?' he asked finally. I told him. His eyebrows lifted. 'And I stay out of it?' he said cautiously. The age of chivalry is not dead.

'Yes,' I said, mentally crossing my fingers. He grunted. I took this for agreement and asked to use his phone.

Bert dumped it in front of me and beat a strategic retreat. He might be going along, but he wasn't going to take any chances of hearing something he shouldn't. This must be what they mean by a sleeping partnership.

I got through to the Aberdeen office, thanked Betty for the papers and said I wanted to see Mike Brown, either late afternoon or early evening, and to get that message to him. She said she would. I rang off and redialled. Jack had managed to fix a meeting. I jotted down the directions.

Bert came back in when I replaced the receiver. I gave him an idea of when I thought I'd be needing him. He said he'd be ready. I left.

Driving north, I cleared my mind and switched on Radio 3. I'd done what I could for the time being. Things would fall into place or they wouldn't. Either way it was too late to worry.

On the outskirts of Aberdeen, I made for my first port of call, the hospital. Hopefully, Helen would let me have a quiet spot where I could take a squint at the papers Donald had left. I had a pretty good idea what I might find there. And I was itching to get at it.

The dragon was still in residence, all set to scare patients away. Must be the latest in cost-cutting exercises. For anyone in need of tender loving care, one look would have been enough, a quick turn around and out the door.

I hustled up to the desk in my crumpled togs ready to take her on. Scowling, I said who I wanted to see. When her mouth opened to give me the runaround, I clipped in, 'She's expecting me.'

It was written all over her physog that she was itching to fob me off. I fixed her with a stare that suggested it wouldn't be worth it. Not unless she wanted me to mess up the regimented order of her person and her fancy desk.

She drew herself up, picked up the phone, spoke into it and put it down. 'You've to go to Mrs MacPherson's office,' she said stiffly. 'She's expecting you.'

I shook my head. And here was me thinking I'd just said that. I marched past without bothering to say thank you. Rudeness is like the plague, highly infectious.

I tapped Helen's door, went in and we exchanged glum faces. She reached into a drawer and came up with a small brown envelope. There couldn't be much in there. I just hoped what there was, was good.

She got up and walked round the desk. 'I have a meeting, Cat. You can use this office.'

'Does your door have to be locked?' I wasn't going to be here when she came back.

She smiled. 'Just close it.' She was quick on the uptake, must've been one of the things Donald liked about her. She handed me a sheet of paper. 'This is everything I could remember. I hope it's a help.'

I smiled to say it would be and put it in my pocket. She disappeared and I sat down at her desk and opened the envelope. Donald's scrawl covered four pages. I got out my glasses and settled down to decipher them.

Coasting

Donald had drawn up a timetable of events and carefully detailed eight accidents, six on the rigs and two on the road, and he'd jotted down comments from the men concerned.

In the first batch, three men had head injuries, two had multiple bruising, the other had been burned. In the second, one car had run out of brakes and hit a wall, the other had been run off the road by an unidentified lorry. The injuries were relatively mild, except the burns, second degree.

The three men with head injuries fitted the details Tomlinson, and Sawers, had provided. But the cases of bruising and burns hadn't appeared on their lists. I needed to find out why.

According to Donald, every man said that prior to these accidents he had refused to carry packages to or from the rigs. That agreed with what I had so far, but I was still missing the whys and wherefores.

I now knew, because I'd drilled the dates into my brain, that all these accidents had taken place within a week of one of Haldane's visits. And there was no way this could be coincidence.

What I needed to know was whether Jack's contact could fill in a bit more of the background, and give me the missing answers. I put these sheets to one side and looked at the third.

Donald had written down his complaints to the company, and why. Not surprisingly Sawers' name kept cropping up. I whizzed over this page. I knew most of it already. I turned it over and picked up the last sheet.

If this was accurate, it was dynamite. Three drug dealers were named and exchanges Donald had witnessed were detailed. He claimed it was high-grade heroin and had been passed on to a rig, hidden for three weeks to a month, and transported back on-shore and distributed.

Although everything was slotting together, I shifted uneasily. After the first burst of excitement I was beginning to feel less than happy. I didn't see how Donald could be sure about the contents of these packages. There was no mention that he'd opened one.

That meant he could be going by word of mouth. All right as far as it went, but there comes a point where hard evidence is needed. And he wasn't offering any.

I poured a coffee from the thermos that Helen had thoughtfully provided, and started to chew things over.

What were the possibilities? One, Donald had seen and identified the drugs but hadn't thought he needed to say so; two, he hadn't seen the drugs and was going on verbals. In the first case, I just needed to prove it; in the second, maybe there was nothing to prove.

I thought some more. Donald was methodical and careful in his work. Were there any circumstances that could explain these slap-dash entries? I found one right away. If you're deep in shit, time is of the essence. You write down the basics. He'd done that.

I still wasn't happy. Okay, think again.

I thought again. Written work is directed to an audience. So who was the audience? A court of law, the police, Yukon Discovery or me, and what was the difference?

I felt myself starting to come round. There was only one situation where Donald didn't have to establish his credentials and detail every point. And that was when he was writing to me, his buddy of long-standing.

I squirmed mentally. Faith's a wonderful thing. But hard data is even better. What's it to be O'Connell?

I've geared myself for years to dismiss gut feelings as the ache you get when you've eaten something that doesn't agree with you. I ran Donald's faults past me like ticker-tape. No worse than mine, but there nevertheless.

I poured another coffee.

By the time I'd finished it, I'd made up my mind. I had nothing to lose by treating Donald's information as accurate. I'd know soon enough if it wasn't.

I tidied up the tray and stuck my half-eaten biscuit in the bin, closed the door quietly behind me, and made for the car. I didn't bother looking at the starched gargoyle. I'd have liked to have seen her turned to stone and stuck on a parapet for eternity, but wish-fulfilment seems to be in short supply these days.

Jack was waiting for me in a pub near the harbour; his contact's choice. If I was as highly nervous as that man was claiming to be, I'd have arranged a meet in the woods, the third tree past the second rabbit hole on the right. I shrugged: mine not to reason why.

I've never seen a shebeen, but this fitted the description: dank, dark and shifty. And the smell – if they weren't making the stuff here, they were washing the floor with it.

My stomach retched. I swallowed hard and asked for a glass of orange, with plenty of ice. Jack went up to the bar. I studied his contact.

The friend of a friend was around six foot, brawny, with heavy dark brows over eyes set too close together; early thirties. He looked the type who would throw something off a lorry, and say he'd found it lying there when he nipped back and picked it up. I didn't feel overly optimistic.

Jack returned, pushed a glassful of orange liquid at me and handed over a pint of beer to our dubious companion. He hung on to a glass of water for himself. 'Cat. This is Johnny.'

Johnny grunted and gulped down some beer. I noticed his hand was shaking. For some reason I wasn't filling him with confidence. His dark eyes ran over me again, the doubt visibly increasing.

I wasn't enthralled by him either, but I think I was better at hiding it. I drummed up a cheerful smile. It didn't seem to work. We stood staring at each other as if war had just been declared, and we weren't quite sure what to do about it.

Jack said impatiently. 'Tell her, Johnny.'

Johnny put the pint glass to his mouth and drew up the beer like a human suction pump. When the last of the brown ambrosia had vanished down his throat, he handed the empty glass to Jack with an expectant stare. Jack took it ruefully and pushed his way to the bar.

Johnny and I engaged in another minute or two of suspended hostility. Then he looked me up and down, shrugged, and started talking. I didn't dare drag out my notebook. I listened, hard.

He'd been working on the rigs on and off for four years, but had only been with Yukon Discovery for eight months. They were good payers. I nodded. Work was easy. I nodded again.

He paused and gave me a suspicious look. I told myself to stop nodding. He started to say something about being on the training course. I interrupted to ask how long he'd been with the company at that point. He said that was at the end of his seventh month, and that he'd been approached by Mike Brown and asked to carry a package off the rig when he went on leave.

He hadn't said yes or no – he squinted at me pugnaciously, a man's got to live – but he'd asked around and what he'd heard he hadn't liked. The word was drugs. Not his scene. He looked over my shoulder as if he was planning his route out.

'So what happened?' I asked quietly.

Johnny muttered out of the corner of his mouth, 'I said no. He said I'd be sorry.' He stuck his chin out. 'I said, not as sorry as he was gonna be if he didn't buck off.'

'And?'

He looked surprised that I needed to ask. He was a big lad, right enough. I began to feel a bit surprised myself.

'I got my cards a couple of weeks after,' he growled viciously. 'If it had just been Brown I'd have sorted him out, but he's got helpers.'

'How did the package get on to the rig in the first place?' He shrugged, dunno. I tried again. 'Has this happened to anyone else?'

He looked at me as if his worst fears had been realised; he was dealing with a porridge brain. 'I've already told Jack.'

'So tell me.'

He clenched his hands. They must feel empty without a pint glass in them. 'You don't know me,' he said mysteriously. It didn't sound like a question.

'Never seen you in my life before,' I agreed affably. He rattled off three names. 'Same situation?' I asked. He nodded. 'Same result?'

He snorted. 'Except Ally. He ended up in hospital with a sore head.' His eyes were roaming freely now. He'd said all he was going to say, and I needed to get somewhere I could note it down.

'Thanks, Johnny.'

'You talkin' to me?' he said coldly.

Who me? Wouldn't dream of it. I pulled down the eye-blinds, finished my drink, and sidled off. I passed Jack without a flicker of recognition. I didn't know him either.

I went back to the car, keeping my radar on full range until I was inside and had the doors securely locked. I took out my pad and noted the who, where and when of the interview, and scribbled underneath the names and dates I'd been given. I already knew they tallied. But I like to keep accurate records.

I felt a buzz. Thanks to Johnny, I thought I now had the connection between the training scheme and the more serious difficulties on the rigs.

Easing out of the alley, I pointed the car uptown. Now for Mike Brown.

*

The minute I barged in, Betty mimed and pointed to the other door; Brown and Sawers were waiting for me. I said thanks, but I wasn't happy about Sawers being there. I knocked and went in. They were lounging at the desk.

Sawers forced himself to his feet. It must still be worth his while to behave half pleasant. He stuck out a hand. 'Miss O'Connell.'

'Ms,' I muttered.

He gave me the sneering once over and acted as if he hadn't heard. He nodded over at Brown. 'Mike Brown. You wanted a word.'

There was a knock on the door and Betty stuck her head in and chirruped, 'Phone call for Mr Brown, on my line.' Brown got up and went after her.

I took the opportunity. 'I was wondering about your stock orders, Mr Sawers. Does Betty handle these for you?'

'She copies out the orders, if that's what you mean.'

I could see that I was seriously upsetting this man by just being here. But he didn't seem bothered by my interest in his ordering procedures.

Brown reappeared. I drew Sawers a bland stare, a put-down would've been a waste of time, and turned to Brown. I suffered the limp handshake and thanked him for coming. Somebody has to set an example.

Now that I was up close, the smell of garlic was overpowering. I imagined myself saying to Thompson: this is the man who tried to break into my flat. And how do you know that, Ms O'Connell? he would say. I'd tell him garlic. And I'd be inside in the blink of an eyelid, for wasting police time.

I looked at Brown. When I'd seen him at Donald's funeral, he'd struck me as a similar type to Sawers. I was wrong. The only thing they had in common was their height and build.

Brown had a thinner face, shifty eyes and a straggle of lank dark hair. He was a walking reminder of what could come out at night. This was a gofer, with teeth.

Sawers had sat himself back down again. I took a deep breath.

'I would like to speak to Mr Brown in private. Is there another office we can use?' I knew he was going to push it. It was written all over his male supremacy.

'I'm afraid not,' Sawers said, waiting to see what I was going to do about it.

I did the only thing possible. I smiled, and said, 'In that case, I'll have to borrow this one.'

I held his gaze and got ready to whip out Tomlinson's letter, or leave. Sawers' eyes hardened. For a minute I thought he was going to refuse, but he got to his feet. The look he gave me would have dented armour.

'Help Miss O'Connell with her inquiries, Mike. Half an hour.' He gave another cold stare. 'I'll be outside.'

I took over his seat and ran through my spiel. What I was doing, and how anything he said would be treated in confidence. Brown's eyes were watchful, his lips wet and pink.

It was ninety-nine per cent certain that Sawers had him primed and I was wasting my time. But even a one per cent chance is better than a slap on the belly with a wet haddock.

I'd already decided that my only hope of coming up with something was to put Brown under a bit of pressure. I started by asking him who he worked for and what he did.

'I'm Mr Sawers' assistant.' A sneer crept round the pink mouth. 'I do what has to be done.'

I just bet you do. 'Good,' I said brightly. 'You'll be able to give me some information on the recent accidents.' I shot out another innocuous grin, 'Just routine.'

He shifted in his chair and looked bored. I started at the top of the list.

'What time did you say this happened?' On to the third. 'This chap wasn't too good a worker?' That's right the man was useless. Back again, a different angle each time, then introduced different names. I hoped to God he was getting confused. I was.

Then I had him. I knew it. My antennae were flapping, telling me so. I smiled across at him. He looked smugly back, relaxed enough to have been filleted.

'Thank you for your help, Mr Brown. Sorry I had to take up your time. But you know how it is, there's always paper to be filled in.' He leered happily. He knew all about these things.

I scribbled a list of points on a sheet of paper and headed it, Information confirmed by Mike Brown, Assistant Safety Officer. I presented it to him. 'If you could check this over and sign it.'

He took the paper, read it through and signed. I was on my feet ready for take off. I wanted out of here before Sawers discovered that his assistant had made a blunder. Brown had provided details of accidents that, according to Sawers, had never happened.

Final questions. I asked him about the discrepancies shown on the list of stock orders Ms Jordan had provided. Brown was uninterested, and unworried. Either he and Sawers were better bluffers than I gave them credit for, or there was something else funny going on here.

I reached the door as it swung open. Sawers. I glared at him as if it had worked out the way he'd intended. A complete waste of time.

That seemed to cheer him. When he looked past me to Brown, sitting smugly at the desk, he cheered up even more. 'I'm glad we were able to help you, Miss O'Connell.'

I went downstairs at a rate of knots and raced along to the car, got in and reversed down the alley. After a couple of rights and lefts, I crept out on to a quiet side road.

I had two things in my favour. One, I was driving a car Sawers wouldn't recognise, and two, I had avoided driving past his office. The fact that I was now lost was the least of my worries. I had something to do – fast.

I saw a sign for Inverness and followed it. The first village I came to I drew up beside a post-box. I wrote a brief explanation on a sheet torn from my notebook, folded it up with the paper Brown had signed, and stuck it in an envelope. I addressed it to myself, care of my lawyer. He was going to love this lot as well.

I nipped out and posted it. And began to breathe a little easier. Hopefully, that was my insurance dealt with. Now to find my bed for the night.

A Lucky Break

Jack had given me an address of a bed and breakfast. I'd said I was looking for a safe haven, off the beaten track; somewhere I didn't need to sit up half the night worrying who was creeping up on me. He'd said he knew just the place.

I drove around for over an hour trying to find it. I was on a particularly bleak stretch of hilly moorland, the sort of place that stirs tribal fears and makes you wish you weren't out and about, when something caught my eye. I reversed back and had another look.

A battered B&B sign, half covered by a piece of sacking, swung limply from the branch of a tree at the entrance to a narrow lane. I got out and shone the torch. I made out ____ Farm, and underneath, MacDou ____. I was looking for the MacDougalls. This must be it.

I went to the car and turned into the lane. The headlights lit up a narrow stretch that looked as if it had come under heavy shell-fire.

Off the beaten track? I'll say.

I eased the car slowly up one side, to avoid the tractor made ruts, and moved along in second, balanced precariously on the verge and central mound. Scraping the exhaust off the car would not please Doreen. It wouldn't do a great deal for my non-existent relationship with Stanley either.

Two miles of bumps and pot-holes followed. I'd almost given up hope of finding signs of life when I reached a farmstead, a three-sided square of low grey stone buildings.

I crawled the car up to what appeared to be the farmhouse. My hands were stuck like claws to the steering wheel. I unclutched, rubbed and straightened them, and got out and battered on the nearest door.

I heard raised voices debating who was going to answer. I shivered, it was a bit parky out here, and gave the door another thumping.

An overhead light switched on, and the door opened. A small sprightly man with reddened weather-beaten cheeks and a shock of white hair faced me up. Ninety if he was a day. He smiled inquiringly.

'Sorry to bother you,' I chittered. 'But I was told that you might have a spare room.'

'A spare room . . .?' He looked puzzled for a minute, then his face brightened. 'Oh, nae lass. We're nae open. Nae in the winter.'

A querulous voice rang out from the depths. 'Fit's that, Erchie?' I grinned. Fit's that. Love it. The voice sounded again, nearer and narkier. 'Fit's that, Erchie?' it yelped again.

He turned, and bawled, 'Nuthin' wumman. Jist a lassie looking fur a bed.' Me, a lassie? I beamed. This was a gentleman.

There was a patter of footsteps and a tiny woman in her eighties shoved out, HAG's *doppelgänger*. There should've been a roll of thunder and flash of lightning. I sprang to attention anyway.

She frazzled me with a pair of sharp blue eyes. 'A bed ye say?' I gazed vacantly: who me? 'Ye'll hae a car?' she snapped. I nodded. 'Pit it in the byre. Erchie'll show ye.' She turned back. 'Ye'll eat whit ye're gaen.'

Since in the circumstances this seemed highly likely, I gave another nod. What did they feed girl babies on eighty-odd years ago? Iron filings?

Erchie and I were left staring at each other. He sprang into action. 'Right, lass. Wee'll awa te the byre,' and zipped past.

I thought about it for a tenth of a second. He lived here. If he thought she who had to be obeyed had to be obeyed quickly, I was with him. I sped back to the car and jumped in.

The byre was a weary edifice listing heavily to one side, its stone walls colonised by the remnants of a variety of hardy weeds. I finally got the car parked to his satisfaction, hard against a wooden stall – the kine can mak 'a hellova mess o' a car, lassie – and we made our way back to the house at the speed of light.

Erchie lifted the latch, swung the door open and ushered me in. I fumbled along in the dark and opened the first door I walked into.

The room was dimly lit and as hot as a furnace. A massive fire set in a black-leaded grate roared up the chimney. A kettle steamed happily on the angle iron. There was a small table to one side of the fire, with a basket of bread and a knife and fork.

I looked around, and my eyes popped. The walls were strewn with claymores, each one gleaming as if it had been used recently. Enough of them here to fight the Battle of Culloden all over again.

Mrs MacDougall turned from the cooker in the corner. 'Sit yersell doon.' I sat, no messing. She walked over bearing a steaming plateful: stovies, eggs and black pudding. 'Eat that up.'

I ate, then wished I'd taken my time. The plate was whisked away and a cup of tea was placed in front of me, along with a sugar bowl and a jug of creamy milk.

'Ye've nae bags?' My mouth started to open. 'Why nae?'

'I didn't expect to be staying over.' The clock had turned back forty years; this was my grandmother when I refused to eat her stringy neeps. 'I live in Glasgow, and I'm up here on business.'

'Frae Glasga ye say? Nae connections this side?'

'I used to live in Dundee,' I said, trying to be helpful.

'Dundae?' She wasn't impressed. 'Nae connections up this wie?'

I searched my brain and looked over at Erchie. He sat by the fire in an oblivion of smoke, puffing thoughtfully, miles away. I was on my own with this one.

'Some cousins?' I proferred, hoping for the best.

'And wha wid thae be?'

I told her. A smile emerged. 'The MacIntyres?' She tutted happily, and said, 'My, thon Dougie MacIntyre wis an awfae man.' I decided I was saying nothing. With more family skeletons than cupboards to keep them in, it was the wisest course. 'An awfae man,' she repeated fondly.

I started to cheer up. If she was happy, I was happy. In the next half hour, I discovered that I was connected to half the population of the north-east of Scotland. And it wasn't the better half. Which was probably why nobody had ever mentioned it before.

I finally managed to get a word in. 'Do you have a telephone?'

'Och, aye.' She pointed at a knitted crinoline lady sitting on the sideboard. 'Ower yon.'

I went ower yon, and checked it out. Under the woollen doll, I discovered a black bakelite telephone, circa 1950. I smiled and picked it up. It appeared to be in working order, there was a dialling tone.

I brought out some legal tender, waved it in her direction, and asked if I could make a few calls. That was fine by her. She sat herself down beside the fire, picked up a heap of patchwork and started stitching. Privacy was clearly a concept that hadn't reached this part of the world.

I pulled up a chair and picked up the phone. I got through to Doreen. Both the car and me were in good condition, I assured her, and would stay that way. HAG next. I was bouncing with health and would keep in touch.

I looked over, they didn't seem to be paying attention. I tried Tomlinson on the mobile and got him at home. I was glad of the crackling interference. It meant I could report that all was well, the last thing I wanted was a search party.

But I managed not to hear him ask where I was phoning

from, and what my plans were for the following day. I hung up feeling relieved.

I was particularly pleased that I'd been able to avoid Tomlinson's questions. I'd been doing a bit of thinking since I left Brown and Sawers, and my confidence in Tomlinson had suffered a severe dent.

He should have known what I'd found out from Brown, so why hadn't he told me? Was it the Haldane business all over again? Or was there a more sinister explanation? Either way I didn't like it.

I went for my last number. I got through. 'Bert,' I said quietly.

'Caithlin, my dear,' he hushed back.

I was going to have to stop speaking to Bert. I was picking up his mannerisms. 'Tomorrow,' I murmured, 'Where we agreed.' The silence reached over the line. 'Bert,' I said sharply. 'You still there?'

'Caithlin.' There was a long pause. 'Are ye sure about this?'

'Course I am,' I barked, my hackles vertical and rising. 'And you'd better be there, Bert. Or I'm in deep sh—' the two elderly heads raised and turned towards me, 'shar-bunkle,' I finished weakly. Sharbunkle? I shrugged to show that I didn't know what it meant either.

I extracted a promise that he would appear, and hung up.

Mrs MacDougall led me upstairs to a small attic bed-room whose floor space was taken up by a narrow single bed. Barely enough room for my big feet. She promised to wake me early and hoped I'd be comfortable.

It may not have been wide but it was handsome, with downy white pillows and sheets and a bright patchwork quilt. There was no doubt about it. I was going to be comfortable.

I crawled under the quilt, stretched out in the coolness of the linen sheets, and stopped thinking.

I sat up, my head buzzing. A roaring and bawling, clattering of hooves and mooing, drifted up from below. I heard the voice again roaring, 'Keep aff that. Git on wi' ye, ye auld buggers.'

I squirmed over to the window and peered out into the beginning of a dark grey dawn. Down below, Erchie was ambling happily alongside a bunch of contented cows. Every few steps, he took his pipe out of his mouth and bawled blood curdling abuse – detailing certain bizarre activities – and returned the pipe with a satisfied puff.

I finally got my watch the right way up – 5 a.m. I shook it and looked again – 5 a.m. Dear God; the middle of the night.

The door opened and a human whirlwind tore in carrying a cup of tea, a biscuit teetering on the saucer, and laid it on the bedside table. I saw it all happen, in silence.

'Ye'll be awake then.' I was unable to agree with her. She stopped in the doorway on her way out. 'Breakfast'll be nigh ready. Ye'll be for getting up.' I grunted weakly. A smile as clear as a sunbeam lit up her face, and she pulled the door shut behind her.

I reached for the tea, took a gulp, and felt it go down. By the time I finished, I was willing to admit that I might be awake. I'd certainly had all the sleep I was going to get.

I picked up the towel and wrapped it round me. Time for a quick bath. The sooner I got back to civilisation the better.

Breakfast. A plate of thick porridge covered with thicker cream was followed by two door-stopper pieces of toast and home-made marmalade and several cups of dark tea.

I reeled from the table, regretting my lack of regular exercise over the past few days, and paid my board. Mrs MacDougall folded it carefully and stuffed it behind the front of her apron. I didn't see Erchie getting his hands on that.

When we reached the outside door, she screeched, 'Erchie!' Erchie answered the summons, appearing from the direction of the byre, shaking his head. I knew how he felt. Mine was numb.

'Whit is it noo wumman?' he shouted.

Since I prefer to be on the winning side, I lined up with the boss. The pair of us stood, arms crossed, watching him cover the last few feet.

'Ye'll need tae help Mrs O'Connell wi' her car, Erchie,'

she nipped, looking at him as if he'd been trying to do a bunk but she was up to all his dodges.

'Di yae think ah dinna ken that wumman?' he roared.

She hmmphed. I winced. She vanished indoors and appeared a second later with a small parcel. She pressed it into my hands.

'A bite o denner.' On a wild impulse, I reached over and gave her a peck on the cheek. She flushed to the roots of her hair and waved me off. 'Och, awa' wi' ye noo.'

I followed Erchie. The car was unscathed, but two curious cows started to wander across to give it the once-over.

'Git oot o' there, ye auld buggers,' Erchie bellowed.

I backed the car out swiftly, in case I heard anything else I shouldn't, tooted the horn and waved. Going down the track, I started to laugh.

When I got to the road, I turned the car towards Aberdeen. And cold reality took over.

A Bridge
Too Far

_____

By the time I reached the outskirts of Aberdeen, I'd been through everything several times over, and I was still chewing over Haldane's connection.

Although Tomlinson and I were both pretty sure that Haldane was up to something, it didn't follow that the game he was playing was the one I was interested in. Some bits fitted, others didn't.

I didn't have any doubts that Sawers and Brown were up to no good, and that they weren't working alone. They liked to pretend differently, but they didn't strike me as the type who made the important decisions.

And Haldane had been unusually supportive of Sawers. He could be repaying services rendered. Or maybe he was just keeping an acolyte in his competitor's camp. In which case, Sawers could be playing a hand that Haldane knew nothing about.

The one damning piece of evidence against Haldane was the association of the accidents with his visits. I knew it couldn't be coincidence. So why was I trying to find reasons for not treating him as the prime suspect?

All right, the records of transatlantic calls to and from the Aberdeen office suggested that Haldane hadn't been the only person in the States in frequent contact with Sawers. Unless he'd been zapping about like a blue-tailed fly. I shook my head. There again, that wasn't impossible.

My thinking was brought short when I ran into Union Street, stop go and a lot of muscular driving. When I found Market Street I was in the wrong lane; I was herded to the left in a one-way, and had to shove over to the right to sneak up on Market Street from the other side.

This time round I made it and headed down. The harbour was on the left. I turned sharp left. Double yellows stretched in front of me like the road to Damascus.

I was at the top before I had the option of turning right. I took it. The road curved steeply downwards. At the foot, I landed back at the harbour. I drove slowly along until I found an open gate. When I didn't find any notice warning of dire retribution, I drove in.

I parked and got out, shrugged myself deeper into the jacket and wandered along. The sun was shining, but the wind was brisk enough to keep me moving.

There were large corrugated-iron storage areas. And I passed three boats, painted bright yellow, with short foredecks and open long sterns. Presumably these were supply ships. I'd expected them to be bigger.

Two tall cranes, bright blue with screaming yellow arms stood on fixed rails. Nearby were large storage tanks, some with red tops and one pillar-box all over. I was beginning to understand Yukon Discovery's logo. The oil business likes colour.

On the opposite quay was a ferry, looking huge. Further along I counted six lifeboats tied up alongside a sign for rescue boat services. Remembering Haldane's comment on the likely survival time in icy water, I shivered. These boats weren't there for show.

I went back to the car, checked the map, and drove towards the South Esplanade. I cruised along at five, looking at the rows of workshops: shipwrights, fabrication, timber, crane and lifting gear, mixed up with offices. The surprise was the fish selling and freezing. I'd thought the fishing industry had moved to Peterhead.

I shrugged, something else to find out. I was going to wake up one morning and find my brain had burst. I went back to the car and drove south up an incline, stopped at the top and got out.

Aberdeen stretched out into the distance. The harbour was directly below me, beyond it was the long golden curve of the bay, glimmering in the sun. Inland, buildings and streets were spread out in an amorphous hollow that rose abruptly on the outskirts.

I looked out to sea. It was a blue pond. The hurricanes must be having a day off. In the distance, I saw the pinnacle of an oil rig, a minute delicate structure squatting defiantly in the midst of the vast watery expanse of the North Sea: David and Goliath.

I'd been brought up beside the sea and I have a healthy respect for it. I've seen storms build up in an hour and engulf boats. And I know that even a placid-looking beach is no guarantee of safety, fast currents can take the feet from you, or sweep in on a high tide and cut you off.

I took a last look at the rig, feeling a sense of awe. You had to hand it to these oil people. But maybe it was time somebody told them they were doing the impossible.

I was turning away when I saw a police car draw up below. Two men got out. I recognised the one with the shoulders right away – DI Thompson. Dear God Almighty. What was he doing here?

I ducked back, in case he looked up, and peered round the edge. He stood for a few minutes listening to the other plain-clothed gent, nodding his head and following the pointing hand. Then the pair of them went into a building that looked like an office.

I thanked my lucky stars that I hadn't wasted any time down there. If Thompson had caught up with me I'd have been pinned against a wall. I went back to the car, thinking furiously.

It was just as well I'd arranged to meet Bert tonight. Looked as if that was going to be all the time I was going to get.

A certain warehouse had cross-referenced with all my informants, and I wanted to look inside. Bert was to be my protection. He didn't know that yet, but he wouldn't have to take part in the breaking and entering, just be around.

I wasn't meeting Bert until six, and by that time Thompson should have returned to his lair. To be on the safe side, I decided to spend the day out of Aberdeen.

I drove down the coast road towards Stonehaven, window open, radio on, trying to feel light-hearted. I was going to have myself a few hours' holiday.

But I couldn't shake off a nagging feeling of urgency.

I forced myself to take a browse round Stonehaven, and lunch in Montrose. By three o'clock I'd had enough, and slowly made my way back towards Aberdeen.

I was a few miles out when I saw a farm road leading towards the sea and, in the distance, the top of what looked like warehouses. There was no sign, but it fitted the description I'd been given. Gulls Cliff, one of the two places I intended visiting with Bert. I stopped at the road end, engine running.

It was getting dark. I spent a minute or two arguing with myself. Safer to have company. On the other hand, it looked quiet enough. I couldn't resist it. I turned in and drove down.

I ended up at a short stretch of warehouses built on a concrete base, all on their ownsome. There was a gravel path leading down to a narrow inlet, and a small beacon tower above it, on my left. As I watched, a flicker of light shot out. Lighting-up time.

I turned back to the warehouses. A discreet sign on the first said this was the property of Acon Suppliers, a larger sign said Keep Out. I swivelled my head – there was nobody around – and walked over to check the large doors. They were securely padlocked.

I felt my way down the side of the building, looking for an entry. When I heard a car crunching over gravel I sank to the ground and froze, my heart beating like a drum.

I heard doors slamming, and voices. I recognised the

voices: Sawers and Brown. I waited ten minutes. When they didn't come any closer, I squirmed back until I could see what was going on.

Sawers was standing by Doreen's Polo, stamping his feet in the cold. I saw Brown squirming out from under the car and stand wiping his hands on a cloth.

Sawers looked at him. 'Is that it fixed?'

Brown nodded, a sly grin appearing on his face, 'Sure is.'

'Let's go.'

'Boss, why don't I take a look round? She's here some-where.'

Sawers stopped. 'Mike, use your head. She takes the car? End of story. If she doesn't, all we have to do is pick her up at the main road. This track is the only way out of here.'

Brown looked along the ten-foot high, thick chain-link fencing that surrounded the property and lined the road out. His face lit up. 'Gee, that's right.'

'Get a move on,' Sawers said sharply. 'It's bloody freez-ing.'

The wheels spun as Brown turned the car, and they moved on to the farm road and out of sight. I sat up shaking. I didn't give a bugger now what was in that warehouse. I wanted out of it, well away.

I spent another fifteen minutes scouting around, looking for a break in the fence. It was new and firm, and capped by rolls of barbed-wire with spikes big enough to skewer a fish.

There was nothing else for it. I knew that the cliffs cut off the inlet, so it had to be up top, using the wire as a horizon-tal safety rope. I started to feel my way along the fence, making for the cliff edge.

By the time I reached the cliffs, I could hardly see where I was going and the light of the beacon was too high to be any help. The roar of waves beating against rocks echoed upwards. They sounded a long way off.

I crouched down and stretched out a hand. There was roughly a foot of ground between the base of the fence and what was probably a sheer drop.

I stood up shakily and took it one step at a time, keeping my feet tight to the base. I hung on to the wire like grim death. A couple of times the ground crumbled, and my feet were left dangling in thin air.

Each time I scrabbled to get a foothold, I determinedly closed off the mental vision of the hungry sea down below, getting ready for its next victim.

My arms ached and sweat poured down my back. I gritted my teeth against the pain, and tried to control the shaking. I had to keep going.

I didn't know how long it had taken me to reach the end of the fence and freedom, but it felt like a lifetime. Taking a fix from the beacon, I stumbled along the rough ground in the dark, on what I hoped was a wide angle from where Sawers and Brown would be waiting.

When I reached the coast road I kept an ear out. If I heard a car, I was going for the ditch. I must have walked a mile before I heard a lorry behind me. I stuck up the thumb. It drew up.

I reeled back from the ripe smell. A fish lorry.

A cheery face peered out. 'Aberdeen harbour. Any good?'

I nodded numbly. Beggars can't be choosers. It took me two tries before I got a foot on the high step and pulled myself up.

He looked quizzically at me. 'You had trouble?'

I felt like crying, but shook my head. 'No . . . uh, yes. Car broke down.'

He shot me a look. 'Bad spot for it to happen.'

He gave me a final curious sidelong glance and drove on in silence. This was a man who didn't believe in meddling in other people's business. And I was grateful for it.

He let me off at the harbour. I struggled along to the pub where I was meeting Bert. It was fairly busy, but I saw him right away and made my way across.

Bert was wearing his green flack jacket, old corduroys, a thick sweater and a shapeless woollen hat, and looked deeply pissed off. When he saw me he jumped up. The face on it would've curdled milk.

'Jasus Christ, Caithlin, where have ye been?' he ranted. 'I've been waiting here over an hour.' He stopped and stared. Maybe I wasn't looking too good. 'Are ye going te sit down or fall down?' I sat. 'What're ye having?'

I told him and slumped back, aching all over. When he stuck the glass of whisky in front of me, I picked it up and threw it down my throat. The raw spirit stung my mouth and set my gullet on fire, but the warm glow when it hit my stomach was worth it.

'I'll have another, Bert,' I wheezed. He stared at me in astonishment, picked up the glass and made his way back to the bar. When he came back, he had a glass of whisky in one hand and a plateful of Ploughman's in the other.

He shoved them in front of me. 'By the look of ye, ye'll need this.'

I smiled, 'Thanks, Bert,' and picked up the glass and threw it back like the first one. Wow! The fumes worked their way up my gullet, backfired, and reeked out of my nose. Vesuvius with heartburn. If Bert brought his lighter any closer we'd both go up in flames.

I got stuck into the food while he chain-smoked. When I pushed the empty plate away and leaned my head back against the wall, there was a satisfying buzz in my head and a comforting warmth in my muscles.

That had helped. Oh my, had that helped. I closed my eyes to enjoy it better. Bert shook me. My eyes shot open.

'Are ye intending spending the night here?' he said crabbily. 'Or are we going te get on with that bit of business ye've dragged me all the way up here for?'

I worked up a cool look. 'In a minute.'

'What is it anyway?'

'A visit to a warehouse.'

Only one now. There was no way I was going anywhere near Gulls Cliff. For all I knew, Sawers and Brown could be still sitting at the road end, waiting for Yours Truly.

'Well, it had better be legit,' Bert pronounced. I stared disbelievingly. He was talking legit? He seemed to take offence. 'I've told ye, Caithlin,' he narked. 'I'm staying away from trouble.'

'What are you doing here then?' I said sourly, too tired to listen to any more of his bleating.

'I'm here te stop you getting inte any more of it yerself,' he snapped back. 'Ye must have a bloody death wish.' He glared. 'And d'ye think I'm an eedjit? Ye wanted me here, because ye think that after the last time these new boys'll stay clear. Fair enough. But this time I'm calling the shots.'

I stared innocently: away ye bum, ye could'na caw time.

'D'ye hear me?' he snapped.

I gave a dutiful nod. 'I hear you, Bert. I hear you.'

He sat back, looking relieved that he'd got that over and done with. 'Right. Where are we for?' I told him. He got up. 'Let's go.'

Outside, he said, 'Where's the motor?'

I didn't feel up to explanations about whose motor was where. And if I told him his was still lying at the airport running up a bill, he'd start whining all over again.

'I had to leave it, it's been doctored.'

His jaw dropped. 'What d'ye mean doctored?'

I pushed him on. 'Forget it, Bert,' I said wearily, 'I'll tell you later.'

We climbed into his old BMW, and I directed him to a side street. Silence the whole way. Bert parked the car, and we got out and made for the harbour. We were half-way along the quay before I found what I was looking for.

I peered up at the board, Acon Suppliers. This was it. 'Wait here, Bert, and keep your eyes open. I'm going round the back.'

He grabbed my arm. 'What're ye going to do?'

I unprised his fingers. 'I'm going to take a look around,' I said, beginning to get a bit narky myself. 'Do you think I've come all the way out here to do the fandango?'

He tried to look decisive. 'Well, ye'd better be quick. I'm not hanging about.'

'Right, Bert, right. Give me ten minutes.' I slipped off before he thought of something else to argue about.

Round the back I found a window I thought I could open and poked at it with my pocket-knife until the latch lifted. I swung it open and looked round for a box I could stand on, so that I could climb in.

I saw two dark shapes in the murk and went over. When

the torch lit them up, I gagged and held my hand over my mouth. Then I ran the light.

Lying on his back, his eyes staring unseeingly at the stars was Sawers. There was a neat hole in his forehead and a trickle of blood running over one eye. I took a deep breath and concentrated.

The gun that had fired the bullet hadn't been pressed against the skin, or there would've been a ragged star-burst wound. And if it had been around ten inches away, there might have been soot or gunpowder marks. No sign of either suggested a professional kill.

Beside him lay Brown, twisted on his side, with the back of his head blown away. It looked as if somebody had used both barrels of a shotgun, close up. Not a pretty sight. Bile rose to my mouth, and I looked away.

I bent over and touched Sawers' neck. The muscles were flaccid, and his head rolled to one side. Feeling the soft warmth under my hand, I recoiled.

The fact that there was no sign of the onset of rigor mortis was no help. Usually evident after four hours, and starting in the face and neck, it can be speeded up by violent exertion before death, or slowed down by cold.

I stood up and tried to think.

All I had to go on was that I had last seen them alive nearly four hours earlier. But if they had been killed soon after, Sawers' body wouldn't be this warm. The icy night temperature would've seen to that.

I staggered back, leaned against the wall of the warehouse, and tried to stop my stomach from heaving. This could've happened when Bert and I were in the pub, and that was too recent for comfort.

After a couple of minutes, I forced myself to go over and check out their pockets. I found a gun in Brown's jacket. I lifted it out gingerly with my fingertips, and hid it under a stone.

I went back to Sawers. In his left trouser pocket, I found a folded up piece of paper. I took it out and retreated to the wall, breathing as if it was my last.

I struggled to get my reading glasses out of my pocket,

cursing under my breath. Half blind, shit-scared, and still here, I must be bloody mad. I shoved the glasses on my nose, unfolded the paper, and shone the torch.

The last piece of the jigsaw had already fallen heavily in place. I knew now what the set-up was, and why. I re-read the note. But this confirmed it and gave me hard evidence.

And if I didn't get back in time with the news, a certain person was going to discover that there were worse problems than a visit from the police.

Feeling strangely sad, I took a last look. They wouldn't be left lying there long. An icy shiver ran down my back. The next stop would be deep water, with heavy weights attached to their feet. And if Bert and I didn't get a move on, we might be joining them.

I felt a hand on my shoulder, and my heart nearly went into spasm. I had my elbow ready for a hefty swing and was turning to deliver, when I heard Bert's voice. I stopped in time, nerve-endings twitching. What the hell was he playing at?

'Caithlin,' he whispered. 'We've got company.'

I straightened up. 'Company?' I whispered back. 'Who?'

'A black Jag's been parked across the exit, and a couple of these new boys are wandering around.'

My blood froze. 'How do you know it's them?'

'Because I've seen them before,' he snarled. I felt the blood rush to my head; he was getting helluva cocky. I was about to snarl back, when I registered the look on his face – caution thinking about turning into panic. 'They're on the look-out for somebody,' he muttered. 'We'd better stay out of sight until they go.'

Bert sounded surprisingly calm. I wondered how calm he'd be if I told him what was lying seven feet away. And how he was going to react, when I mentioned that we were the somebodies the new boys were on the look-out for.

If Sawers' and Brown's sticky end was a result of me escaping the net, as I suspected it was, some people wanted me out of the way pretty badly. That meant these boys would be keen. And if Bert started exercising his injured squeal, we were both done for.

I gave a grim smile. Bert is a much tougher cookie than he makes out, but his instinct for self-preservation is paramount. This gives him a knee-jerk reaction to trouble: one whiff of it, and he's off. And he was looking restive. But I had to tell him.

I grabbed oxygen from the air, relished it, and took another few intakes, while I thought about how to phrase the news. 'They're not going to go, Bert,' I said finally. 'We're the people they're looking for.'

His head whirled round. I saw the white of his eyes in the moonlight. 'Don't be ridiculous,' he muttered. 'We haven't done anything te them. Why should they . . .?' He developed the stare of a man whose wife has forgotten to post his winning coupon, knowing his worst fears have been realised and hating to admit it. 'How do you know?' he squeaked.

'Believe me, Bert, I know.' I took a grip of his arm. 'Come on, down this way. And be quiet.'

He didn't even argue. I took a shifty. He looked as if he'd gone into shock. I gave him a nudge to get him going, and we started moving.

We crept along the length of the quay behind outbuildings, acting like mice avoiding the cat. A wait, then a silent rush for the next dark shadow. We wore a powder puff on each foot. And we gave up on breathing.

I knew where we were going, the only place we could go. But I'd no intention of telling Bert until we got there.

He was going to like it even less than I did.

Rough Justice

The moon came out from behind the clouds. Bert took one look at the small boat bobbing about below us in the black oily water. He took another at the way down: a rope ladder disappearing over the edge of the quay. Then he looked at me.

An expression of profound disbelief spread over his face, and he did an abrupt about turn. I'd seen it coming. I grabbed him by the jacket and dug my heels in.

He kept going. At this rate we'd soon be back where we'd started. I didn't want to have to tell him what I'd found behind the warehouse, but I would if I had to – in techni-colour. Summoning up the last of my strength, I counted to three and pulled.

'Bert,' I hissed. 'We've got to take that boat. It's our only way out of here.'

'Caithlin, for Gawd's sake,' he gasped, jerked to a halt. He loosened my grip and straightened the jacket. 'Ye can't ask a man my age te climb down there. Inte that.'

'If I can do it, you can do it,' I snarled. He didn't budge. I went for the jugular, 'And I'm a woman.' He shot me a cynical look: some woman. Cheeky bugger. 'Bert,' I said, between clenched teeth, 'If you don't climb down, I'm gonna throw you down.'

Something convinced him. Could've been the insane stare. He moved back huffily and over to the edge. I followed, real close.

Taking a hold of the ladder, he swung over and started to lower himself, muttering under his breath. He paused, face suspended above the quay, to deliver his parting shot.

'Ye're a thrawn besom, Caithlin O'Connell, just like yer mother. And she has a lot te answer for. Gave yer father the life of a dog.'

The face disappeared and I heard a thump as he landed in the boat. A string of curses emerged from the gloom, all related to his opinion of my nature and my antecedents. I wasn't all that interested.

I sent a snarling whisper down after him, 'And you can bloody well get that effin' engine started. I'll see to the ropes.'

There was a scrabbling sound, and I looked round to see Bert's face reappearing, black with rage. 'Ye'll mind ye'r language when ye speak te me, Caithlin O'Connell.'

His gaze shifted to the heavy rope-end I had in my hands, and he shut the mouth and disappeared as quickly as he'd come.

The muttering went on down below as I struggled to untie the last rope. Several more choice curses floated up from the darkness, accompanied by several loud thuds. It sounded as if he was kicking the hell out of the motor. But Bert has a way with engines.

Then a sweet-sounding roar, quickly throttled back to a quiet purr. We were in business. I lowered myself over the side and jumped. I wasn't a minute too soon, bloody swine would've gone without me.

Rocking violently, the boat puttered away from the quay into the darkness. Bert stood at the wheel like an old salt, eyes straight ahead, his weight shifting with each movement.

I wondered if the sea-dog act meant that he knew something about boats. I hoped so, because all I knew was that they were meant to stay on top of the water.

— 227 —

Bert shivered and pulled the sides of his woollen hat down and around his ears, stuck his shoulders up, and peered into the black night. Now he looked like a cross between the SAS and a down-and-out.

'Maybe ye're ready to tell me where we're going. And how we're going te get there.' He swivelled round and added sarcastically. 'Not that I want ye to put yerself to any trouble.'

I tried to visualise the map I'd looked at earlier, and relate it to the pitch black that surrounded us. Somehow, we had to get round the quay into the inlet further south. Nobody would expect me to go back there. Anyway, Sawers and Brown were out of the running, and I had to get Doreen's Polo.

We couldn't stay in too close or we'd run foul of the fishing boats. Too far out, and we'd be waving goodbye to land and hitting the open sea. In this boat, that probably meant waving goodbye to living.

Bert squirmed round again and hissed furiously, 'For Gawd's sake, Caithlin, will ye tell me where the hell I'm supposed te be going?'

I explained as best as I could. Pointing out that he was supposed to avoid other boats, rocks and any such impedimenta to our progress. And that the general idea was to hug the coastline, not kiss it.

'And maybe you can use some of the low cunning of these bloody Irish ancestors you're always going on about,' I sneered. 'And get us out of this mess.'

He whipped round. 'I've te get us out of this mess?' He took his hands off the wheel and thumped himself on the chest. 'Me?' The face filled with indignation. 'This isn't my mess,' he bawled. 'And I didn't get us into it.'

The boat took a mad dive to the right. I saw white water looming up straight ahead, and pointed at it, fatalistically.

'Bert,' I said, quietly. He was too busy huffing and puffing to notice. 'Bert,' I repeated, raising my voice, 'look.'

He looked. 'Jasus Christ!' he roared. He grabbed the wheel and started turning. The white water swirled past us with the sad whoosh of a predator cheated of its prey. He sagged on to the wheel. 'Jasus bloody Christ.'

I gave him a disgruntled look. A fat lot of good that was going to do. And we didn't even have a cigarette between us. I searched my pockets again just to make sure. At this point in time, lung cancer was the least of my worries.

I found a crumpled paper tube and scraped it out. The fisherman's friend. One of these might shut him up. I struggled over. 'Here, have one.'

Still staring dementedly into the darkness, he scraped a mint from the paper and stuck it in his mouth. 'Christ almighty,' he mumbled. I could see it wasn't working. He shifted the mint to the other side. 'Christ all-bloody-mighty.'

I gave up. I was fed up listening to his dirge, and craning into the dark was pointless, since my eyes were even worse than his. I stumbled back, and flopped down in the stern to await my fate.

The world went up and down. I felt more and more squeamish. And if I got any colder I'd have to be chipped free. Maybe surviving wasn't all it was cracked up to be.

'Caithlin,' Bert hissed, 'is this it?'

I struggled forward again. There was a light on our right. It could be the beacon at the inlet. It had better be, I couldn't take any more of this. 'That's it,' I hissed back, 'Slowly and quietly now.'

He throttled back to a low putter. 'What happens next?'

I told him about the car, and the keys that were nestling snugly in my pocket. He turned a horrified face in my direction. 'But I thought ye told me it had been doctored, and that was why ye left it there?'

'You'll just have to un-doctor it then, Bert. Won't you?' I said tightly. 'After all, you're the motor man.'

If looks could kill, I'd have dropped on the spot. He turned away, huff written all over the muff, and gave me the stony-back treatment.

We grounded the boat on shingle and crunched along in silence until we reached a path. I sagged with relief. I knew where I was now. We struggled up the steep slope. Another hundred metres and we were home and dry.

Well almost. First, Bert had to find whatever had been

planted on the car. Then he had to remove it. Preferably without blowing us up in the process.

A mere bagatelle.

I had my hand on the handle, ready to open the car door. We'd been over the hassle of this wasn't his car, so where was his? And Bert had just crawled out from under with a small package which he deposited delicately into a drum half-filled with water.

He whispered that there was a bigger one further in. And that if I thought he was going to try to deal with that one in the dark my head must be filled with sawdust.

I could tell that he was putting on his running shoes, and was wondering what to do about it, when the torchlight got us between the eyes. Blinded, we clung together like Hansel and Gretel.

'Well, well. This is a surprise. If it isn't Ms O'Connell. And you've brought a friend with you. The one who knows about motors.'

The snide voice was confident, and unrecognisable. I felt a stab of fear. My first instinct was to run. But what about Bert? He'd used up his speed reserves years ago.

In the time I wasted thinking, footsteps drew closer. Then it was too late. The moon re-emerged to show us our visitors, two of them, dressed in fisherman's gear. And I'd never seen either of them before in my life.

If these were the new boys, I hoped they'd recognise Bert and remember that he had powerful friends; people that it didn't pay to upset.

The one behind was a dark blur, big but unremarkable. The front man was a little over average height, slim, looked as if he could move quickly, and had a thin smooth face, deadpan features, dead eyes. He had the torch. He switched it off and stuck it in his pocket and smiled, showing sharp canines.

'Good of you to deal with Mr Brown's package for us. Since the police are taking an uncomfortable interest in our activities, it's time for us to bow out. So we'll take the car. Save us having to hang around.' The voice was flat, this was routine. He held out a hand. 'The keys, Ms O'Connell.' He waited half a second and snapped his fingers. 'Give.'

Bert stepped forward as if he was about to say something. I wanted him to hold his tongue until I'd worked out what to do. I shot him a warning frown, and made as if I was digging my elbow into his midriff.

Bert caught the look, and rode the elbow. I watched him, gasping and doubling over, and thanked the Lord for sly old play-actors.

Dead-eyes took it all in, looking unperturbed. I began to get really worried. This man was chock full of confidence, king of the heap. If he was into megalomania, that could turn out to be very bad news.

'Your friends don't seem able to mind their own business, Ms O'Connell.'

I chilled. 'My friends?'

'Yes. Your Dr Grant was just the same,' he said silkily. 'Couldn't take a telling.'

'Dr Grant?' I felt icier than permafrost. 'What do you know about him?'

He shrugged indifferently. 'Let's just say he had to be dealt with.' Expressionless, he reached inside his jacket and brought out a gun. He pointed it at me. It looked like a cannon. He jerked his head to one side. 'Away from the car. I'll have the keys.'

Things were adding up so quickly that I felt as if I was going to hyperventilate. I slowed myself down by looking him over. A bunch of nothing. The man wants the keys? He can have them.

I held out the jangle of metal. 'Sorry, Bert,' I said. 'No choice.' Dead-eyes smiled coldly, reached out and grabbed.

Bert stopped his wheezing, took one look at the gun, and lunged forward. Stupid bugger. The fist with the gun in it swept forward and mashed into him. This time Bert bounced back and landed on the ground, retching and coughing, and settled into a moaning huddle.

I felt sick with anger. I breathed deeply and moved backwards, very slowly. Reality was beating my worst imaginings into a paper bag. I edged towards Bert.

The two of them got in the car, the big one going to the back, and the windows nearest us were wound down. It wasn't hard to work out what they intended to do next. Still moving as if I was walking on eggs, I reached Bert and got ready to help him up.

What we needed was time. And a little help from above. I glared at Bert. With the effort he puts into communicating with the Almighty, if we weren't in with a shout, we bloody should be.

I checked him over. He was breathing and his eyes were open. I dragged him to his feet and inched away, pulling him with me, and strained to see what they were up to.

The dead-eyed one was in the driving seat. He leaned forward as if he was putting the key in the ignition, then he switched on the lights and turned to say something to his mate.

When he leaned forward again, I tensed and pumped adrenaline. Grabbing Bert, I pushed him and myself into the darkness, and bawled, 'Dow-ow-own.'

There was a booming crump, and something punched me in the back and sent me tumbling over and over. And everything went dark.

When I came to, the place was lit up like a carnival and I was engulfed in heat. I lay on my back in a silent world, gasping like a fish. By the time oxygen reached my lungs I'd almost given up hope. I wheezed it in gratefully, even though it burned all the way down.

Another wave of heat rolled over me and I heard the roar of flames. I smelled smoke. I was on fire. I struggled to sit up, and beat at the smouldering patches on my jacket. I touched my face, then my hair. Bits of sizzle fell off.

I sat slumped, my arms barely managing to hold me up. The car was an inferno. Where was Bert?

I saw him lying a few metres away and dragged myself over. I had to stop every couple of moves to hold my arms up against the heat. By the time I got there he was stirring.

I took a grip on his arm and started to pull him away.

Tears ran down my face, nipping my skin. My muscles were like jelly, I couldn't go any further.

I propped him up and leaned against him, back to back. I don't know how long we sat like that. But I remember being violently sick, and looking at the puke as if it belonged to somebody else.

Bert tugged at me. I struggled to my feet and we went back to leaning on each other, this time standing up. Too shocked to speak, we stood and stared at what was left of the car.

It was a twisted, blazing wreck, with two dark shapes in it that didn't look human; and the smell. I bent over; my body did its best to be sick again but all I could produce was bile. I started to shiver.

'Caithlin.' Bert hugged me. 'Are ye all right, lass?'

I looked at him. His face was sooty, with paler streaks running down his cheeks. A mass of blood was pouring from above his left eye. He was a mess. If I looked like that, I didn't want to know about it.

Am I all right? Jesus Christ. 'Yeah. I'm fine, Bert.'

We took a last look and turned away without speaking. I was tottering, weak as a kitten. Bert looked shaky on his pins as well.

'Ye should've told them, Caithlin.'

I couldn't believe my ears. I stopped and looked at him. He was wearing his judgemental face. And how he can judge anybody else, ever, is beyond me. It lit a fuse I thought had been burned out.

'Told them?' I shouted. 'Are you mad?' I was slavering with rage. 'They knew about it, you fool. It was their mate that put it there in the first place.'

He gave me an offended glare that said he was nobody's fool, and bawled back, 'But they thought we'd fixed it. Ye heard them.' He grabbed me to stop me falling over, and stood looking at me as if I'd sprouted horns. 'What've ye done, Caithlin lass?' He shook his head sorrowfully. 'What've ye done?'

What had I done? What the hell did he think they'd done? And that gun hadn't carried blanks. When they'd got round to sticking it out the window to wave us goodbye, it would have been a permanent leave-taking they had in mind.

I shook my head, pointless arguing.

I stuck my hands in my pockets to stop them shaking, and turned to take a last fix on the burning car. Did I feel guilty? Not bloody likely.

That realisation made me feel even colder. I hunched my shoulders, and started to walk away. Looked as if I was going to have to live with it.

Bert pulled at my arm. I turned, ready for a fight. 'The Dr Grant he was talking about was ye'r friend, Donald?' I nodded, stiff-faced. Don't give me any more aggro Bert. He linked his arm into mine. 'Come on, Caithlin, lass. Let's go home.'

I grinned weakly, and we started a wavering walk. Two beat-up dead-beats heading for civilisation.

About a mile along the road, Bert disappeared into the bushes saying he needed a pee. I think he was just having a look to see that all his bits were still hanging in there. I collapsed on to the verge to wait.

I heard a car coming fast. The scream of a siren broke the air and headlights landed, spot on. I saw Bert hit the dirt. I decided not to worry about him. If he wanted a lift in a nice police car, all he had to do was step out of the bushes.

The car screeched to a halt, doors opened, and they came out running. When I saw who was out in front, I buried my head in my hands.

An
Offshore Wind

I was keeling over when Thompson reached me. He made a grab and propped me up. In the glare of the head-lights, the texture of his coat magnified in front of my eyes into a loose grey weave, dotted with minute coloured flecks. I started to count them.

He shook me, and shouted, 'You on your own?' I nodded weakly. Another siren screamed alongside. Thompson bawled over his shoulder, 'Get those medics over here.' Turning back he gave a glare that said he'd like to give me a good going over, and didn't mind joining the queue. 'That blaze down there can be seen for miles,' he said, between clenched teeth. 'You start it?'

I tried to shake my head. 'Not exactly,' I mumbled. My mouth opened and spewed out a stream of watery gunge. It just missed Thompson. Pity.

Two medics pushed their way in.

'See to her,' Thompson ordered, 'but she goes nowhere till I get back.' He gave me a sour glare, shouted some more, and he and his gang went for the car at a run. The back wheels spun as it careered off.

The leading medic unzipped a small bag, and dragged out the paraphernalia. He shrugged sympathetically. If it was up to him he would've whisked me away to a comfortable hospital bed, but what could he do? Yeah, I know. It's tough all over.

The pair of them started to check me out. I lay back and let them get on with it. They could check anything they liked. When they'd satisfied themselves that I'd no broken bones, deep wounds or had consumed anything that might be poisonous, a blanket was wrapped round my shoulders, and I was given fruit juice in a plastic cup.

I was still supping when the heavy mob returned. The steam had gone out of their action. They must've run out of things to chase.

Thompson marched over, frowning. 'How is she?'

'We'll take her to hospital, to be on the safe side,' the medic said. 'But after a couple of days in bed, she'll be as good as new.' I squinted up at him. He must be joking.

'Let's get going then.' The medic looked surprised. Thompson produced the wolfish grin, and leaned over. 'I'm keeping her company, son. Police business.'

I was lifted in, and laid out. As the door was firmly closed on the medic, I thought I saw another spasm of sympathy on his face. I sighed. It's amazing the number of people who would like to help you. If only they could.

The ambulance crawled slowly off. Thompson pulled out the seat from under the bed and settled himself down. I had a feeling of *déjà vu*. A couple of inches lower and he'd be nibbling my ear.

'Let's have it, O'Connell,' he growled. 'From the top.'

The top, where was the top? All I knew was that I was at the bottom, and my head was swimming. I closed my eyes, and sent up a prayer.

He shook me. 'This is important. Stay with it.'

A warm lethargy crept up my legs and along my arms, and started to spread through my body. It was getting no argument from me.

Something cold and wet slapped on my forehead, my eyes shot open and I yelped. Police brutality. Another shove and

I saw a sponge come up, dripping. I lifted a limp hand, Aw gie's a break.

'Talk, O'Connell,' he growled. 'And I want names.'

I talked. I gave him all the names I could think of. He recorded it, the lot, every last gasp. I ended up by scraping the crumpled note from my pocket, handing it over, and saying that I'd posted papers to my lawyer. He perked up when he saw the note, and I told him what was in the papers.

He wanted to know my lawyer's home address. I gave it. He stood up and banged on the glass divide. The ambulance stopped and he got out. He came back stuffing a mobile phone into his pocket. The door was slammed shut, and we were off again.

As I started to go under, I felt him take my hand. I hadn't the energy for a fight, so I left it there. And fell asleep.

When I wakened it was lunch-time, and I was in a six-bedded ward with pretty floral curtains. The tubular iron beds had white sheets topped with faded green covers; beside each was a steel locker, and two red plastic chairs.

Only the two furthest away beds were occupied, and both women were busy eating. I rang the bell. A young nurse raced up five minutes later, and insisted on taking my pulse and temperature before she went to look for the lunch trolley.

She came back with a plateful of tepid mince, potatoes and watery sprouts. Pudding was off. I was disgusted. And more meat, at this rate my teeth would be growing points. I ate the lot.

Replenished, I eased back. What I wanted to do was go straight back to sleep. What I had to do was find out what had happened to Bert.

I have every faith in Bert's devious capacity for survival. I should do, he's been at it long enough. But the last I'd seen had been him hitting the dirt. What if the cantankerous old goat was lying in a ditch somewhere?

Bert would never forgive me if I went to the police. That left Jack Baker. With his contacts there was a chance he could come up with something.

I needed a telephone.

I belled for attention. The same young nurse scurried to the bed, looking rushed off her feet. I put my request, while she piled up the pillows. She grabbed the tray and promised she'd bring a phone, when there was one available, and she had the time to wheel it round.

I unravelled myself from the bedclothes, and hirpled along to the loo. There was no mirror. Probably just as well. I got a cup of tea after that, and some magazines, and settled down to wait.

Ten minutes later, the phone arrived and was plugged in. I thanked the nurse for her trouble, and dialled. When Jack's cheerful voice came over the wire, I fielded the questions and got straight to the point.

'Would you do something for me, Jack? It's important.'

'Sure,' he breezed.

I gave him a description of Bert, and told him when and where we'd parted company. 'I think he might have thumbed a lift to Aberdeen. Could you ask around, find out if anyone has seen him. The state he was in,' I said acidly, 'he'd be difficult to forget.'

Jack sounded amused. 'Is he in some sort of trouble?'

Not yet, but he would be when I caught up with him. 'I just want to make sure that he's all right, Jack.'

'Wait a minute,' he said slowly. 'There was a car blown up around there.' I had to agree there was a connection. 'Does that mean he's hurt?'

'Could be,' I admitted reluctantly. I had been between Bert and the blast, so he hadn't taken the full force. But he was no spring chicken.

'I'll get on to it right away,' Jack said reassuringly. 'How do I get back to you?'

I explained that I was temporarily occupying a hospital bed, but was fighting fit. He laughed, said he was glad to hear it, and told me not to worry. Easy said.

Wishing myself back to the certainties of youth, I hung up and turned my attention to the next problem. Tomlinson would have been contacted, so I could expect a visit. He'd be looking for answers. And I had to be ready.

Everything I'd collected on drug trafficking between the States and Aberdeen was now in the hands of the police. And I didn't need Thompson breathing down my neck to tell me that was where it had better stay. I was obliged to tell Tomlinson about the activities of his staff, nothing more.

I had mixed feelings about Tomlinson. I'd got him what he wanted, the names of the main players in Yukon Discovery, and hard evidence. But it had carried a heavy price tag. And I couldn't help feeling that if he had been honest with me from the start, that might have been avoided.

As it was, I'd been lucky. I got a breakthrough. And I'd survived.

The breakthrough had come with Sawers trying to cover up the extent of the 'accidents', and Brown forgetting which ones he wasn't supposed to mention.

And the final piece of evidence was the note I had found in Sawers' pocket, itemising earlier payments and naming contacts, which had been prepared by Ms Jordan.

By that point, I'd figured things out, but recognising her distinctive upright script, from the letter she'd sent with the stock entries, had still come as a shock.

I decided it was time I took a rest from thinking, and dozed off and on for the rest of the afternoon.

I sat up at the arrival of the tea trolley, feeling rejuvenated. When I took a sip of tea, my jaws clamped in. This was HAG's idea of a good cuppa, it wasn't mine. Seconds later, a tall steel cabinet clanked into sight, delivered plates, and clattered off. The speed things are done here, you'd think there was a war on.

I studied my delivery suspiciously, and stole a look at my distant companions. They were stuffing it down.

The cheerful woman caught my eye. I could tell she was an optimist. She was going to look on the bright side, if it killed her. The figure in the other bed had a glum face, and an aura of misery. I aimed a weak smile, looked away, and ate. I was going to have to ask for my clothes back. So I could get out of here.

The trolley returned, the dishes were rolled off, and the place went quiet. The lull before the storm. I lay back to enjoy it.

I was relaxing nicely, when a bustle announced visitors. Tomlinson was walking swiftly up the ward, his face preoccupied. A debriefing was heading in my direction. I thought of the money, and dug up a welcoming smile.

Tomlinson reached the bed, and stopped and stared. 'I heard you'd been hurt, Cat. But I didn't think it was this bad.' Looking concerned, he flopped a bunch of flowers on the bed. 'Maybe I should come back later.'

I shook my head, I wanted this over with. 'Don't worry, Edward. Now is as good a time as any.'

He opened his overcoat, and pulled up a seat. 'You're quite sure you're up to it?' I didn't bother answering. Daft question. He stared some more, and shook his head. 'You look as if you've been in a fire.'

That got me going. Was he trying to be funny? 'What do you mean?'

'Well, you're missing a lot of hair, and your face is peeling.'

My hands shot up to check the damage. I felt over my head, all that was left was a crisp sizzled layer. I was bald. My fingers hit the painful gunge on my nose, and bounced off raw cheeks. I put my hands down. There are certain realities I prefer not to face.

'The police told me you were here,' Tomlinson said, getting down to business. 'Dragged me out of bed in the early hours to open the office, and took some papers. It was a shock hearing about Joe Sawers and Mike Brown.' He looked at me sceptically, 'But Ms Jordan?' His eyes hardened. 'And where does Haldane fit in?'

I gave him a blank stare.

Remembering his manners, he took a minute to commiserate with my plight, and say that I'd done a good job. 'Right,' he said leaning back. 'Tell me about Ms Jordan, and Haldane.'

'It's a long story.'

'I'm listening,' he said icily.

To my delight, Jack materialised at Tomlinson's shoulder,

dressed in jeans and a bomber jacket. 'Sorry to interrupt.'

I introduced them. Tomlinson wasn't pleased, and didn't try to hide it. I couldn't care less. I concentrated on Jack, trying to gauge whether I was in for good news, or bad.

Jack's only comment on my appearance was a rueful shake of the head. 'That information you wanted, Cat. One of the men from the market gave a lift to a man answering that description, and dropped him off in Aberdeen.' He grinned. 'I'm told he was pretty lively. Narked the whole way in.'

I laughed. There couldn't be two like that in this world. The Devil looks after his own, right enough. 'Thanks Jack,' I said warmly. 'I'm very grateful.' I waved him goodbye with a promise to keep in touch.

Tomlinson's steely blue eyes saw him off the premises, then focused on me. His internal information processor was waiting for an input of data, and it was getting impatient.

I lay back, and started to get my thoughts in order.

Harbour-lights

Tomlinson edged his chair nearer the bed, his eyes intent. I decided to start at the beginning.

'Ms Jordan found a way of making some easy money,' I said. 'And I don't think she realised what she was mixed up in until it was too late.'

'Easy money?' he interrupted tersely. 'For doing what?'

'She was paid to provide the names of workers who might be persuaded to carry certain packages between the rigs and shore, without asking awkward questions. Her access to the files allowed her to target the most likely candidates. The new training course provided the route.'

He stiffened. 'The course?'

'Her best bet was the longer serving workers, because they were familiar faces, and that was the catchment group for the new course.' He didn't look convinced. I spelled it out. 'Security tends to be less stringent when men are attending for training, especially if they are old hands.'

'Security follows strict procedures at all times,' he replied coldly. But the look on his face said there was going to be some changes in Yukon Discovery, and that heads would roll. It was the cleaning ladies I felt sorry for.

These constant interruptions were tiring. 'Do you want me to give you a report, or not, Edward?'

Tomlinson nodded, crossed his arms, and looked as if he was ready to listen this time. False assumption. He had been chewing things over, and he didn't like the taste. 'Who did Ms Jordan give the names to?' he rapped out.

I shook my head. 'I'm afraid I can't say. That's police business now.'

There was a flash of irritation, then the urbane exterior slipped back into place. 'Presumably you can tell me,' he said caustically, 'what made you suspect her in the first place?'

I took my time answering. There had been Ms Jordan's reluctance to meet me, her nervousness when she did, and her attempt to put the finger on Sawers and Brown. But the warning bell had only rung when she described Donald as nice. And there was no way I could explain that to Tomlinson.

I mentioned the first three, and her expensive taste in clothes, and how she'd tried to explain them away by making her affair with Haldane public, and picked up the tale from there.

'Ms Jordan co-opted Sawers and Brown, to be on the spot and see to the merchandise. She made the money, gave them a cut, and everybody was happy. Then things turned sour. Probably because Sawers didn't like taking instructions from a woman,' I said wryly, 'or maybe he just got greedy. Anyway, he started using muscle instead of persuasion, and that was when the "accidents" started.'

What I didn't say was that Sawers had also started dealing direct. That much was clear from the transatlantic calls to and from the Aberdeen office, geographically too widespread to have been down to Haldane, the official company contact.

I would've seen it sooner, if Tomlinson hadn't got me so hung up on Haldane being the guilty party.

'Brown just did as he was told,' I ended. Tomlinson was

staring thoughtfully into the distance. I took a deep breath. 'When Donald asked . . .'

'Donald?' he said quietly. 'You mean your friend, Dr Grant?'

'Yes,' I said, my throat tight. I started again, 'When Donald asked too many questions, Sawers warned him off. When he persisted, Sawers arranged the enforced sick leave.' I swallowed hard. 'That should've been enough. After all, Donald was effectively discredited, and off the scene.'

'Why wasn't it?'

Because I came along, I thought miserably. The threat of an official investigation meant loose ends had to be tidied up, and Donald had been top of the list. I gave a bitter shrug. If wishes were horses, beggars would ride.

'It was decided that Donald had to be taken care of, permanently,' I said, side-stepping. 'And they tried to do the same with me.' I went on to tell him about Sawers and Brown fixing the car.

I didn't tell him that they were carrying out instructions. Nor did I mention cold eyes and his bulky companion and their cleaning up process, or how they had ended up. That was Thompson's stamping ground.

Tomlinson's face had tightened into a mask. 'Did Ms Jordan have anything to do with any of this?'

I shook my head. 'No. But she was pretty certain that Donald's death hadn't been an accident, and was afraid of what might happen next. She wanted out. To protect herself, she tried to set up Sawers and Brown for fraud.'

'She altered these stock entries?' When I nodded, he murmured, 'I thought Haldane could have talked his way out of that, which was why I left it alone.'

'I know, you told me. And that was one of my first clues, because I couldn't see any reason for you to let it ride.' Other than you were part of it, I thought, but that was something else I was keeping to myself. 'When I sounded out Sawers and Brown, I was convinced that they didn't know anything.'

Tomlinson leaned forward. 'So where does Haldane fit in?'

'He wasn't involved,' I said calmly.

He gave a belligerent glare. 'What makes you so sure?'

I sighed. Tomlinson and Haldane's professional animosity had blinded them to what was really going on, and made things more difficult for me. And he still wasn't letting up.

'Haldane was genuinely concerned about the training scheme,' I said, determined he would hear me out. 'One, because that's his line of business and he takes it seriously. Two, he didn't want his reputation as a go-getter to take a nose dive, when he was getting near a seat on the board.'

'The biggest problem I had,' I went on, 'was the time link between the accidents and Haldane's visits.'

Tomlinson stared. 'Surely that proves that he had a hand in it?'

'No,' I said shortly. 'It was arranged that way, to muddy the waters,' I shot a look at Tomlinson. 'And Haldane's attempts to undermine you, by supporting Sawers, played right into their hands.'

The last sight I'd had of Sawers and Brown flashed chillingly to mind. 'Sawers had big plans,' I reflected sombrely, 'but he was out of his league.'

Tomlinson said sharply, 'Out of his league?'

In the middle of wishing that I'd held my tongue, I felt a draught on my back. Right down the space that hospital gowns leave open to the elements.

Thompson's growl hit my ears like an air-raid warning. 'Good evening, Ms O'Connell.'

I hit the pillows and lay as stiff as a board. How long had he been standing there?

Thompson reached across the bed, shook hands with Tomlinson and exchanged the time of day. From the look of him, sleep had been off the menu for weeks. I sent a distasteful look at the dark spiky growth covering the lower half of his face. Thank God I wasn't likely to get close to that.

Thompson whirled a chair round, straddled it, and leaned over the back. 'And how are we today, Ms O'Connell?'

I scowled. I'm another woman Thompson has a peculiar effect on. But in my case, a bell rings and I come out fighting. If we'd been alone I'd have told him to beat it.

'Fine,' I snapped.

'That's good. Because I thought you might like to hear how everything turned out.' I peered at him. He was going to tell me something. What was he after?

The wolfish grin widened. 'We've picked up Ms Jordan and two of her dealer friends. She has admitted everything, and is helping with our inquiries. Those papers of yours came in very useful.'

Money instantly re-entered my consciousness. Yukon Discovery still owed me the balance of my fee, and I wouldn't get it until I submitted my written report. For that, I needed these papers.

'I want those papers back,' I said quickly.

'Don't worry, you'll get them.' He stared as if he'd just noticed something. 'You look a mess.'

Charming. He wasn't much to look at himself. Only I was too polite to say so. I worked up an icy glare, and gave it him right between the eyes.

Thompson lifted his lip as if he was trying out a smile. 'I've arranged a lift for you tomorrow, Ms O'Connell. In a nice police car, all the way to Glasgow. The Superintendent wants a word, at the station.'

'What about?' I barked.

'This and that.' He unravelled himself from the chair. 'If you're ready, Mr Tomlinson, we'll take your statement now.'

'Certainly, Inspector.' Tomlinson turned to me, 'See you later, Cat. Enjoy your rest.' I nodded, Given half a chance. He took a sly look at me and Thompson, smiled, and walked off.

Thompson waited until he was out of earshot. 'Maybe I'll call in and see you one of these days, O'Connell,' he said quietly. 'When I'm passing.' His dark eyes held mine, If you get my drift.

I got his drift all right. The cheeky bugger. But if he thought he was coming around knocking on my door, he had another think coming. I was sick of the lot of them. And him in particular.

'Don't bother,' I snarled, 'It wouldn't be worth your while.'

'Oh, I don't know.' The wolfish grin reached his ears. 'We'll have to wait and see, won't we?'

The sheer effrontery reduced me to speechlessness.

He swaggered off, his back looking the happiest I'd seen it. I watched as he caught up with Tomlinson, chatted for a minute, and they walked out bosom friends. Right in front of my eyes, male bonding.

I lay back, feeling worse than when they'd brought me in. My head was a jumble of worries, and they were all pushing and shoving for attention.

I had to face Doreen and try to explain how the Polo had got blown up. Stanley was going to love that. I had to smooth down HAG and Bert, which would take some doing, say goodbye to Martin, and visit Donald's father.

And Allan was going in to the Australian outback. Plenty of mileage there for maternal worry beads and sleepless nights.

I lay back, coopered.

What the hell had happened to all this fun I'd promised myself? That was what I wanted to know.

After a good night's sleep and a mediocre breakfast, I got up, showered and dressed. Feeling more like my old self, I made my way to the front entrance. The nice police car was waiting.

My own clothes had been consigned to the bin, and I was togged out in stiff black jeans, a heavy brown sweater and a pair of plimsolls; all purchased for me that morning. None of these items were to my taste.

The journey back to Glasgow was uneventful, the driver and the WPC polite but distant. When we reached the police station, I was ushered in as if I was a human being. Made a change from the last time.

My interview with the Superintendant was brief and to the point. A tall burly man with beetle brows and piercing grey eyes, he read me the riot act about not providing the police with information sooner. I pleaded the pace of events, and we both agreed it wouldn't happen again.

He unbent sufficiently to thank me for my assistance, and offer a brief resumé of the wider picture.

Because of the crackdown in southern Florida over the

past year, he explained, there had been an influx of heroin from the States. British Customs were working closely with the police to ensure that any route that started up was closed down.

The one I'd stumbled on involved a complicated exchange, whereby drugs were transferred by coastal shipping to Aberdeen, and the rigs. After a rest period, they were distributed inland. The people involved, he confided, were not nice to know.

If he'd told me this to show me how much trouble I could have been in, he needn't have bothered. I already knew.

I came out of the station with my ears ringing, and stood and looked around. The few pedestrians in sight were keeping carefully to the other side of the road, probably scared they'd get dragged in. Traffic was steady.

I shivered, stuck my hands in the pockets of the baggy jeans, and ran my eyes up the battered tenement opposite until I found the sky; bright blue.

I totted up my blessings: I was alive, it was a beautiful day, and there was no sign of Thompson. I grinned and flagged a taxi.

Life was quite good really.

Books by post

Virago Books are available through mail order or from your local bookshop. Other books which might be of interest include:–

☐	An Imperfect Spy	Amanda Cross	£14.99
☐	Face Value	Lia Marera	£9.99
☐	Poisoned Hearts	Elizabeth Wilson	£6.99
☐	Burn Marks	Sara Paretsky	£5.99
☐	Catnap	Gillian Slovo	£5.99
☐	The Dog Collar Murders	Barbara Wilson	£5.99

Please send Cheque/Eurocheque/Postal Order (sterling only), Access, Visa or Mastercard:

☐☐☐☐☐☐☐☐☐☐☐☐☐☐☐☐

Expiry Date: ——————— *Signature:* ———————

Please allow 75 pence per book for post and packaging in U.K. Overseas customers please allow £1.00 per copy for post and packing.

All orders to:
Virago Press, Book Service by Post, P.O. Box 29, Douglas, Isle of Man, IM99 1BQ. Tel: 01624 675137. Fax: 01624 670923.

Name: ————————————————————

Address: —————————————————

——————————————————————

Please allow 20 days for delivery.
Please tick box if you would like to receive a free stock list ☐
Please tick box if you do not wish to receive any additional information ☐

Prices and availability subject to change without notice.